From My Lips To God's Ears

M.A. Walker

Library of Congress Control Number: 2009904244
ISBN: Hardcover 978-1-4415-3337-1
Softcover 978-1-4415-3336-4

This book was printed in the United States of America.

To order additional copies of this book, contact:
Xlibris Corporation
1-888-795-4274
www.Xlibris.com
Orders@Xlibris.com
58978

Dedication

With much love and gratitude to my parents whose love and acceptance never wavered. Supporting me in bad times and rejoicing with me in the good times, wrapping me in the security of their unconditional love.

And to my friends, *"friends are the pillars on your porch. Sometimes they hold you up, sometimes they lean on you and sometimes it's just enough to know that they are standing by."* Angelic quote

Profound thanks to my parents and friends for their unfailing love, patience, encouragement, and rooting along the way.

Author's Note

I know that nearly everyone who visits a therapist or psychiatrist can identify with being thrown into confusion over love, one way or another. Each has a story to tell of love lost or denied, love twisted or betrayed, love perverted or shackled to violence – our need to comprehend an ultimate human mystery – *how people who seem so ordinary can possess the hearts and minds of monsters?*

Love, what is this small one-syllable word that's not clearly expressed or defined that comes in many guises and strengths. A vague and confusing word that we use it for an idea extremely great and powerful or we use it in such a careless way that it can mean almost nothing or absolutely everything. I have heard it said that *love* is a positive force that somehow exalts the one feeling it. It commands a vast array of moods, but it cannot be explained, measured or mapped exactly. But yet, to give and receive love is a global human need, something integral to each person's life, something beautiful, and something natural.

I have treated it as if it were an obscenity, reluctantly admitting to it, an emotion that scared me more than cruelty, more than violence, more than hatred. Why did I have this painful feeling of being lowered and shamed of an emotion everyone admits is so wonderful and necessary? How inhibited I have been about love. Afraid to face it head on, allowing myself to be foiled by the vagueness of the word. After all, doesn't love require the highest degree of vulnerability?

Love seems rare nonetheless, always catches one by surprise and cannot be taught. Each child rediscovers it, each couple redefines it, and each parent reinvents it.

Language helps us to define our feelings, but many of my moods and tempers could not be articulated. My memory provided me with a circus of shortcomings when I was younger, in dire straits, frightened or less wise. I assumed no one on earth had erratic behaviors or had an obsession with certain unrealistic ideas or no one was as uniquely flawed.

Throughout my life, I have felt trapped by family, society, age, gender, and job. Also by many intangibles: tradition, religious teachings, and my own, and others' expectations of myself.

But, love had become my greatest intangible, an imponderable force. Inconsistent, full of contradictions, a strengthening and disabling emotion, not easily or clearly expressed, defined or grasped by my mind; a vague statement, a vague notion, a vague longing. I wasn't consciously looking for love, but I was constantly hurt by love or losing love. In short, I was charmed, troubled, and lead astray by love. Nothing began with so much excitement and hope or failed as often as love.

It is said that everyone has at least one good book in them; I believe that this is true. Each of us is special and has unique life experiences and views of the world; our souls appointed means of growth.

So the one I know best is myself; my past and my present, my thoughts, and my emotions. Yet, it's probably the subject I try hardest to avoid.

Now I can hardly believe what a liberating journey I have embarked on. I never had the nerve before, I always was afraid to try. I didn't think I had permission or to believe in the validity of my life. But, I realize I can no longer be eager to please. I am writing for myself. The physical act of writing is a powerful search mechanism. I'm often amazed, dipping into my past to find some wholly forgotten incident, clicking into place just when I need it. My memory is almost always good for material when my other wells go dry.

The details of people, places, events, anecdotes, ideas, emotions took me where I wanted to go . . . deeply to the root of a personal experience . . . to all the drama and humor, and unexpectedness of life . . . to some corner of my past that was unusually intense . . . the editor of my own life, imposing on an untidy sprawl of half-remembered events, a narrative shape, and an organizing idea . . . the art of inventing the truth . . . so, I'm giving myself permission to write about myself.

Most of the events in, *From My Lips to God's Ears* have taken place in my life over the years. Though names and characters are used fictitiously, I experienced *nearly* every word, feeling, and incident experienced by Elizabeth "*Liz*" Sulis.

M.A. Walker

"Far away in the sunshine are my highest aspirations. I may not reach them, but I can look up and see their beauty, believe in them, and try to follow where they lead."

Louis May Alcott:
An American novelist best known
for the novel Little Women (1868)

FROM MY LIPS TO GOD'S EARS

Preface

I had an ideal love, a one and only, a person that made me whole, a Mr. Right, my one true love, that special someone, my significant other. I didn't have to wait in suspense until the handsome Prince arrived with an invigorating kiss. I didn't have to wait for the knight in shining armour to ride by. Nor did I have to wait for karma, fate or destiny or some other temporal God to send a likely partner my way or use Cupid's arrow. We didn't need a powerful love potion to be brewed or drank, while thirsty and unaware, to make us fall in love . . . Geoffrey and I were already absolutely joined by love, inseparable at heart, soul, and flesh. But, what went wrong?

"What did I do wrong, Liz? No more empty excuses, *please tell me!*"

After all these years, Geoff just couldn't understand why or put his finger on it. Nothing made any sense. If it was something he had done, he wanted to know. This time he was going to be persistent, relentless if he had to be, in order to get to the truth, why I had given up on us. What was so bad or why couldn't I trust him enough to tell him? He was baiting me, trying to get me to talk about it.

"What does it matter, Geoff?"

"It matters to me because I want to know. I need to know. *Damn it, Liz!*"

Another heated argument ensued and the words at some point inadvertently rolled off my tongue. It seemed like an eternity had passed as we sat there, both motionless. I just wanted to go home; he got what he wanted, the truth.

~

Everything, as I knew it, changed. With so many alternatives that promised so much, but delivered so little, the search for answers seemed hopeless.

It has been said countless times; life is what you make of it. You are your own destiny. Living is a wonderful thing, what a privilege. You know stumbling blocks, bumps in the road, and frustrations are all part of life, how else is one to learn. Isn't it taking what life throws at you and making the best of it?

That one moment in time, which altered everything, sending my world into a tailspin, my future unfathomable. Losing a part of myself as to who I was and the positive direction my life seemed to have been headed in. Dreams and aspirations I once had *shattered*.

The simplicity of adolescence made it easy to fool, snatching away my innocence. How could I cope with everything coming at me when I was so young, naïve, and vulnerable? How was I to deal with this incident and emotions far beyond my years, and put it all behind me, let go?

How does a person reach out and ask for help from a *saviour*, a person who saves or rescues when everything seems to be at a loss? Would I even recognize a helping hand reaching out to me to help? Who would become my saviour?

What revenge is there? Revenge, is that really what I wanted? Was there revenge in my heart, getting even? Is there such a thing as a moral equalizer to such a demoralizing wrong? Or, was I holding back with baited breath in the hopes of, or grasping for, an acknowledgement of the wrong that had been done? An apology even?

It only took one or two things to go wrong, and it was all too easy for me to fall into a negative mindset that spiraled out of control. Self doubt or outside influences intervened, and I wound up getting sidelined, believing that I didn't deserve to triumph after all.

No one really knew or had any idea. How could they? In a way, I went from being an extrovert to an introvert over night. I remembered my mother alluding to the fact that they had noticed significant changes taking place, but there were no apparent reasons for my sudden loss in my zest for life. I simply disengaged. Usually, there's a reason like bad health or some sort of emotional trauma.

Why was I shutting down and shutting everyone out? Everyone seemed to be grasping at straws. I was unable to care about myself and give or receive love. No one heard my silent cries for help, but I wouldn't let anyone in. I became a loner of sorts, pretending everything was perfectly fine on the outside. My mind was on basic survival. I definitely didn't want to feel what I was feeling, trying desperately to forget, hoping someday I wouldn't remember. Thinking, eventually, it wouldn't affect my beliefs, thought patterns or my rationalization of things that I could grow up, mature, and lead a normal life and be happy.

My parents were doing the best they could at the time, frantically searching for some sort of answer. False diagnosis and assumptions started. The expert's diagnosis was a reading and comprehension learning disability. Solid comprehension skills are necessary for any person's personal and professional growth.

I remembered being told that I wouldn't amount to much or even be able to handle a secondary education. Any criticism when I was feeling vulnerable at such a young age limited my ability to learn. Or, the way I was taught and what I believed about my abilities determined what I could learn or do. During this time in my life, I often made decisions that seemed logical to me, but perhaps were not logical from an adult perspective. What did I care? What was going on inside me? What did anyone know back then?

I was a teenager who became an expert at being closemouthed, even under the best of circumstances. Oddly enough, I truly believed I was protecting my family from what actually took place by not saying anything. I didn't want to make more of a mess than what I felt already was unfixable. By saying nothing, I wouldn't be a disgrace to the family. The fear of any reproach that I deserved it would have been unbearable humiliation. I never could understand or comprehend the why part for what had happened, and probably would never know.

My parents refused to give up and their love for me was unconditional. I took the missed diagnoses and assumptions, having few fond memories of these years, never being nostalgic about my past. I urgently needed to get away from what I believed were those curious, pitying eyes of people who knew me.

Was I being punished for my relationship with Geoff? What we had was it wrong, forbidden love? What did I do wrong to deserve this? I didn't want anyone to know, especially my family or friends, let alone Geoff. Who would have believed me?

During my adult life, I had been struggling to find myself. Very few people can single-handedly determine the deep reasons for their despair, much less chase them away. You would think, after forty plus years, I would get it right. But, what were the fears, insecurities and troubles still lurking in the shadows of my subconscious mind, but not really consciously felt or recognized?

It is not healthy to wallow in painful emotions all the time. Everyone needs a healthy balance in his or her own life, living in the present moment, and enjoying life. I had to become free to live and live happily, by caring for my spirit, nurturing my unique potential, and celebrating life's many blessings. Therefore, increasing my self-esteem, understanding myself, and making myself physically, and emotionally stronger.

Unforgiveness . . . unforgiveness contaminates. Out of anything, one thing was a must; I had to learn to forgive unconditionally. Somehow, I had to find a way to rise above all of my disappointments, hurts, and failures. I had to free myself from this heavy burden created by the negative mindset I had been accumulating for so many years. I needed a trustful faith, a faith to believe in myself. Putting a stop to punishing myself for what had happened. To open the floodgates of forgiveness, a spirit that wanted to be healed, releases for my inner healing to begin.

There are those of us who were sheltered from harms way, able to handle stumbling blocks, bumps in the road, and frustrations. But, bad things can happen that you cannot be protected from.

Many of us are going to fail, but we don't have to remain in our failures. The bondage and pain of past suffering *does not* have to be today's reality.

This is for all the ordinary men, women, and children who became heroes when confronted with extraordinary circumstances.

Elizabeth 'Liz' Sulis

Chapter One

The *future* – that vast uncharted sea of the unknown, holding joy or terror, comfort or pain, love or loneliness. Some people fear the days to come, wondering what evils lurk in the shadows; others consult seers and future-telling charlatans, trying desperately to discover its secrets.-Author Unknown-

~

It's not an uncommon thing for many to have come from a traditional military family background. I'm no exception. My Dad, Robert, who recently turned 85, in retrospect, spins an engaging personal account of a young man coming out of the depression years with his grandmother, mother, brother, and sister, and growing up at sea. A witness to the drama of a deadly serious fight for supremacy during the Second World War and the War in the Pacific – and commemorates with genuine affection, the dedicated men with whom he served, and the loss of some of his best friends, and the fighting navy, which shaped them . . . looking beyond the sensational acts of cruelty, to ponder the horror of man's inhumanity to man, and the examples of heroism in the midst of savagery . . . all a preamble to where my story actually begins.

By 1939, Hitler was a mad genius with tremendous political ability and considerable talent in developing military strategy. He was a danger to the world. The arming of Germany was accelerated. The Third Reich had arrived. The Nazis were in charge and the path to the Second World War lay ahead. A war that would claim approximately 60 million + lives.

In 1942, during the Second World War, Canadian Naval Radio Station Albro Lake was built during the height of the Battle of the Atlantic, and served as a naval radio communications station for the Atlantic coast. The Battle of the Atlantic was a battle primarily pitting the North Atlantic German submarines, known as U-boats, and armed merchantmen of the German Navy, Kriegsmarine, against allied convoys, in particular, the Royal Canadian Navy.

The U-boat campaign had gained momentum all through the latter half of 1942. By November, Canadian and Allied shipping losses reached a new wartime high. Kudos' to foul weather in December and January, which gave the Canadians and their Allies some respite. Good intelligence kept losses down in February 1943, but the increasing number of U-boats being deployed in the mid-ocean made it painfully clear that the worst was yet to come.

The German's had changed their codes and during the first three weeks of March 1943, 22 percent of all the ships sailing in the main trans-Atlantic Allied convoys never reached their destination. A disproportionate number of Canadian escorts however, were in refit in early 1943. This was a time that the battle was passing through its most crucial phase. The change of events at sea would prove to be the only time the German Wolf Packs would achieve any success of the Battle of the Atlantic.

The British considered abandoning the convoy system, in desperation, a desperate move indeed, since there was no viable alternative. But, by April and May 1943, the combination of excellent intelligence, recently arrived support groups, and extended air-cover dealt a death blow to the German Wolf Packs, and would eliminate the serious threat to the main North Atlantic convoys for the rest of the war.

The Canadian Northwest Atlantic Command was established. This command, which controlled defence of merchant shipping north of Maine to the edge of the Grand Banks of Newfoundland, and the mouth of the St. Lawrence River, was the only Allied theater of war commanded by a Canadian, Rear Admiral L.W. Murray. The Royal Canadian Navy would also cooperate with the Americans, preventing the Japanese submarines from penetrating coastal waters off Alaska in the northeastern Pacific.

~

The Canadian Naval Radio Station Albro Lake sat on a hill that overlooked Big Albro Lake, one of two lakes that were located in the north end of Dartmouth, and named after one of Halifax's prominent early settlers, John Albro. Its sister lake being Little Albro.

Permanent Married Quarter dwellers were located a short distance, adjacent to the Naval Radio Station. Though the price tag to build this station was a hefty one [$6 million], in those days it would prove to be an invaluable weapon in allied shipping saved.

The station was divided into a receiving site at Albro Lake and a transmitter site, 50 Kilometres northwest, near the rural hamlet of Brooklyn, in the St. Croix River valley, in Newport Corner, Nova Scotia. Its signal could be heard and read from Murmansk to the Falklands and half way around the world.

Murmansk is located in the extreme northwest of Russia, the largest city within the Arctic Circle and not far from Russia's borders with Norway, and Finland. Its seaport is on the Kola Gulf, 12 kilometres from the Barents Sea on the northern shore of the Kola Peninsula. Its port is warmed by the waters of the Gulf Stream and is ice-free. During the Second World War it served as a transit point for weapons and other supplies entering the Soviet Union from other allied nations.

Uncle Bruce was four years older than Dad and had already been serving in the Canadian Navy since 1937. He too, was part of the Murmansk run to Russia, when merchant ships steamed into the stormy Arctic with supplies for the Russian front. They faced a relentless enemy as they fought through the Barents Sea and the White Sea to reach the distant Russian supply ports of Archangel and Murmansk. This supply route was absolutely vital to the Russians if they were to hold out against the Nazi offensive. Without the Allied ships that made the voyage with products from the American war arsenal, the Russians may well not have beaten back the German invasion.

The voyage to North Russia was never a routine affair, for there were always hazards of storms and Arctic ice, whether or not the ship faced enemy attack. But they did. During the short northern summer, 24 hours of daylight made it possible for German aircraft to attack continuously from the time ships came within striking range. Throughout the rest of the year, the merchantmen and their escorts, especially the destroyers, and smaller craft, had the worst weather to contend with. Spray froze the topside surfaces, blinding snow, driving sleet, and violent storms tossed ships about, and hopelessly scattered convoys.

By 1944, HMCS ships would be escorting all of the main transatlantic convoys, which would make up 40 percent of the Allied antisubmarine forces in British waters. Canadian destroyers served with the British fleet and HMCS torpedo boats would operate in the English Channel, and the Canadian minesweepers cleared the approaches to the beaches at Normandy, in preparation for D-Day, which they would put Canadian soldiers ashore to participate in the Normandy invasion.

Although the Second World War continued in the Pacific, the war in Europe ended on May 7, 1945. The Port of Halifax and Bedford Basin had hosted transport ships, tankers, warships of all types, and merchant marine cargo vessels, all supplying materials, and personnel for the war effort. They gathered in Halifax from all along the eastern seaboard of the United States, as well as from other Canadian ports.

There was always the fear, in this seaport community, of a repetition of the huge explosion on December 6, 1917. The ammunition ship Mont Blanc steamed up from the harbour mouth where she had anchored overnight. Her cargo consisted of TNT, tons of picric acid, and a deck load of benzol drums. About the same time, the Norwegian steamer Imo, chartered for Belgian relief purposes came out of Bedford Basin. At the Narrows, the two collided. The result was the largest man-made explosion, prior to Hiroshima, with over 1,600 deaths recorded, and the destruction of thousands of homes.

Albert Einstein, an American theoretical physicist, was born a German Jew. As many know, he would later be recognized as one of the greatest physicists of all time. Hitler's climb to power, brining official support of vicious anti-Semitism, was making the position of Jews and other opponents of Nazism impossible.

After Einstein left Germany, in 1932, he never returned. In March 1933, he once again renounced German citizenship. In 1934, his remaining property in Germany was confiscated, and his name appeared on the first Nazi list of people stripped of their citizenship.

Many universities abroad were eager to invite the renowned, 1922, Nobel Prize recipient, in physics, but he accepted an offer to hold a post at the Institute for Advanced Study in Princeton, New Jersey. He arrived in the United States, in October 1933, and in 1940, became an American citizen.

In 1939, Einstein was approached by his friend Szilard about new research into atomic power and sent a message to Roosevelt, urging him to investigate the possible use of atomic energy in bombs.

Otto Hahan and Fritz Strassmann's discovery of Uranium Fission in 1938 steered Germany toward developing an atomic weapon. This motivated the United States to launch the Manhattan Project. By 1941, the Germans were leading the race for the atomic bomb. They had a heavy-water plant, high-grade uranium compounds, a nearly complete cyclotron, capable scientists, and engineers, and the greatest chemical engineering industry in the world.

Between 1941-1945, factors including internal struggles, a major scientific error, and the devastation of total war, compromised any successful research toward a German atom bomb. Unlike the American program, the Germans never had a clear mission under continuously unified leadership.

In 1942, at the University of Chicago reactor, Enrico Fermi, friend and colleague of Einstein's, and Szilard, oversaw the first controlled energy release from the nucleus of the atom. After intense effort in 1945, the Y-12 plant in Oak Ridge, Tennessee, began to produce bomb-grade U-235, which was shipped to Los Alamos, New Mexico.

By March 1945, with victory nearly at hand, Franklin Roosevelt had been President for more than twelve years, but the war, and the office were taking their toll on his health. Physically crippled by polio, he exuded confidence and vitality as he led the country through many of its darkest hours. And the nation responded in kind, re-electing him to office by wide margins of victory – even when, in 1944, his failing health suggested that he might not live long enough to complete his term. As long as the U.S. remained at war with Germany and Japan, the American people were determined to stick by their commander-in-chief.

Recognizing his ailing condition, Roosevelt decided to leave for a vacation to the *little White House* in Warm Springs Georgia, a spot that usually improved his health. He arrived there on the afternoon of March 30, 1945. The Georgia air seemed to invigorate the President and soon he settled into a balanced routine of work, and pleasure.

On Monday, April 9, 1945, Lucy Rutherford, accompanied by her painter friend, Elizabeth Shoumatoff, arrived to spend the final week of the vacation with the President. Lucy and Roosevelt met when he was assistant secretary of the navy and FDR became quite smitten with her. Lucy brought Shoumatoff with her to paint a portrait of FDR during their stay.

At around 1200 hours EST, on April 12, 1945, Shoumatoff had begun working on FDR's portrait, as he sat in the living room dressed in a double-breasted gray suit, and crimson tie, sifting through a stack of papers as she sketched. Lucy and a few others were present. At 1300 hours, the butler brought FDR and his guests their lunch. At that moment, Roosevelt seemed agitated and flinched in his chair. An assistant asked the President if he needed help. FDR's head went forward. He gripped his head with his left hand and said, *"I have a terrific headache."* They would be his last words. The President collapsed and lost consciousness.

At 1747 hours, EST., Americans were jolted by broadcast interruptions.

> *"Good evening ladies and gentlemen. This is Fulton Lewis, Jr., speaking from the Mutual Studio's in New York City... This nation has suffered this day, a staggering loss. At this moment, at Warm Springs Georgia, President Franklin D. Roosevelt lies with the problems of the nation finally lifted from his shoulders. Stricken late this afternoon with Cerebral Hemorrhage, he passed away before his physicians could be of any assistance, if assistance, in such a case is possible at all. Vice-President Harry Truman, who from here on will be President Truman, went immediately to the White House. A special Cabinet meeting was called and we should know more about what is going to happen in*

Washington, as the evening wears on. But, Franklin D. Roosevelt, the first President to be elected for four terms in the White House, has passed away, and that, is the overshadowing of all news events that have happened or can happen . . . for quite awhile" [http://www.otr.com/lewis.html. Radio Days – biography of Fulton Lewis, Jr. – Death of FDR].

People of every walk of life struggled to come to terms with it. For the millions who adored FDR, an America without him seemed almost inconceivable. The sudden death, of President Roosevelt, shocked the world. Allied world leaders paid tribute to the President.

Though as an ardent pacifist, Einstein was opposed to the use of the atomic bomb. But, it was as a result of Fermi's, Szilard's, and Einstein's work that the 32nd President of the United States, Harry S. Truman, decided to use the A-bomb. Knowing that the Japanese military leaders were prepared to fight a conventional war to the last man, Truman felt he had no other choice.

After six months of intense firebombing of 67 other Japanese cities, the nuclear weapon *Little Boy* was dropped on the city of Hiroshima, August 6, 1945, followed on August 9, 1945, by the detonation of the *Fat Man* nuclear bomb over Nagasaki. U-235 was used in the Little Boy bomb and plutonium was used in the Fat Man bomb, produced at Los Alamos, New Mexico. The bombs killed over 140,000 people in Hiroshima and 80,000 in Nagasaki by the end of 1945. Thousands of more died from injuries or illness attributed to exposure to radiation, released by the bombs. The majority of the dead in both cities were civilians.

Six days after the detonation over Nagasaki, on August 15, 1945, Japan announced its surrender to the Allied powers, signing the Instrument of Surrender on September 2, 1945. This officially ended the Pacific War and therefore, the Second World War. Germany had already signed its Instrument of Surrender on May 7, 1945.

Spud Roscoe of Halifax tells the following story about his friend George who was on duty during the Halifax ammunition explosion of 1945.

The Victory in Europe [VE Day] riots had caused strife between the service personnel and citizens of Halifax, but the city was working hard to put that in the past. Troopships were bringing the forces home and naval vessels were coming home to be removed from service. But, before the many naval vessels could be decommissioned, the key job was to de-ammunition them. Like the Halifax Explosion of 1917, there had been several other close calls, largely unknown to Haligonians.

For two months, naval craft of all sorts had passed up the harbour and put ashore their ammunition. By July 18, 1945 the Bedford Basin Magazine held an inordinate quantity of shells, bombs, mines, torpedoes, depth charges, and other powerful materials.

This should have been a slow process, as safety rules allowed only one at a time to unload its lethal cargo on the jetty at the large ammunition storage Magazine at Burnside, above Dartmouth, on the Bedford Basin. However, it was politically important to get the servicemen home as quickly as possible and the regulations with respect to the handling of ammunition were bent, despite protests.

In an inordinate rush, three vessels' stocks of ammo were on the jetties at a time. The large, carefully designed Magazines in the rocky hillside on the wooded far side of the Basin were very safe . . . when the rules were observed. The Magazines had been built in 1927, for the joint use of the army, navy, and air force. *The possibility of another explosion preyed on the minds of Dartmouthians and Haligonians. Not surprisingly, everyone assumed the worse.*

Inevitably, their fears once again turned to terror when trouble came at supper hour, on July 18, 1945, toward the close of what had been a hot summer's day. An ignition of a high powered explosive on a jetty at the Bedford Magazine set off a series of fires, followed quickly by a big bang. The ground shook for kilometres around and the jetty and the barge tied alongside disappeared. A high mushroom like cloud rose above the Magazine that could be seen from distances well beyond the populated areas surrounding the Bedford Basin.

The ammunition depot was less than 4.8 kilometres west of the Albro Lake Naval Radio Station. Trained Operator Telegraphist, George D. Crowell was working the Atlantic Broadcast at the Albro Lake Naval Radio Station on the evening shift, July 18, 1945. Around 1830 hours local time there was a lull in this broadcast, so George got up to walk around and chat with any of those on duty who were not busy.

George was also the Telegraphist who received the message on May 9, 1945 from U-858, the first German U-boat to surrender on the Western side of the Atlantic. She was ordered to proceed to Fort Miles, Delaware, where she would arrive and surrender to the Americans, on May 14, 1945.

What timing! When George stood up, he happened to look out the window towards the Magazine and immediately saw the mushroom cloud from the explosion. He yelled "explosion" and instructed everyone to hit the deck. He dove in under a desk with Janie the dog, the station's mascot. One of the staff, believed to be Quigley had been on the Murmansk run to Russia and brought Janie back. They claimed she was a Russian wolfhound, but George said she looked like a Staffordshire terrier.

When the blast struck the Albro Lake Naval Radio Station, it blew in all the windows, and also severed the control lines from Albro Lake to the Newport Corner transmitter site. These lines ran past the Magazine. Albro Lake had been left with receiving, but no transmitting capability.

Lieutenant Dill was in command of the Albro Lake station and was on the premises when this explosion took place. He ordered George to contact Newport Corner using the Canadian Marconi CM11 transmitter. It was designated to communicate with the Newport Corner transmitter site in case of an emergency. Communicating via Morse code, with its familiar dots and dashes or dits and dahs required Telegraphist to send a message for help.

George kept calling and calling, but couldn't make any contact. It was the perception that the duty watch at Newport Corner was not paying attention; no one was actually keying the transmitters.

All Albro Lake personnel were to head to the dormitory on the upper floor of the Operations building, collect their personal effects, and prepare to abandon the station. It was late in the evening and quite dark when a few of them boarded an army truck. This truck took them to an army camp past the RCAF station at Eastern Passage, having to spend the night in an army hut with no bunks or cots, having to sleep on the floor.

Eastern Passage is located at the southeastern edge of Halifax Harbour, fronting the Atlantic Ocean.

George and several others of the Albro Lake personnel were taken to the RCAF Station Gorsebrook on South Street, on the south side of Halifax. The air force had loaned them a couple transmitters. Jointly, they managed to set up a temporary radio station for a few days until the control lines could be repaired, windows replaced, and the building at Albro Lake made ready for their return.

George couldn't remember what happened to Janie the dog. He just figured that someone must have located her and took her to the camp. Most dogs in this area were traumatized whenever they heard thunder-like sounds.

Minor explosions continued however, throughout the night, until approximately at 0400 hours on July 19, 1945 another huge blast shattered windows, shook foundations, blew off roofs, and rattled walls of major buildings throughout the area. The danger passed, but not before thousands of refugees evacuated to the parks, protected streets, gardens, and villages surrounding Dartmouth, and Halifax.

Dartmouth became a ghost town. With limited roadways leading from Halifax, particularly to the South Shore, traffic was slow and tiring. Service personnel were on full alert. Rescue and support systems were organized to give whatever aid might be required and to dispense sandwiches and coffee. Hospitals prepared for casualties. Children, adults, and seniors suffered not only physical hardships, but also mental anguish, and fear of what might yet come. This was the situation prior to the initial explosion. Halifax and its environs were sitting on a powder keg.

Fortunately, only one patrolman was killed, but it was vigilance by service personnel and volunteer forces that bravely, and without regard to their own safety, battled the flames at the Magazine. They saved Dartmouth and Halifax from an explosion with the potential to wipe both cities and its surrounding neighbourhoods off the face of the earth [http://jproc.ca/rrp/albro_lake.html - The Explosion of 1945/Albro Lake].

Chapter Two

Dad's parents, Wilfred Sulis, and his mother, Hazel, had been living in Boston, Massachusetts. Wilfred's family roots were originally from Clementsport, Nova Scotia, located in the Annapolis Royal – Bridgetown region of the Evangeline Trail, Annapolis County, where Wilfred's father had been a sea captain. These were difficult times in the twenties. Over time, for the most part, many of the Sulis family connections and ties had been relocating in the Eastern parts of the United States, in search of employment, earning better money than in rural Nova Scotia.

While Wilfred remained in the States, working as a bus driver, Dad's mother Hazel, brother Bruce, and sister Millie came home from the New England States for a visit. Hazel needed the warmth of her mother and some quiet-time, as she was pregnant with Dad. Hazel was one of those unfortunate women who became ill each day of her pregnancies. The visit lingered on. It wasn't intended for Dad to be born in Deep Brook, but Hazel, and her two children remained with Grammie and Pup during her difficult pregnancy. Then WOW, 12 pound Robert was welcomed into the world on a lovely spring day, in the home of his grandparents.

Grammie was over protective of her children, especially her first child Hazel. She really wanted them to stay home with her and Pup, and succeeded in doing that. Grammie raised the children. Hazel, who had good skills, went to the States to work. She always sent money home to help Grammie with the needs of the children, including regular visits to the dentist. Hazel always came home for a two-week vacation each summer; and, as Grammie would say, "To spoil the children, then leave for me to straighten them out." Probably the happiest employment Hazel had in the United States was as Secretary/Companion to a lovely lady of means. Sometime during these years, Wilfred and Hazel divorced.

The Great Depression was one of the greatest economic collapses of the Western World. Until the outbreak of the Second World War, the economies of Western countries were struggling, and poverty was commonplace. In actual times of war, like these, it was not an uncommon thing for many young men, of age, and wanting to answer the call to fight, and defend their country, signed up as Volunteer Reservists; taking up the cause along side other permanent forces personnel. But, for many, this also meant fighting in a distant war with little idea of what it would entail.

On Friday, May 23, 1941, Dad and his mother boarded the train from Deep Brook, Annapolis County, Nova Scotia, bound for Halifax, two days before his 17th birthday. There were no trains on the weekend to Halifax. Dad was to report to the Naval Base on Monday, immediately being whisked away for humiliating basic training at the Canadian Forces Base in Esquimalt, British Columbia.

Hazel moved to Halifax, the entrance and exit point of most military personnel, to feel near her children. Hazel easily made friends in Halifax, working at the Conservatory of Music. A woman of faith and prayer; praying for each of her son's and the rest of the ships crew's protection, while at sea and for their safe return, for an all too brief shore leave.

~

By the time fall/winter of 1941 rolled around, Dad was in the Pacific on HMCS Prince Robert, as a Telegraphist [Radioman]. HMCS Prince Robert had been one of three Canadian National Railway passenger steamship liners that were purchased in 1939 – 1940, and extensively converted to Armed Merchant Cruiser's, for the task of intercepting merchant traffic and convoy escorts. The two others were HMCS Prince David and HMCS Prince Henry.

After HMCS Prince Robert was refitted at Esquimalt B.C., during the summer of 1941, it was dispatched to escort the Australian, HMAS Awatea to Kowloon, Hong Kong. HMCS Prince Robert carried four officers and 105 ranks of the Royal Rifles, from Quebec, while HMAS Awatea carried the remainder, along with the Winnipeg Grenadiers from Manitoba. The total contingent, Force C, consisted of 96 officers, 1,877 other ranks, two Auxiliary Service Supervisors, and one stowaway.

A few weeks earlier, the Canadian Government, at London's request, had agreed to send two battalions to Kowloon, Hong Kong. In the face of the growing Japanese threat, the British Staff had convinced Prime Minister, Winston Churchill, to dispatch reinforcements to the British colony in Kowloon, which would be doomed in advance if it were attacked. London, which was short of resources, regarded Canadian participation as a way of strengthening the spirit of unity within the British Empire. Canada, without requesting an analysis of the military situation had quickly agreed. Ottawa had been told that its two battalions would be limited to maintaining a garrison.

HMCS Prince Robert and HMAS Awatea set sail the night of October 27, 1941, via Honolulu and Manila, where the British light cruiser, HMS Danae was added to the escort. When they arrived in Kowloon, Hong Kong, on November 16, 1941, the Canadians discovered the charms of the Orient and looked on their assignment as a gift from heaven. The risk of combat seemed minimal and an ordinary soldier could live like a king in Hong Kong.

Dad couldn't really remember, which port they had been in while in the South Pacific, but someone managed to bring a monkey on board. They built a cage for him and kept him back on the quarterdeck. When the monkey was let out in the mornings, he would head straight for the fo'c's'le [forecastle], run down the Hawse Pipe, and sit on the anchor. Another set of eyes perhaps, keeping watch for any enemy submarines. Anyone who had been bitten by the monkey was to report to the ship's medic.

I couldn't help but laugh, when Dad was laughing at his memory of seeing how close the ocean would rise, to almost meet the monkey's *arse*, as he put it, as the ship sailed through the ocean waters. The monkey didn't flinch. Of course no one could reach him. He just sat on the anchor, until either someone tried to entice him with some food, whatever they could get their hands on, such as a piece of lettuce or he would eventually scurry back up on deck, on his own accord. Dad couldn't remember what name they gave the monkey, but he became an ordinary seaman monkey, and no doubt, the only monkey who would know what it was like to become a sailor.

About one week later, once HMCS Prince Robert's mission was complete in Kowloon, Hong Kong, she returned to sea. She had passed through Honolulu December 3, 1941, to pick up supplies, without an inkling of the Japanese task force already on the way to Pearl Harbour. There were of course rumors [much after the fact] of mystifying signals picked up, but since it is now known that the Japanese task force steamed through the North Pacific under strict radio silence, the rumors are laid.

Just four hours after the Pearl Harbour attack, a message was received aboard HMCS Prince Robert that the U.S. Navy transport, Cynthia Olsen had been torpedoed, about 209 kilometres south of HMCS Prince Robert's position. She diverted, searched the sea, but found nothing. Despite this message, they had received, while at sea, communication technologies were not yet developed. So HMCS Prince Robert and its crew had no idea of the attack on Pearl Harbour, until their return home to Esquimalt B.C.

The following day of the raid on Pearl Harbour, December 7, 1941, The British Colony of Kowloon, Hong Kong would also suffer a surprise attack by the Japanese. After seventeen days of bitter fighting, the Canadians battalions, along with their British, Chinese, and Indian Allies, surrendered on Christmas night, 1941. Nearly 300 of Canadian soldiers had been killed and 500 wounded. The losses would have been less heavy if the Japanese had not killed injured men and prisoners. The survivors subsequently were faced with the disgusting conditions that prevailed in the prison camps.

They were assigned to construction of a landing strip at Kai Tak, in Hong Kong or to work in the coalmines of Niigata, about 250 kilometres northwest of Tokyo or at the Yokohama shipyard. Suffering from malnutrition, disease, and the violence of their guards, 260 Canadians perished from neglect or from the harsh treatment they received from their executioners.

After the bombing of Pearl Harbour and up until now, the three Canadian Prince ships were equipped with only rudimentary radar, which made navigation a source of constant danger. The Prince ships were also not equipped to defend themselves or their charges against well-armed enemy ships that it was feared may begin to operate off the West Coast. In 1942, HMCS Prince David and HMCS Prince Henry were converted into Landing Ships Infantry, in preparation for the coming invasion in Europe. HMCS Prince Robert's conversion was an anti-aircraft cruiser, to help protect Allied convoys from German air attacks.

They took up defensive duties in the Pacific Northeast, off British Columbia – providing protection to shipping in the region, reassuring the public by their presence, and to satisfy American demands for a Canadian naval force in the area. Late August of 1942, the three Prince ships and the corvettes HMCS Dawson, and HMCS Vancouver, were ordered to cooperate with American forces, to escort convoys between Kodiak, and Dutch Harbor, Alaska, now Unalaska, as part of the Aleutian Islands campaign [http://www.airmuseum.ca/prstory04.html – Hong Kong 1941—Prince Robert Story, Hillman WW II Scrapbook HMCS Prince Robert].

They soon realized that whatever the perils of the North Atlantic, and my Dad would often say, nothing compared with the sudden gales, erratic currents, and uncharted shoals of the North Pacific. The monkey was probably the only monkey to have seen snow and didn't seem to be overly impressed with it. Of course, he wasn't alone on that one. It might have been a mystery of how he came to be on board HMCS Prince Robert, but no mystery how he left the ship. He was given away to the U.S. Marines, somewhere in the Aleutian Islands.

Some time, in late 1942, Dad was sent to Prince Rupert, northern British Columbia's Naval Shore Radio Station, and remained there for approximately six months. During the war years, Naval Communications

Telegraphist either manned ships or manned naval radio stations. He was then sent to the Canadian Naval Communications School in St. Hyacinth, Quebec, for three months of training, to become a Leading Telegraphist, *same as Petty Officer 2nd class today*, for the British Communications Systems. At this time, the Canadian Navy didn't have their-own Communications Systems. Upon completion of this training and in the early fall of 1943, he got his orders back to sea, on HMCS Timmons Corvette, as a Leading Telegraphist.

The design adopted of these vessels was based upon a whale-catcher built in a port, in Middlesbrough UK, northeast of England, and one of the United Kingdom's three largest ports. One hundred and forty-five of these *Flower-Class* Corvettes were built in the UK and they, led by a few non-fleet destroyers, formed the bulk of the escorting warships, which fought in the Battle of the Atlantic. These Flower-Class Corvette convoy escort vessels were capable of being built quickly, of mounting, the then, available anti-submarine equipment, surviving the heavy seas around the British Isles, and of matching U-Boat speeds. HMCS Timmons was one of 80 Canadian Flower-Class Corvette's.

Their short length and shallow draught made them uncomfortable ships to live in, even when they were modified after the fall of France, to enable them to counter the extended range of the German Wolf Packs.

Transatlantic convoy duty tended to exhaust all who sailed in them. Service aboard was tedious, wearying, and debilitating for long periods, either because of the need for constant vigilance in the face of those twin dangers, the sea and the enemy, or because of, in the North Atlantic at least, the cold. Dad never talked about his wartime experiences until later years, he believed, what you don't experience, you can't understand.

There were two types of corvettes – short fo'c's'le and extended fo'c's'le. Life in the cramped quarters of a rolling ship held few comforts. Officers lived "aft", Chief and Petty Officers Mid-ship – and crew fo'c's'le. Officers had stewards to look after them – meals – general housekeeping duties, while Chief and Petty Officers usually had a Messman. Remainder of crew looked after themselves. Living facilities were referred to as a Mess, each having two to three tables – lockers [clothes etc.] were on one side of each table, and a bench on the other. Duty *cook-of-the-mess* had to draw meals from the galley, scrub the deck, etc. Short fo'c's'le corvettes meant that the cook of the mess had to go out on the upper deck to the galley to draw the meal, foul weather or not . . . so you can only imagine the salt water he had to travel through. All crewmembers, except officers, slept in hammocks, which had to be lashed up and stowed prior to breakfast. Upper deck personnel were all those who had to work on the main deck and above, while the lower deck was primarily engine room personnel. Washrooms were generally fitted with three sinks and three toilets. Water was rationed and was turned on for twenty-minute intervals two or three times daily – doing laundry in a bucket or often not able to change clothes for days. Electric razors were not allowed. Winter clothing was at a premium. Signalmen had one sheepskin coat and it was turned over upon being relieved; during rough trips it was seldom dry. *The crew was not fitted with proper winter clothing until the later part of the war.* Clocks were put ahead during daylight hours and set back during the night watches. No corvettes were fitted with stabilizers, a device to keep the ship from rolling.

Home-leaves were possible, only when the ship was refitting or cleaning boilers, but local leave was liberally granted on both sides of the ocean, at the end of convoy duties.

On April 15, 1945, just three weeks before the end of the Second World War, HMCS Timmons was docked at a Halifax jetty. Dad was able to take an early evening shore leave, to visit with his mother, before going to see a movie at a local Halifax theatre. As he was leaving the movie theatre and walking back towards the ship, he met up with a friend that was a sailor on HMCS Esquimalt. They spent some time chatting together at a little Halifax café, before returning to their respective ships.

In the following early morning hours, on April 16, 1945, HMCS Esquimalt and its sister ship, HMCS Sarnia, both left Halifax Harbour to search for German U-boats. HMCS Esquimalt was a diesel-powered Bangor-class minesweeper, but operated primarily as an anti-submarine escort. HMCS Esquimalt went over to the east side, while HMCS Sarnia went over to the west. In the morning rendezvous, both ships agreed to meet at 0800 hours, off Chebucto Head, at Buoy C.

German U-boats, although out-numbered and out-classed by this stage of the war, fought to the end. The days when they had aggressively hunted in Wolf Packs on the surface had long since passed. Now they operated singly and stayed submerged. The loss of German bases in France prevented U-boats from operating much farther a field than the east coast of North America.

U-boat 190 had sailed from Norway on February 21, 1945, bound for the coast of Nova Scotia, under the command of 25-year old, Lieutenant Hans-Edwin Reith. It was his second cruise in command. U-190 travelled, submerged, to evade detection by radar or aircraft, using the snorkel to breathe. Reith intended to operate in the approaches to Halifax, where other snorkel-boats had met with success. Just a few months earlier, U-806 had sunk HMCS Clayoquot and escaped undetected, in spite of a determined search. Poor sonar conditions off Halifax made the detection of submerged or bottomed U-boats difficult, at the best of times.

U-190 arrived off Nova Scotia in early April 1945 and sighted two merchant ships on April 12, 1945. But, their torpedoes missed both vessels, which then disappeared from view. Reith moved in close to Halifax, during the night of April 15, 1945, in search of targets.

Towards dawn, Lieutenant John Smart, the Watch Officer and Royal Canadian Navy Volunteer Reservist [RCNVR], ordered the depth charge crews to their stations without sounding general action stations. The sea was calm, with a long, low swell, and visibility was good in the morning sunrise. There was no need for radar. Halifax East Light Vessel and the shoreline were clearly visible. All eyes on the bridge were directed toward the vicinity of the stationary light ship, about 4.8 kilometres away. The depth charge crews stood down from the alert at 0610 hours and the watch was relieved.

Nearby, U-190 heard the pinging sound of HMCS Esquimalt's sonar, which had failed to make contact. Below the surface, the Germans listened intently, as HMCS Esquimalt circled above at 10 knots and passed overhead two or three times. When no attack followed, Reith took U-190 up to periscope depth for a quick look around. He observed the warship through the periscope at a range of between 1,000 and 2,000 metres. HMCS Esquimalt suddenly turned towards him and closed rapidly. Reith ordered the fire of an acoustic homing torpedo from a stern tube. HMCS Esquimalt carried an anti-homing torpedo decoy, known as CAT gear, but was not streaming it. Nor was the minesweeper zigzagging.

At 0630 hours, the German U-190's torpedo struck HMCS Esquimalt. It ripped a gaping hole in the starboard quarter and that's where the depth charges were stored, blowing up the stern of the ship. The explosion knocked out the power instantly, preventing the radio room from sending a distress signal. HMCS Esquimalt listed heavily to starboard, threatening to sink at any moment and the emergency lighting failed.

Reith had watched his victim sink through the periscope and then put some distance between him and the position of the sinking. He moved into shallower water, reasoning that Canadian forces would expect him to move out to deeper water to escape.

Commanding Officer, Robert Cunningham MacMillan emerged from below and made his way to the bridge, where he gave the order to abandon ship. The explosion had stunned the signalman and no one else had the presence of mind to fire flares. The heavy list to starboard pushed the lifeboat under water before the crew could release it from the davits. They succeeded in getting four carley floats cleared off the ship and plunged into the icy water after them.

Some of the crew were trapped in the wreckage of the ship, but most of the crew made it into the water alive. HMCS Esquimalt sank stern first, less than four minutes after she had been torpedoed.

The survivors huddled together, 14 or 15 to a carley float. Many of them were clad lightly and only those who had been on watch were wearing their protective weather suits. An aircraft flew overhead ten minutes later and sighted the carley floats, but thought they were fishing boats, and made no report. The sun rose higher in the sky, shining brightly. At first, the men sang to keep their spirits up; later MacMillan led them in prayer. Gradually, many would succumb to the cold water.

The Port War Signal Station had contacted HMCS Esquimalt at 0627 hours, a few minutes before the torpedoing. The station could not raise her on the radio at 0741 hours, but did not suspect anything was amiss and the changing of the watch delayed further action. HMCS Esquimalt did not appear at the rendezvous, off Chebucto Head, at 0800 hours, and the forenoon watch operator didn't try again until 0901 hours. The failure to raise the ship was noted and passed up the line without apparently, any sense of urgency. Two minesweepers, on their daily sweep, closed to within 3.2 kilometres at 0930 hours, but moved on without seeing the survivors or hearing their desperate calls for help. HMCS Sarnia radioed her absence at 0950 hours to shore authorities.

Lieutenant Robert Douty, RCNVR, the Commanding Officer of HMCS Sarnia, then set about looking for the missing escort when Sarnia made sonar contact at 1000 hours, about 15.3 kilometres west of the position where HMCS Esquimalt sank. He now suspected that HMCS Esquimalt had been torpedoed and reported the contact to shore, but his first duty was to counter-attack, not search for survivors. HMCS Sarnia carried out two depth charge attacks on the contact, without effect. The Germans heard the explosions of the depth charges in the distance, too far away to cause any damage to the U-boat. Douty lost sonar contact after the second attack and did not regain it during a brief search. At 1125 hours, he gave up the hunt and went to search for his missing consort.

One carley float had started out with 13 men, but they were slowly dying, one by one, from exposure, until only six were left. The six survivors paddled their carley float towards the Halifax East Light Vessel, waving a white shirt. They had closed the distance to a half-mile, when the light ship and HMCS Sarnia noticed them. A boat from the light ship picked them up and they directed HMCS Sarnia to the position of the other carley floats.

By now, the shore establishment in Halifax had finally come to life and realized that HMCS Esquimalt was missing. An aircraft, sent out to search, sighted the other carley floats and flashed their location by signal lamp to HMCS Sarnia. Douty and his crew came upon the survivors at 1230 hours; six hours after HMCS Esquimalt had been hit. He lowered the whaler to pick up the men from one raft, while he steamed toward the others. The minesweeper's crew climbed down the scramble nets to pull the nearly frozen to death and exhausted survivors from the icy water.

HMCS Sarnia rescued 21 men and recovered the bodies of 16 others. The survivors were revived with rum aboard HMCS Sarnia and taken to the RCN hospital in Halifax, as were the six men rescued on the Halifax East Light Vessel. Most of the men suffered swollen legs from immersion; few could walk. In total, 27 men survived and 44 perished. Men either died from being blown up on deck, were trapped in the ship as it sunk or died of exhaustion, and exposure, while waiting six hours to be rescued in the frigid Atlantic [http://www.familyheritage.ca/Articles/esquimalt1.html. Robert C. Fisher, 1997 – Within Sight of Shore: The Sinking of the HMCS Esquimalt, 16 April 1945].

Dad's friend that he had met up with the night before was one of the men trapped in the ship as it sunk. War certainly can bring a lot of grief and death. In a blink of an eye, it can be all over.

When the war with Germany was over, attention-focused on Japan. Some Royal Canadian Navy ships were deployed with the British Pacific Fleet, joining the many Canadian personnel already serving with the Royal Navy in the Pacific War. The war in the Pacific was expected to culminate with a massive invasion of Japan itself and this would need a different navy than that required in the Atlantic. Many Volunteer Reservists, however, were heading home. Only those who volunteered to go to the Pacific went, including RCN permanent personnel. Ottawa expanded the Royal Canadian Navy's capabilities beyond its anti-submarine orientation. At this time, Dad had been transferred from HMCS Timmons to a Russian minesweeper, as a liaison, helping it to navigate through other Canadian waters. The Canadian Government had been building wooden minesweepers to help the Russians during the end of the Second World War.

Dad had volunteered to go to the Pacific, but, before he could go, he had to go back to the Naval Communications School in St. Hyacinth, Quebec to learn the codes of the American Communication Systems. All Telegraphists needed to know the American Communication codes, for communication purposes in the Pacific.

Britain was nearly bankrupt after the five and a half years of war, and was looking to shrink its military somewhat, especially since the United States was now the dominant power in the Pacific. With this in mind, the Royal Canadian Navy and the Royal Australian and New Zealand Navies were to receive many ships considered surplus to the British Royal Navy's needs, with the end goal being a powerful Commonwealth fleet of Australian, British, Canadian, and New Zealand ships alongside the United States Navy.

However, the war in the Pacific ended before any of these plans came to fruition. Japan's will to fight evaporated with the dropping of the nuclear bombs on Hiroshima and Nagasaki.

The return of HMCS Prince Robert and the Empress of Australia entered the Port of Kowloon on August 31, 1945. The crews were on the alert for they had learned that the garrison was completely in the dark about the Japanese surrender. The men of HMCS Prince Robert quickly liberated the 1,500 Canadian and Allied prisoners in Sham Shui Po Camp, which was abandoned by it guards. They also had to maintain order in Kowloon, where Chinese pillagers were taking advantage of the chaos. No serious incidents were reported, other than a few warning shots. In the days following, a group of sailors, commanded by PO2 Paul-Henri Bouchard, seized the Commanding Officer of the Sham Shui Po Camp. Col. Tokunaga was taken aboard a launch to the Port of Kowloon where, flanked by his officers, he simply gave himself up. Japanese soldiers were captured without incident by Canadian sailors, who proceeded with a weapon in one hand and an English-Japanese lexicon on the other. The Japanese garrison did not officially surrender until September 16, 1945, but it did so, fortunately, without a fight.

Admiral Cecil Harcourt received the surrender from Vice-Admiral Fujita and Major General Tanaka. Later, Fujita and Tanaka were sentenced to 20 years imprisonment for war crimes. The Commanding Officer of HMCS Prince Robert, Captain Wallace Creery, represented Canada at the ceremony. That very night, the event was marked by a gigantic fireworks display. The war was really over!

The former Canadian prisoners were welcomed aboard HMCS Prince Robert and HMAS Empress, along with half a score of Roman Catholic Church missionaries, who had also been held captive by the Japanese.

After trading in their rags for new uniforms, they headed for Canada with great relief. On the voyage home, the crew quickly fraternized with their infantry comrades, who had been through a horrific ordeal. On board, the soldiers, who were nothing but skin and bones, were only thinking about filling their stomachs. Despite orders and despite the risk the ex-prisoners took, by stuffing themselves, the sailors let them eat their fill. Although, many Canadian soldiers did not get off without numerous vomiting episodes, none had his life endangered by eating so much rich and wholesome food. After a stop in Manila, the ships reached Esquimalt, B.C. The American warship USS Wisconsin meanwhile had repatriated the Canadian prisoners from Yokohama and Niigata.

Hundreds of families gathered together to welcome the ex-prisoners home. Many of their family members had been worried sick, for they had not received any news since December 1941. As though they had not suffered enough already, the soldiers then had the painful task of informing many families that the one they were waiting for would not be coming back. Thus, one of the first missions of HMCS Prince Robert had been to carry these fighters to hell and now, by an ironic twist of fate, its last mission was to bring back the survivors who, in the course of this ordeal, had discovered that greatness and the low of the human soul [http://www.airmuseum.ca/prstory04.html—Hong Kong 1941—Prince Robert Story, Hillman WW II Scrapbook HMCS Prince Robert].

Dad got his new orders and was sent to HMCS Miramichi, a Bangor-Class Minesweeper. Its small size gave it poor sea handling abilities, very wet, worse even than the Flower-Class Corvettes in a high sea state. The diesel-engine versions were considered to have poorer handling characteristics than the slow-speed reciprocating-engine versions. The shallow draft made it unstable and its short hull tended to bury the bow when operating in a head sea. Over 90 enlisted sailors and six officers were often crowded, crammed into the vessel, which was originally intended for only a total of 40 officers and sailors.

The expected mine threat in home waters never materialized and these ships were instead used primarily as coastal anti-submarine escorts, and received the appropriate weaponry. In general, the armament fitted, varied from ship to ship, based on what was available at the time.

A number of these ships had been transferred to the United Kingdom to sweep the approaches to Normandy on D-Day and their armament was altered for this purpose. Very few of these ships saw post-war service with the Canadian Navy, although several were sold to foreign navies. Upon returning to his homeport in Halifax, Dad was stationed at the Albro Lake Naval Radio Station, as a Chief Petty Officer Telegraphist 1st Class.

By the outbreak of war in September 1939, the Royal Canadian Navy only had six destroyers and a handful of smaller ships. By the end of the Battle of the Atlantic, the Royal Canadian Navy was the primary navy in the northwest sector of the Atlantic Ocean and was responsible for the safe escort of innumerable convoys, and the destruction of many German U-boats. Similarly, a massive building program, for a nation of only 11 million, saw newer and faster frigates, the Canadian Flower-Class Corvettes, such as HMCS Timmons, gave way, in the Atlantic, to the newer *Castle-Class* Corvettes, and other escort vessels built in shipyards on both coasts, and on the Great Lakes. Following the end of the Second World War and the War in the Pacific, the Canadian Royal Navy was the third-largest navy in the world, behind the United States, and the United Kingdom.

After five and half years of violence, Germany had paid the price for starting the war, as they lay virtually destroyed. They had won early battles, but, in the end, the Second World War had been a disaster for Germany. The nightmare Hitler had unleashed was over . . .

Chapter Three

Dad was able to track down his sister Millie after the war, with help from Uncle Norman Merritt. Uncle Norman was their mother Hazel's baby brother, who lived alone in the old family home, in Smith's Cove, Digby County, Nova Scotia. A man, usually of very few words, but as a youngster, my Dad recalls the many good times he had spent with his Uncle Norman on his fishing boat or the times they sat around the kitchen table, playing a game of cribbage, and Dad getting soundly trounced.

Uncle Norman had been the one who told Hazel, Bruce and Millie that their father, Wilfred Sulis, was still alive.

During the war, Millie had joined the Air Force; eventually marrying a guy named Fred, and was living in Trenton Ontario, raising their three children, Teddy, John, and Janet. Millie had also been in the process of trying to build a relationship with their father Wilfred and his second wife Alma.

Having his sister Millie's address, Dad was able to write a letter, initiating contact. Millie and Dad kept writing back and forth until her death in the late 1990's. Uncle Bruce passed away unexpectedly in 1979.

Jean, my Mom, was from Saint John, New Brunswick. In 1947, at age 18, she was offered a summer relief job in Halifax as a Teletype Operator for Canadian Pacific Telegraph. This would be the first time Mom was away from home. Her stepmother travelled with her by train to Halifax, making sure she had a decent place to live and once settled, knowing she would be okay, she returned home. Mom was able to board with a private family and enjoyed walking through the Halifax Public Gardens each day, on her way to work.

There was a communication line between CP and the Albro Lake Naval Radio Station in North Dartmouth. When fellow co-workers planned a summer BBQ, inviting several known Albro Lake sailors, Sally Standfield invited Mom too. This is how she met Dad, who was stationed at Albro Lake. Nothing really came-about from this outing, however, Mom returned to Saint John once the summer vacations were over. Upon returning to New Brunswick, Mom took a job in the office of a furniture company for the winter, and in the spring, she was called back to Halifax and told that this may lead into a permanent position. The pay was very good!

The same day Mom started work, she was called to Albro Lake line that someone wanted to speak to her. It was Dad, inviting her to a hockey banquet. He didn't even know she had not been in Halifax the past several months. The day of the banquet, Dad called for Mom, and both thought they were the *cats' meows*. Dad had a new suit, topcoat, and hat, and Mom had purchased a new dress, and matching shoes at D'Allairds in Saint John, just before leaving for Halifax.

Dad was always punctual for any dates they went on after that night. In fact, Mom remembers the time he turned up on her doorstep an hour earlier than expected for one of their dates. Mom answered the door with curlers in her hair. She was mortified! They wed July 20, 1949.

The long awaited link between Halifax and Dartmouth, the Angus L. MacDonald Bridge, one of Canada's longest suspension bridges, was opened in 1955, ushering in an unprecedented increase in suburban development. The Naval Radio Station was renamed NRS Albro Lake in 1956. It served under the name until communication conditions deteriorated, due to the rapid growth in the town and suburbs by industrial and housing expansions, creating problems for receiving radio signals at Albro Lake.

Interference increased to the point where decreased capability and performance deemed it necessary for a replacement station. Dartmouth annexed several of its suburban areas and became a city in 1961, the year I was born.

The Navy decided to relocate the Albro Lake Naval Radio Station 88 Kilometres southwest of Halifax, in the Blanford Peninsula, a relatively isolated area, free of man-made interference. Over 4,000 acres of land were purchased for the new site.

Similar to the Albro Lake area, the new property embraced dense woodland, several lakes, and was adjacent to a bird sanctuary. Canadian Forces Station Mill Cove offered the best solution and once completed was commissioned in late 1967.

When all communications facilities were transferred from Albro Lake to Mill Cove, the Albro Lake Radio Station was closed in mid 1968. A second traffic crossing, the A. Murray MacKay Bridge, was opened in 1970 and the Highway 111 Circumferential expressway was built around this city of lakes.

Military brats or military dependents usually grow up and experience a different world compared to their civilian counterparts. Being a child raised in today's society is tough, but being a child raised back then, in a military family, was equally as tough, if not perhaps, somewhat tougher. When a parent serves in the military, it isn't just a job, it is a lifestyle, where a parent's devotion to military duty dictates the life of the family, and has a direct influence on the lives of their children.

My brothers knew first hand what being military brats were all about. Due to our father either being drafted or called to serve overseas, on several different occasions or being stationed elsewhere on military land bases, Mom, and the boys had to pull-up stakes and move. Things were perhaps more regimented or strict for my brothers. Luckily, being the baby of the family, a distant third in birthing order, which Dad was home for, I didn't have to adjust to the constant change of different schools, loss of friendships or anything else relating to military nomadic lifestyle, such as my brothers had experienced for a time.

I was the apple of my father's eye, the only girl, his little girl, and the spoiled one. Perhaps things weren't so regimented or strict when he was home, like they had been for my older brothers.

As an Operations Officer, at the time of the Albro Lake Naval Radio Station closure, Dad chose not to take the transfer to the new station at Mill Cove. Our family moved from the Albro Lake PMQs into a bungalow across the street from the neighbouring homes that encircled Little Albro

Lake. He accepted his orders back to sea, on HMCS Bonaventure, also known as the *Bonnie*.

Dad had been offered a civilian job, one of the reasons he had decided to retire from the navy, in 1970, as a lieutenant. But, due to political influence, the job didn't materialize. It was very disappointing. However, as fate would have it, he would become an Oceanographic Technician for the next 17 years at one of the world's leading Oceanography Research Institutes, the Bedford Institute of Oceanography.

> *Located on the shores of the Bedford Basin in Dartmouth, not far from the Bedford Basin Magazine Ammunition Depot, BIO was established in 1962 by the Canadian Federal Government. Following the Second World War, Canada recognized that it needed dedicated multi-disciplinary oceanographic research institutes and vessels to address issues such as sovereignty, defence, environmental protection, and fisheries.*
>
> *In the 1970's, the Institute considerably expanded its study of the ocean ecosystems and their resources – a trend that has continued to this day, making it Canada's largest centre for ocean research.*

~

In 1972, Mom took a challenging job at the same institute. She was one of five ladies who were trained by the Micro-Paleontologists to recognize and pick all the foraminifera from the core samples prepared for picking, in search of offshore oil. It was tedious work, with powerful microscopes, working with them for five hours per day. I would go to a neighbour for lunch and my mother would be home when I returned from school in the afternoon.

The main floor of our new bungalow consisted of three bedrooms, a full bath, kitchen, and a living room with a bay window. Looking out from the kitchen to the back of the house was a deck extending from side to side. It was great for lounging, sunbathing or BBQs. A portion of the deck and opposite end to the kitchen had an overhang extension. It was enclosed with Plexiglas siding, shading the flowerbed beneath, and added protection from those incumbent days of precipitation.

The ocean waters made the climate one that is moderated by warm moist air in winter and cool sea breezes on hot summer days. Winter storms brought snow changing to rain, with a mixture of freezing precipitation during the change over. Foggy days were the norm in spring. There were no barriers to stop wind, waves and weather from lashing the shoreline when ocean storms were in the vicinity. The ocean's store of summer warmth was enough to make autumn one of our finest seasons.

Over time, Dad had turned our ugly concrete basement floor into an attractive, comfortable surface, with sub-basement flooring and shaggy carpets, which were the in-thing at the time. To complete the basement renovations, he had added-on a bedroom and private, half-bath, which were separate from the laundry facilities, and his workbench area. Dad loved to fiddle around with his woodworking; he could build just about anything.

My brothers were 11 and 10 years older. They were never unkind to me, they just ignored me a great deal of the time, as older brothers would I suppose. But, being the baby of the family, I had to be patient and wait in pecking order for the downstairs, which I quickly laid claim to once they both left the roost for university. What more could a young girl ask for. My parents then converted my upstairs bedroom into a dining room, with an opening adjacent to the kitchen, and a patio door that led out onto the deck. The kitchen was also enlarged with a solarium that extended the kitchen out onto the deck.

From an early age I wasn't into dolls or anything that girls liked. I had quite the collection of Tonka trucks, dinkies, and GI Joe's, a full-fledged tomboy. The boys in the neighbourhood would come a-callin for me to come out and play. A gravel street next to our house was a great place to play with my collection, the dirtier or muddier I got, the better.

Remembering one day, as I was outside playing, Dad had returned home from being overseas. He had a present for me. I was so excited to think I was going to get a new toy to add to my collection. I quickly tore into the wrapping paper to get to the present, wanting to take it out to show the boys, who were still playing.

When opened, I stood holding onto a doll. Looking rather bewildered and perplexed, I looked it over, asking what I was to do with the doll. I couldn't take this out to play with, what would I do with a doll?

"Liz, this is something that any little girl would love to have," exclaimed my mother. I pleaded. "Then give it to one of them." Mom led me to the front door step.

"Here, sit there and play with your doll. We want you to try and play with the doll, Elizabeth."

She went back inside, at first peeking out occasionally, to see how I was doing, I suppose. I sat for sometime, pondering what to do.

Good thing the boys couldn't see me now. An overhang sheltered the front steps of the house, with the living room and bay window jetting out on the right side, blocking from view the boys who were still in the street playing with my toys.

I sat on the doorstep looking around, hearing, but not seeing the boys. I didn't want anyone to see me.

I began to dismantle the doll, pulling the legs and arms off frantically, then the head, but keeping the sleeveless cotton dress the doll was wearing intact on the body, along with the matching hair accessories and shoes. The dress had pink flowers and a pink satin ribbon sash that was tied in the back.

To the left and below the doorstep was my Mom's flowerbed. It was made of brick with an arrangement of geraniums, adding color to the front of the house. I took the pieces of the doll, burying each piece as deep as I could, in different spots. Once I rid myself from the dirt, I ran inside the house, giving a performance of a lifetime.

With crocodile tears, I told my parents that a couple of bullies walked by, saw me playing with the doll and stole it out of my hands, and ran off down the street. It wasn't until years later when my mother would discover what had actually happened to that doll.

Chapter Four

Everyone was still enjoying being off from school due to the Holidays. It was a bone-chilling, windy, wintry day, somewhere between Christmas and New Year's 1973. The snow, which fell heavily the night before, left a crisp, white blanket across the frozen expanse of Little Albro Lake. According to the meteorologist, this cold snap we were experiencing wasn't about to let up anytime soon. The weather wasn't about to deter any of us from donning our skates for an innocent game of hockey, on one of nature's own outdoor skating rinks.

Friends and acquaintances from school or the surrounding neighbourhood gathered on the lake to have fun, wanting to play hockey. Coin tosses decided on the two-team captains. Back and forth, the two captains took their turns, methodically choosing each team member, keeping in mind both sides had to be equally divvied-up with girls. Once that was done, the shovelling began.

Everyone participated in the clearing off of an arduous, large patch of snow. When the game actually started, sounds of laughter and cheers soon filled the air. The guys couldn't resist chuckling at the sight of the girl's who were rather clumsy and desperately trying to remain upright, let alone skate. It didn't take much for the guys to bowl them over. Yes, those were the days when everything was innocent fun.

Some sparks were flying that winter's day. They do say that opposites do attract. If there were any sparks flying, they were probably coming from me. Not the opposites attract kind of sparks, more like the ready-to-rumble type of sparks.

Geoffrey O'Donnell was on the opposing team. My cloud of suspicion grew as the game proceeded that somehow he strategically planned it this way. Every time I had the puck, he was bound and determined to pick me up and dump me in the snow bank. So much for body checking or stick handling to simply get the puck away from me.

He was persistent, holding obstinately to a purpose and unyielding. Of course we didn't have any referees. But what was his purpose? Or why was he so *hell* bent in trying to get my attention and keep me distracted? Increasingly and annoyingly against my disapproval, his actions were embarrassing me.

My frustration and competitiveness were beginning to shine through. Good thing there were no referees or we both would have probably spent most of the time in the penalty box, if for any reason, delay of game.

My girlfriends kept teasing me, taunting me that he was interested in me. I figured it was amusing to them and they were all getting their jollies. I told them they were all crazy, chalking it up to me being a pretty good female hockey player. At least I could skate. The guys must not have wanted me to out-shine them. It was a conspiracy on ice and this meant war.

I usually thrived on the camaraderie and rivalry, always trying to be a good sport if my team lost. If you had fun while playing your best that was the important thing. That's what Dad kept trying to tell me.

However, I was becoming rather perplexed from this so-called innocent game of hockey. Having to take the time to brush off the snow Geoff kept dumping me in. It couldn't mean he was actually interested in me, could it?

After the game, the girls and I were changing our footwear, while sitting on one of the wharves that jetted out from the shore of Little Albro. Geoff came over and plunked himself down next to me, trying to strike up a conversation, which for the most part ended up being one-sided.

I was still brewing over what he did to me during the game and was unsure how to take him seriously. He sure was obstinate to say the least. But then, much to my surprise, he began to stumble over his words when he tried to ask me if I would like to hangout. It was the first sign of him acting coy, lacking the confidence he portrayed earlier.

That's how I remembered it anyway and asking someone to hangout was like asking someone out on a date, of sorts. Back then, hanging out as buddies was the thing to do. Who had money, unless one counted their allowance their parents gave them or perhaps the money one earned from the newspaper route they might have had.

Geoff's words of a contrite apology, dumping me in the snow bank were more of a confession at his attempt of literally wanting to sweep me off my feet. But, what was meant to be humorous didn't seem that way to me.

I was wrong, my friends were right. He was definitely interested in me. He had made his true intentions known. There was no turning back now. Anticipating an immediate rejection, it came as a shock to him and everyone else around me, when I had said yes. I hadn't even flinched, a rather subdued yes perhaps, but it was a yes.

Good Lord! I had no real explanation or answer as to why I had said yes, next to a momentary touch of lunacy perhaps. There had to have been some sort of attraction or misguided impulse that compelled me to say yes.

Gazing at me with a puzzled look and his mouth drooped open, I quickly gave him a stern, but witty reply.

"Close your mouth, Geoff. You're not going to catch any flies at this time of the year, and no more stunts like the one you pulled earlier!"

Geoff and I had known of each other since the first grade and our older brothers played hockey together. Other than that, we never really had any other connection, until that day on the lake.

It didn't take much time for our relationship to blossom. Changes were taking place in both of us.

~

At first, being very callow or naïve, coupled with unbridled curiosity, I wasn't quite sure what to make of it or what to do. Neither of us had experienced this sort of thing before, but we were going to explore it together.

Something magical happened that hurled us both outside the realm of guilt or sin, good or evil, above morality. I never saw it clearly. Something about him put my hormones in a dither. We threw ourselves upon the experience, instead of waiting for it to happen.

I couldn't explain or understand the forces that drove me to Geoffrey. I was predisposed to love him, too focused, and wrought up to notice the world around me. True love, something wonderful, something morally good.

He seemed to have caught on quickly, which most guys probably did. I had never been with a guy in this way before. It was exhilarating for me just to be around him.

My need for him intensified when he held me close and made love to me. I closed my eyes the moment I surrendered to him, letting love 'be blind, innocent and tenderly true.

Teasing my lips with his and the sensitive lobe of my ear caused me to quiver with delight.

We belonged to each other completely. He gave love endlessly. Our lovemaking was becoming a habit this girl could get used to.

Geoff would curl himself around me; his front to my back, and hold me in his arms as we rested. Rather than feeling imprisoned, I felt his protective strength pleasing, safe, and secure in the world we were creating for ourselves. Behind my closed eyelids, dreamy thoughts raced through my mind.

When I opened my eyes, we laid still joined. I was in the same position facing away from him, my hands next to my face on my pillow. He was still snuggled up next to me with a leg and arm draped over me. I could have stayed like this forever. I didn't want to get up, but Geoff had other plans.

I turned my head and caught Geoff smiling at me. He stroked my arm and laid a soft kiss on my shoulder as he threw back the bed sheets, and jumped to his feet.

"How about a shower, Liz?"

I was too comfortable and didn't really want to get up yet. I groaned, reaching for the blankets and as I pulled them back up over myself, I suggested for him to go take a cold shower.

That wasn't quite what Geoff had on his mind at that particular moment. He pulled the sheets off me again, extending his hands, motioning for me to get up.

When he helped me to my feet, he held on to my hands making sure I wouldn't crawl back into bed. As he held my hands, I protested following him into the shower.

It didn't take long for me to wake up to my senses. The shower was a time for leisurely explorations. I couldn't get enough of his kisses.

Geoff and I did pretty much everything together as time passed, taking time whenever we could, just to be alone. He had quite a vivid imagination. Many of our risqué rendezvous were just that, risqué, but romantic, unique, and unforgettable.

Our sensuous summer trysts, making love out-doors at our secret hideaway, a secluded part of Big Albro Lake, was convenient when it came to skinny dipping. He personally knew how I loved the water and definitely knew how to sweep this girl off her feet. We didn't care; we just wanted to be together.

Both of us had many friends and hung around different crowds at times, due to different curricular activities, and sports we participated in during the school year. We went to different junior high schools. He had his friends and I had mine, but we also had friends we knew together, and chummed around with.

CHAPTER FIVE

Mom and Dad were in the midst of preparing for the move into my brother James, and his wife Bridgette's recently built home on Lake Banook. Not the ideal time of the year to move perhaps, it could snow anytime; it was nearing the end of November 1990. Mom and Dad's house went on the market in July, but the real estate market was soft, however, after a few open houses the house had eventually sold.

Banook means 'First Lake' in the Mi'kmaq dialect. Mi'kmaq Indians were the first to navigate Lake Banook and the Dartmouth lake system as they traveled across the province. In 1828, officers of the British army played the first ice hockey game in Canada on Lake Banook, and a seaplane carrying the first airmail shipment from Ottawa to Halifax landed on the lake in 1929.

Lake Banook hosted hundreds of local regional regattas since the late 1800's and boasts a world-class paddling course where regattas are held each weekend in July and August, ranking it as one of the best lakes in the world for paddling competitions. It hosted national and international events for the past 20 years, such as the World Junior Canoe Championships in 1989; the first time the event was held outside Europe. My brother James had become a prominent paddler.

James, Bridgette, and their two boys, Troy and Trevor, had only been living in the house for a year before James took a transfer to Ontario with the company he was working for. They didn't want to sell the house, in the hopes of returning someday to retire. Knowing full well, if they were to sell the house now, the chances of them ever getting to buy it back when they wanted it, would be highly improbable. So, they struck a deal with our parents for them to sell their house and move into their home.

Besides, this new house wouldn't have been as difficult to maintain as the older house. Saying that, any home usually doesn't go without needing some sort of up-keep, repairs, maintenance, or perhaps renovations.

During the process of the selling of our parent's home, the house inspector commented that builders today sure don't make houses like they use to. Alluding to the fact that houses built 30 years ago were well built and structurally sturdier. Their home was one of those and it was well maintained. It would be a great starter home for any young couple. Location was a great selling feature too. The house was close to schools and all other amenities. The only thing the inspector suggested, for safety reasons, was for a handrail to be added to the stairwell leading downstairs.

Thinking back to the time I had the accident on the stairs, Dad took the inspector's advice and installed one. Not that a handrail would have prevented me from falling or have helped me out any, at the time of my accident.

Prior to Dad completing the renovations to the basement, I had taken quite a nasty tumble. I did it in style too—head first, from the top of the stairs to the concrete floors below.

It happened in the midst of their Silver Wedding Anniversary celebrations in 1974. I received scrapes, bruising, and some strained muscles, along with a grotesque lump that protruded from the left side of my forehead. The doctor referred to it as a goose egg. More like the actual size of an ostrich egg. All I wanted to do was bury my head to avoid any onlooker's startled stare. To make matters worse, my brother James couldn't resist from poking fun.

"Sis, you're like a Timex watch. You take a good beating, but you keep on ticking."

Without my brother realizing it, there was some irony to that particular expression of wit he had used. To me, it had some element of a hidden truth.

After years of engaging in academic pursuits and achievements, Donny became a National Defence Research Scientist for the Federal Government in a Defence lab here in Dartmouth. Less than two years prior to James and Bridgette's move, Donny accepted a new position, a promotion, which meant transferring to the National Defence Lab in Ottawa.

Donny, his wife Carol, daughter Melissa and their two boys, David and Michael, were now well adjusted in our nation's capital. Though the summers were a lot hotter than they were accustomed to, having an air-conditioned house with an in-ground-pool in the backyard helped ease any humid and hot weather-related sufferings.

The winter temperatures are generally more frigid in Ottawa, compared to the Maritimes. As far as snow goes, that nasty white stuff is unavoidable just about anywhere you go in Canada. Those who can migrate to the south for the winter usually do, while the rest of us tough it out. There are many winter sports or activities that one could participate in, other than just shovelling snow. Yes, shovelling snow in these parts tend to be a great cardiovascular workout.

Maritimers can generally breathe a sigh of relief from not getting the many other weather-related storms or freaks of Mother Nature that cause havoc and destruction in many parts of the world. Our storms are tame, docile or mitigated for the most part. But, the great news is that we don't get any of those ugly, tropical, creepy, crawly, poisonous critters that can crawl, climb, leap, fly, swim and bite. It's nice to know that our weather isn't conducive to their liking or habitat.

As Melissa, David and Michael were able to adapt quickly to living in a new environment, going to a new school, and were able to make new friends, James and Bridgette wanted the same for their boys. The school season had recently started, so pulling Troy and Trevor out of school and away from their friends would hopefully not affect them too much.

James' company was faced with a sharp downturn in its sales growth. The same fate all companies such as his, in the electronic industry were dealing with at the time. As the saying went, "It's hard times in the Maritimes."

Most companies were laying off people in significant numbers. The obvious solution was to follow its competitors and lay off ten percent of the work force. However, top management in his company was committed to trying to avoid layoffs.

Careful advance planning would eliminate much of the need to do excess downsizing, the costs incurred by the people involved, and the company was sufficient to make this a least favored option.

A key part of his company's business strategy was based on trying to maintain a strong corporate culture, an organizational culture that was conducive to success and profits.

Most companies more often focused solely on making a short-term profit, viewed employees as disposable commodities, and created unadaptive cultures. A high turnover would have made it almost impossible to keep a consistent set of values and objectives that were followed up and down the ranks. A ten percent layoff would have severely dented this culture. Most likely, it would have plagued the company for years, impeding growth plans, and would have added to the overall personnel costs.

However, there were those who were offered, and took through attrition, adequate financial and benefit severances, and/or early retirement packages; insuring that all were provided in a way that preserved their dignity.

The company took this responsibility very seriously. Partially out of a humanitarian concern, wanting to do their best to avoid both the human resources lost and the human costs associated with layoffs. And partially to avoid censure from the community, in which they operated, and to help preserve the loyalty of those who remained.

Through the company's restructuring and knowing that his days as regional manager were numbered, James was not sure what to expect. His was one of the positions that the company was considering to flatten from their hierarchy. It was to his great surprise when he was offered a promotion, to be President and General Manager of the local office.

After some consideration, discussion with his wife Bridgette, weighing all the pros and cons, and the added stress and headaches associated with this type of position, he decided to decline the offer and let the chips fall where they may. The company appreciated his decision, however, they were reluctant to lose who they considered to be an invaluable employee. Another offer was made, a transfer to another office. Unfortunately, the only regional manager positions that were not on the chopping block, as such, were either in Toronto or Calgary. Bridgette didn't want to have to move for various reasons, but knew a move was inevitable, if James was to remain with Hewlet Packard. A company he liked working with and for.

They accepted the transfer to Toronto. At least James could keep the same position he held here as a regional manager. Calgary was too far away from family and friends. Bridgette, being from London, England, didn't want to live in a large city such as Toronto.

They hunted for a house, finding one in Oakville, a town on Lake Ontario in southern Ontario, part of the Greater Toronto area metropolitan community. It lays midway between Toronto, about 31 kilometres away, and Hamilton, about 20 kilometres away. James could commute back and forth to work.

It wasn't long before the moving began. One never knows or realizes just how much stuff can be collected or accumulates over the years, until one actually prepares to move. This seemed to be the case with our parents.

The company incurred many of the expenses of both moves. Once their things were transferred to their new home in Ontario, Bridgette returned to help with Mom and Dad's move to the house on Lake Banook.

Mom wanted to make sure, before handing over the keys to the new owners that the house was left immaculately clean. So, after their things were moved out, Bridgette and I helped with the cleaning.

Mom had unearthed her flowerbed and, much to her surprise, discovered the pieces of the doll that had met its fateful demise and been buried for quite sometime.

Bridgette and I were downstairs cleaning, Mom called out. "Oh Elizabeth, would you come up here for a moment please!"

As I reached the landing at the top of the stairs, I could see the pieces of the doll lying on the kitchen floor, where she had purposely placed them.

The little pink flowered cotton dress that the doll had been wearing was rather dirty, tattered and torn. I didn't recall tearing the dress, but the hair accessories and shoes were still intact and in good condition, considering the length of time it had been buried.

"So, some bullies came by and stole the doll, huh, Elizabeth?"

I tried desperately to stop from laughing, trying to keep a straight face, and thinking fast to come up with a good response.

"Where did you ever find that, Mom?" I asked, knowing full well I had been caught red-handed.

"Oh, as I was cleaning out the earth from my flowerbed, lo 'n behold . . ."

"Well, imagine that, Mom. Those bullies were something else."

I was grinning from ear to ear, giggling as I reminisced as to what I had done. It had happened so long ago, I had forgotten about it, until I saw the pieces of the doll lying on the floor.

Chapter Six

During the summer of 1974, I was very active, and learning how to canoe and kayak in the competitive amateur paddling environment at a local boat club on Lake Banook. Following in the footsteps of my brother James.

This lake provided an excellent location for recreation, as well as attractive vistas, such as hosting the Down East Old Time Fiddling Contest, which takes place in mid-July, or hosting the city's birthday celebrations, a civic holiday known as Natal Day.

City Counsellors decided to combine their sister cities birthday celebrations to help cut costs and so, on the first weekend in August, both sides of the harbour come alive with a Natal Day parade, concerts, and fireworks.

Dartmouth was founded in 1750, a year after its neighbouring sister city Halifax, and capital of the province. It was settled by Colonel Edward Cornwallis, and [2,500 others] who christened 'Halifax' in honour of Lord Halifax, President of the British Board of Trade in 1749.

Dartmouth is Nova Scotia's second-largest city and located on the eastern side of the Halifax Harbour, a tranquil, ice-free, deep saltwater harbour. It is a myriad of lakes and streams, boasting a chain of 23 lakes within its boundaries that form part of the Shubenacadie Canal, thus dubbed the 'City of Lakes.' There are five other supervised freshwater beaches located in Dartmouth.

No one had to go too far for a good time at a beach. It depended on what one wanted, fresh-water or the sea. I loved the water, revisiting the many nights Dad had to come to fish me out. I was like a fish in the water. The lakes were popular, a recreational haven.

Dartmouth has the oldest saltwater ferry system in North America. A large rowboat with a sail began service in 1752. Present day, Dartmouth's waterfront has boardwalks that lead east and west from the Dartmouth Ferry Terminal. Anyone can take a scenic ferry ride back and forth across the harbour.

When looking out toward the harbor's entrance as you cross provides excellent views of George's Island, McNab's Island and Lawlor's Island. Lawlor's Island is primarily undeveloped woodland, the protected home of deer and osprey.

The islands played a key role in the harbor's defence system for almost 200 years. Also located on the Dartmouth waterfront is the Dartmouth Events Plaza, which accommodates a variety of special events, such as the Nova Scotia Multi-cultural Festival and the first of July Canada Day celebrations.

There's plenty of living history here. Evergreen House is a restored historic residence, formerly the home of the famous Nova Scotia Folklorist, Dr. Helen Creighton. For history buffs, Evergreen House is the current site of the Dartmouth Heritage Museum, which tells the story of Dartmouth from pre-colonial times to the present.

The four bodies of water, the Atlantic Ocean, the Bay of Fundy, the Northumberland Strait, and the Gulf of St. Lawrence, surround this province's 580-kilometre-long peninsula. If it weren't for the piece of land that joins Nova Scotia with New Brunswick, Nova Scotia would be an island. The Bay of Fundy is a world-renowned natural phenomenon. The highest tides on earth fill the Bay with over 100 billion tons of seawater – waters as high as a four-storey building, attracting one of the world's greatest concentrations of whales, seabirds, and other marine life. Only hours later, you can walk on the seabed at low tide. What makes this ecological wonder so unique is that it happens twice a day, every day.

No part of the province is more than 56 kilometres from the sea. Its indented shoreline stretches 10,424 kilometres, great for the avid surfer or scuba diver too, Canada's ocean playground.

Along with my two older brothers, I had many male influences in the neighbourhood for sports, most of whom I had played with in the gravel and mud with my Tonka trucks, dinkies, and GI Joe's years before.

Dad was very active in the provincial Junior A Hockey League, eventually becoming the President of the local Dartmouth team. One could say he got the *hockey bug* when he had put a land-based naval hockey team together in the league for ships, when stationed at Albro Lake. Each year the land-based teams, Shearwater, Stadacona, and Albro Lake competed for the right to face off against the winner of the ship-based teams.

In the hockey season finale, prior to the Albro Lake Naval Radio Station closure, the covenant Naval Hockey League's championship game pitted my father's team against the members of the *Magnificent*. Dad couldn't actually remember what the final score was, but it was close, a nail-bitter, with the team of the Magnificent being victorious, and getting to claim bragging rights as the overall league champs.

During age eligibility, James and Donald, along with Geoff's older brothers, Stephen and Richard, played on our Dad's team. It was easy to get hooked on the sport, a favorite pass-time for many players and spectators.

There was a time I was considered to be a well-rounded athlete, excelling in school sports such as track and field, volleyball, ringette and softball. However, the problems that developed with my feet during fifth grade would continue, and interfere, keeping me sidelined, and in a cast a great deal of the time. But as a kid or teenager I was resilient and always managed to bounce back. Corrective surgery eventually helped to eradicate any further problems.

I remember the time Donny and I were injured while participating in the final championship game of our respective sports, lacrosse and floor ringette. Mom was attending my game, while Dad was at Donny's game.

During my game, there was a pile-up and I ended-up with a fractured left foot. Donny was in a similar scrimmage around his goaltender and the goaltender accidentally fell on his right ankle.

Shortly after my mother brought me home from the emergency, Donny was soon to follow, being helped into the house. Donny and I sat together with our legs elevated, sporting casts.

Or the time when Donny and James were playing a friendly game of flag football, no tackling, but as Donny leaped to catch the football he was accidentally flipped head-over-heels, landing on his collarbone, and dislocating it.

Mom refused to attend any further sporting events, believing she brought us bad luck. It was evident to Mom that we only received an injury when she was a spectator. Of course no one believed this to be the case. Besides, she wasn't attending Donny's lacrosse game.

It wasn't an uncommon thing for accidents and injuries to occur in the Sulis clan. Nope, not at all, next to broken bones, bruises, black eyes, cuts needing stitches, sprains or even to lose the occasional tooth or two, was a way we kept the doctors and orthodontist gainfully employed.

It wasn't funny at the time, but Donny was the one who ended up spending most of his time as a kid in the orthodontist chair, as I recall. Come to think of it, he was the one who seemed to suffer the most, plagued with injuries playing sports. Grant it, I was a close runner-up, sustaining my share of injuries too. Donny's injuries no doubt cost the most. I'm sure that's how our parents viewed it

Orthodontist didn't come cheap. Of course, most of the sports equipment that we needed didn't come without a cost either. James seemed to go somewhat unscathed. He must have had a four-leaf-clover or a horse shoe somewhere?

Anyway, one winter while Donny was playing a game of hockey on Little Albro Lake, he fell on the ice. They say he had only fallen, but it looked more like he tried to stop a puck with his mouth. Either way, he had done a great job of cracking his front tooth and having to get a gold peg put in.

The following summer, Donny was playing baseball and while at bat, he swung at the ball, it ricochet off the bat hitting the base, and bounced back up hitting him square in the mouth. Ouch! Not only did he lose the gold pegged tooth, but he had also cracked the tooth next to it, above the gum line.

It was the nature of the contact sports we loved to be apart of, the thrill, the adrenalin rush, and the challenge. Perhaps we were gluttons for punishment or accident prone, coincidental if any mishap occurred while our mother watched from the sidelines.

I had also been taking private piano lessons since I started school. Whether or not I actually practiced, Mom dug her heals in, not giving up, and carted me off to my lessons. I always remembered hearing Dad's words ringing in my ears.

"I don't know how you manage to learn to play the way you do, Elizabeth. You only practice five minutes before your mother takes you to your lesson."

I snickered. "Good teachers with lots of patience, I'm sure, Dad."

The piano actually became my solace of sorts. It empowered me to temporarily hide from my problems. I had always been told I played with emotion. Playing the piano was a way I could somehow escape and express myself in my music.

One of my private piano teachers, Mrs. Nicholson, a former neighbour, understood I only wanted to learn to play for my own enjoyment. I didn't feel any pressure, no doubt a reason I continued taking lessons, even if Mrs. Nicholson had to make deals with me to get me to play at a recital. It was the only thing I hated having to do, I laugh at it now. In order for me to play what I wanted, Mrs. Nicholson told me she wanted me to be the one to play the National Anthem and God Save the Queen, formalities. The recitals were a confidence builder, where in other areas of my life I had been starting to show signs of lacking that same degree of confidence and self-esteem I had for learning to play the piano.

I had a mentor at Senior High School. After following in Kevin Marshall's footsteps for two years, he graduated, and in my senior year, I became what seemed to be the school's primary piano player, leaving me with little or no time for playing sports.

Anticipating hearing the principle's secretary's gruff voice being piped into the classroom, over the PA system, was becoming almost a daily ritual; telling me that my presence was needed after school in the music room.

I had discovered that I loved to play the piano, I liked the sound and that other people liked it too. Playing the piano was one thing that I could learn and be good at. I was a sought after accompanist. It was as if I came to life when I played. But I was never one for taking compliments very well, as I was feeling less than adequate for others' praises. It was another avenue for me to beat up on myself.

I naturally became a very critical person of myself. Believing it to be the truth that I would never really amount to much, berating myself for a lot that went on in my life.

Sometimes, I would try to imagine my future, but I couldn't. There was a blank screen, no husband, no children, nothing. I painted a portrait of myself as a lonely, excluded outsider; the fact is I was part of the scene. If not the most popular or recognized as the most talented, friends surrounded me, and during my senior year I was kept pretty busy playing for many singers and musical ensembles.

~

Geoffrey and Michel were very close. They hung around each other, even when I was in the picture. I thought Michel was my friend, too. He appeared to be a nice guy with a French background. He was cute, a looker, and many girls vied for his attention. He could have had anyone he wanted. Just not me, I was going with his best friend.

I usually loved parties, hosting a few of our gatherings. They might have been a little risqué perhaps than they should have been. We played spin the bottle, a game called chicken, and lots of dancing to the hit tunes of the times. We were young, just having fun, but nothing ever went too far at these parties. What others did on their own was just that, on their own.

I tried to enjoy my emerging sexuality without judging it or comparing it to what other people were experiencing or what I thought I should be experiencing. But Geoff and I were living on the edge, thinking that we could handle our unbridled intimacy without anyone knowing or finding out. That was a challenge we both excelled in, becoming completely absorbed in each other.

I was totally given to passion, commitment and love. I trusted Geoff. He meant everything to me and treated me special. I had never been unfaithful, either in body or in spirit. It was easy for me to love Geoff, expressing to him just how deeply I cared for him and how much he meant to me.

He was an exceptional guy; a great part of his charm was his sharp wit and humor. Friends had us pegged to someday getting married. One could say we were the boy and girl next door. Geoff and I were happy and well suited. *There was a time I believed this all to be true.*

One night, Geoff and I were with another couple, friends of ours—Sara and Jason. We were taking it easy and watching a movie. I excused myself and went to the washroom. As I was coming out, Geoff was there; he took me by the hand, led me back into the washroom, placed his arms around me, lifted me up, and sat me on the bathroom vanity.

"Geoff! What are you doing?" He chuckled and smiled.

"I have something I need to say to you, Liz, and this is as good a time as any."

"In the bathroom?"

"Yes! It's a good a place for us to be alone in here for a moment."

I thought to myself, this must be important, to tell me in the washroom while I sat on the vanity. He certainly got my undivided attention.

Geoff and I had recently gotten back together, on and off again relationship, due to my warped beliefs, hang-ups, and my inability to commit to more than I was already giving. Whenever Geoff wanted to ante-up our relationship, I simply shut down or broke it off.

That night, Geoff wanted to make a commitment to me. He knew he was taking a risk, but his need to tell me and show me that he was in love with me, hoping that some day I would consider marrying him, was a risk he was willing to take.

I was caught off guard. I really didn't see this coming. However, I had an inkling something was up. Earlier in the day, Sara, who was out in the living room pretending to watch the movie with Jason, had mentioned something about a surprise for me. I had shrugged it off because I knew Sara liked to dangle tidbits of information, but she never actually would spill the beans. At this point, I was sure Sara wished she were a fly on the wall, the suspense must have been killing her.

Geoff knew I wasn't really ready for marriage. We were only 19, but it really had nothing to do with our age. He just wanted to make a promise to me that he would wait until I was ready. He even had a ring to give me, a promise ring.

I glanced over my shoulder, catching sight of myself in the bathroom mirror. Not liking what I saw in the mirror and what I felt I had to do and was about to do, I scrambled for some sort of composure, knowing I would probably someday regret my response.

I knew I was a fool, taking the ring, placing it back in his hand, and closing his fingers over it. With my quivering hands holding on to his, I mustered up enough courage to look him straight in his eyes. It was then I felt my heart start to cry and tremble inside. I uttered the words I couldn't accept it at this time and wasn't sure if I would ever be able to accept it.

If the truth were known, beneath my severely serious exterior, I really wanted to say yes, but ended up saying no. I would always remember that look of dejection on his face. I could tell he was crushed. And for that, I felt I couldn't blame him if he wanted to leave me once and for all.

Geoff told me he wasn't going to stop trying. I admit Geoff had the patience of *Job*, not to mention a lot of perseverance. He never wanted to give up on our relationship. I remembered Geoff telling me that, no matter what it was that I was having difficulty with, we would work through it somehow. But, I had to *trust* him enough and let him in to help.

I was the one with problems, fear blindsided me. Fear, the demon that led me to do what I considered right, alienated me further from Geoff's love.

I couldn't let him in to help, trust, and commitment was not going to be one of my fortes. Besides, he wouldn't have wanted to be with me really, if he ever found out the truth. In my eyes, I was damaged goods—inadequate and unworthy of his love.

Chapter Seven

Time had passed, things were definitely not like they use to be. We had broken up again, but this time it was different. The chances of Geoff and I ever getting back together were dismal.

Another woman was in the picture. I couldn't really blame Geoff for getting involved with another woman. I believed that she got pregnant deliberately to trap him and I wasn't surprised when this had proven to be the case.

A few of our close-knit friends knew his heart was elsewhere, still with me. Not knowing who she was, I wanted to keep it that way, but I knew Geoff would marry her. I hoped she could make him happy.

Emotionally, I was unable to cope and had been shutting down my emotions, not wanting to feel. I didn't want to ruin anything else. Whoever she was, she was pregnant. Geoff was going to be a father. It just wasn't going to be ours.

Unbeknownst to his wife-to-be and before I high tailed it away, Geoff pleaded with me to meet with him. For some reason, I granted him his wish.

Geoff was working at a local garage as a mechanic for a friend of his. He asked me to meet him that night, after he finished work. They would be closed and no one would be around. His boss left him the keys to lock up. I was leaving the next day with my friend, Alexis.

Alexis Bannerman was average height, a body to die for, with a vivacious smile that would light up the night. People would stop and take notice of her. Looks that others dreamed of having, which I was sure if there was any way possible, may have hoped that Alexis' good looks might rub off on them. Despite her beauty, she had a personality to boot. An unthreatening way about her; a joyous, loving spirit that made it easy and fun for just about anyone to be around her.

I was a good friend with her sister Joanna. We were classmates in a secretarial course I had taken after high school. She had introduced me to Alexis a few months back while a bunch of us were out one night at a bar. We started to hang around together. In many ways, Alexis and I were like night and day, but we both got along great. We had big plans for our future and were going to see them through together as friends.

Geoff and I didn't get too far. I didn't expect we would end up sitting in my car inside one of the garage bays talking. It was just the two of us. At least, it was warmer in the garage than on the outside. It was the middle of October and there was a chill in the air.

I was expecting Geoff to lock up the garage and we would go somewhere for a coffee and talk. That was not the case. Geoff asked me if my car was ready for our trip. He offered to check it over, but I pleasantly declined his offer, telling him it was already serviced, which it had been.

I was sure Geoff was a very reliable mechanic, but foolishly, the thought did cross my mind that he might remove something from under the hood. Something I wouldn't be the wiser for until it came time for Alexis and me to leave the next day. Inwardly, I laughed at myself for thinking such a thing, but knowing Geoff, I wouldn't have put it past him to do something like that. I just thought it was better to be safe than sorry.

More idol chitchat ensued, we were both feeling awkward and I knew I was nervous. We were alone, sitting in my car. Thinking, what am I doing here? I realized the compromising position I had just placed myself in, a fine predicament. I needed to get back to my parents house and try to get some rest as the next day Alexis and I had a long journey ahead of us. I broke the ice, asking Geoff to tell me what it was he wanted to talk to me about?

"Well, for starters, Liz," Geoff paused and reached into his pocket. "Here, this if for you, I want you to have it, you can accept it as a birthday gift. Happy Birthday, Liz!"

I was surprised, I hadn't thought of my birthday, but Geoff never forgot it.

I recognized the small velvet box he was holding. He took my hands and placed the box in them. This time, he wrapped his hands around mine as I held on to it. I was stunned, what was he doing?

"It's the ring I tried to give you before, Liz. But before you say no, I want you to have it, I got it for you, it belongs to you, and it was a token of my love for you." Geoff's voice softened. "It still is, Liz."

My eyes swiftly and tightly closed. "Look at me, Liz." He commanded. I couldn't look at him as I was desperately battling back tears. My lips quivered when I felt the touch of his hand on my shoulder. In a moment, the tears began to run from beneath my closed eyelids, I could no longer control them or stop them – Geoff saw the tears, reaching to wipe them away.

"What did I do wrong, Liz? No more empty excuses, please tell me!"

After all these years, Geoff just couldn't understand why or put his finger on it. Nothing made any sense. If it was something he had done, he wanted to know. This time he was going to be persistent, relentless if he had to be, in order to get to the truth why I had given up on us. What was so bad or why couldn't I trust him enough to tell him?

"I need to make it clear to you, Liz, that I'm only marrying her because she's pregnant. You had shut me out of your life before I met Pam. I never meant for her to get pregnant, Liz. You got to believe me; I'm still in love with you."

Thinking to myself, what a funny way of showing me that he was still in love with me. Sarcastically I said. "As you keep telling me."

"Under the circumstances, Liz, I feel you have left me no choice but to do the right thing and marry her."

I looked at him with a wry grin. "Wait one minute! What do you mean I left you no choice?" Now I was riled up and on a roll, wanting to lash out at him for trying to put the blame on me.

Next thing I knew, I threw the box with the ring at him; it bounced off his chest and somehow landed in his lap.

"I'm not the one responsible for whomever it is you choose to sleep with, Geoff. You know the risks involved and the consequences; it takes two to tango. I don't own you, Geoff, and never will. Didn't she ever hear about birth control? Or didn't either of you ever stop to think? I doubt that the thought even crossed either of your minds to use protection, I guess not, eh? But, then again, and from what I have heard, she wanted to get pregnant. I thought you would have been smarter than that Geoff . . . than to have had unprotected sex?"

Suddenly, I caught myself for what I was doing and saying. I was a ranting and raving lunatic who was scolding him, sounding like I was a jolted lover, a jealous jolted lover. What they do is none of my business. I really was loosing it. My body was shaking uncontrollably from how upset I was and now I began to feel nauseous.

His eyes were transfixed on me. "You are right, Liz. I didn't respect her nor myself enough, and yes, yes I was stupid, and yes I made a huge mistake, sex was sex . . . except with you! I was so lost, angry, and alone after you gave up on our love. It never made any sense to me. It hurt me deeply, so I tried desperately to get you out of my head and heart, but the truth is, I couldn't . . . and I still can't."

"Geoff, we can't ever go back and recapture the past. You have to forget . . . the way that I've already forgotten. Whatever we had is over and it's best if we keep it that way."

Realistically, we couldn't change the fact he was getting married, she was pregnant, and I was moving away.

"We both have to move on with our lives, Geoff . . . apart."

I don't think he took in what I had just said or he turned deaf ears to it. Removing the box and ring from his lap, he leaned forward, and placed it on the dash. Then adjusted and repositioned his body to be nearer to me, settling his left arm and hand over my headrest, while reaching with his other hand and taking hold of one of mine.

"Listen to me, Liz. I wanted to be alone with you. I want to know the truth, and we can sit here, even if that means arguing. But until you tell me the truth, you're not going anywhere."

Somehow, I knew he meant every word. He was focused on getting to the bottom of things and he was going to be relentless and keep me captive. We were not going anywhere. He wanted the truth out of me, once and for all. He was baiting me, trying to get me to talk about it.

"What does it matter, Geoff?"

"It matters to me because I want to know. I need to know. *Damn it, Liz!*"

I felt trapped and angered by his tenacity and the fact he had backed me into a corner, literally and emotionally. I remembered shouting, "God, you never give up!"

Another heated argument ensued and the words at some point inadvertently rolled off my tongue. Once it did, silence filled the air. I couldn't believe I just blurted it out.

I bit my lip as the first pangs of regret struck without mercy. I had promised myself to never tell anyone, especially Geoff. I thought I was stronger than that. He had penetrated my tough exterior. I was unprepared for this. If I knew this was going to happen, I would never have agreed to meet with him.

It seemed like an eternity had passed as we sat there, both motionless. I just wanted to go home, he got what he wanted, the truth.

I was terrified what he would say or do after the information I had just blurted out had sunken in. Now I was really overwhelmed and frantically wanting him to get out of the car . . . and open the bay doors so I could leave.

Next thing I knew, he grabbed me and put his arms around me, telling me he was so sorry. In his voice was all the sorrow and remorse that mere words couldn't express. He really didn't have a clue, his face frowning and eyes misty. Geoff's altruistic personality was passionate, concerned and caring in nature. He wore his heart on his sleeve. He was overcome with his emotions. Now Geoff had a clearer understanding of those invisible walls I erected every time he got too close to me. But couldn't understand why I punished myself for something that he said wasn't my fault, realizing also that I didn't quite see it that way.

I tried to wiggle out of Geoff's embrace. He didn't want to let me go. Now he was faced with something I had been dealing with for a very long time, and his best friend wasn't who he thought he was.

Contrary to what I had expected, Geoff's expression wasn't anger, but grief. His eyes weren't hard with annoyance, but soft with compassion. Geoff didn't want me to see his anger, but I knew it was there. At that moment, he was more concerned about me, and somehow he wanted to comfort me, to focus on me.

He had covered my hands with his, holding them captive against him. I pleaded with him to promise me not to breathe a word of this to anyone, nor say or do anything to Michel. I didn't want anyone else to find out, but my greatest fear was what Geoff would do to Michel. Who was I kidding, for now he would promise me, but I knew that promise would be short-lived once he would catch up with Michel, his so called best friend.

I could feel his heart racing beneath my hands. I withdrew my hands from beneath his. He quickly pulled me into a closer embrace, holding me firmly against him. Placing a hand on the back of my head, he drew his face closer to mine. All I could see was his mouth. I knew a kiss was imminent.

At that moment, it felt too good. He brushed his lips with mine, the very next moment he was kissing me tenderly. Something that was partly peace and partly fire took possession of me, and for a few rapturous seconds I responded to the pressure of his warm mouth on mine, then, with a horrified gasp, I tore myself free.

"Geoff, we can't!" My voice was weak and not altogether steady. He paused, then, his eyes fixed on my face, coolly saying.

"You haven't forgotten after all, Liz. That kiss just now, it was quite something you know."

When he had kissed me, for a few incredible seconds, it hadn't been all one-sided. Obviously, he felt that. Man could he kiss. I marveled at his determination and the power of his kiss. No surprise that it made my mind and body surge with gorgeous sensations. I had to stop myself from returning his kiss, but I had wanted to. The reaction was a self-imposed conditioned reflex, part of that control I was so hung up on. I shrank from his touch. I knew I was in deep, deep trouble.

It was a blast from the past since he held me in his arms. I was flushed and breathless, and excitement still pulsed. He still had me in his embrace.

"I know you still love me, Liz; prove me wrong."

His lips hovered above mine, giving me an opportunity to protest again. I couldn't summon the will to fight any longer. The heat and desire his touch caused overwhelmed me so quickly that I surrendered, reaching up to clutch his head, drawing his mouth back to mine. I kissed back wildly and hungrily this time, returning kiss for kiss, and caress for caress. So much for proving him wrong, but he wasn't wrong.

Up until now, I couldn't let him get this close. I got caught up in the heat of the moment and the memories of how it used to be, the pleasures we once shared.

This time I gave myself over to it, desire finally unleashed. I was accessible, submissive, yielding in a mild, utterly feminine way. Geoff's hands seemed to be everywhere. My head kept saying no, but the rest of me was like putty in his hands. I couldn't stop myself. I just let it happen.

He let go of me, pulling his shirt over his head and when we embraced again, he just had to tell me.

"I miss you so much, Liz. I need you. Let me know that your love is still mine. Let me back through the door to your heart. I have always been in love with you, Liz, and always will." I heard the urgent passion and longing deepening his voice. I immediately forgot everything, but the need to yield to him, and to my own desire for him, at least for this moment in time.

Wanting sex and wanting Geoff were two completely different things. I knew now and wondered within the hidden passion-dense fog of my brain what he would have said or done if I had told him that I was still in love with him. I just couldn't bring myself to vocalize it.

I had never been either ashamed or proud of my body, it was just part of who I was. I had been physically fit due to the sports I participated in before. I just didn't need to wear anything under a baggy warm sweater or my jeans. Besides, I wasn't expecting this.

The heat and desire his touch caused overwhelmed me that I became both tearful and bold, emotionally begging him for more than he was giving.

"Please, Geoff, make love to me, do it now!"

He whispered hoarsely. "Yes, sweetheart, yes."

I seized the moment, freely letting Geoff make incredible love to me. Right now, my actions had to be speaking louder than words.

How could I feel so guilty, confused, and lost after I let him make love to me again? I shouldn't have let it happen. He didn't want to let me go, or for me to leave the next day.

He looked at me with a puzzled look on his face and quietly said, "You're sorry we made love? We didn't do anything wrong, Liz. Please, don't think that we did."

We both were finished dressing, I cleared my throat. It felt as if something was lodged in it. I asked for him to open the bay door so I could go and mumbled a *"sorry"* as I was fumbling for my keys, and battling back tears, but somehow managed to start the car. He heard me say sorry.

"Don't say you're sorry, Liz, for letting yourself feel something."

Easier said than done, I had gone too far, and knew it.

"I'm not trying to make you stay. But I want you to, Liz, because there's something here that can't compare with any other as long as we both live. There's no one who loves you or cares about you the way I do. I'm the one who loves you, Liz."

Battling tears, resenting Geoff one minute, and my own mindless response to him the next, I backed out, leaving the garage, and Geoff behind. I don't really recall driving home that night and I knew I wouldn't get much sleep.

~

As I laid awake for most of the night, I confess, I willed him to come after me, to grab me, and pull me into his arms, and tell me he loved me too much to let anything – even Michel or Pam – ever come between us again. But, he didn't and it was pointless to even think that he would. Besides, how could we work anything out? What a mess. She was pregnant, he was going to be a father, and they were getting married, and I was leaving. I had to go. We couldn't talk or see each other again.

I started the water for a bath, splashing in a generous measure of bath beads, hoping the warm water would make me sleepy. But I emerged as wide awake as before, the impressions of the evening still filling my head, and thinking about what had happened, and reflecting back to the last several months of our relationship, before the initial break up. I hadn't permitted Geoff to slip through the impenetrable fortress guarding my heart and mind. Whatever intimacy there had been between us was more one-sided. I had turned myself off. I knew I was in love with Geoff. There was no denying it. He definitely knew how to show his love, but I couldn't, and didn't reciprocate his passion, and lovemaking, not in the physical sense . . . at least not until earlier tonight.

I had tried to date a short time after our initial break up. I had met Tim Collins at a hockey game. I was asked to help out with selling tickets from the president of our senior mens hockey team and if I could get a couple more friends to help.

The first night, Tim had come rushing in, wearing a team jersey, sweat pants, and ball cap, with a 5 o'clock shadow. Hoping to make it before the second period had started. He hated being late, such a loyal fan, but work sometimes would prevent him from making the first period.

For the following week of home games, he had made sure he came to the booth where I would be selling tickets. The first few home games we were giving away free beer steins with the team's logo on them, to the first few hundred fans that came. The second night, Tim had asked me if I would mind putting one aside for him for the following night, since he wouldn't make it until sometime after the first period.

Sara and Stephanie helped out, selling tickets in the booths at the back doors to the Sportsplex that led into the rink. I sold tickets at the front door, near the box office.

Sara and Stephanie picked up on our display of innocent bantering and flirtation that went on between us during intermissions. Tim would come out and chat with me, having a beer or two.

Sara and Stephanie both approached me at one point, telling me that it was evident to them that Tim sure had the hots for me. Of course, I told them it was just some innocent carrying on. They assured me that as far as they could see, it was far from being anything that they or anyone else, for that matter, would consider innocent. They even made mention that Geoff was noticing it, too. I wasn't going there. Geoff and I were finished.

My lips pinched at the memory of that horrible moment when she and I had stood staring at each other. She was wearing Tim's pajamas. I had, of course, been an unexpected visitor. I thought I would surprise him, but I guess I was the one who got a surprise, a big surprise. He had just returned from spending two weeks in the Caribbean with his grandfather. I, perhaps, should have called first.

Tim was in the apartment, I knew, because I'd heard him call out. I panicked. I felt suddenly as though I couldn't bare him to come to the door and find me standing there. Instead of asking to see him I'd mumbled. "Terribly sorry, wrong address!"

I bolted before the other girl could speak. There had been a cold sickness at the pit of my stomach and I had to swallow repeatedly to stave off tears or nausea.

Sara had warned me that Tim was something of a philanderer.

"Mark my words, Liz. He'll break your heart if you give him half a chance." Of course, Sara was still upset in how things turned out between Geoff and I. She absolutely adored him, telling me that I was a fool to push him away, and right into the arms of another woman. I could understand how things must have looked to her, but she certainly wasn't wrong about Tim. In fact, she was dead on about him.

He was definitely a charmer. I must admit he definitely had changed in his appearance for our first date, wearing a shirt and tie, black dress pants, leather black shoes, and a brown suede jacket. His hair was wavy, thick, and blonde. His eyes were a deep blue. His jersey and sweat pants certainly didn't do him any justice.

It was criminal though, in how I was feeling. Now I felt stupid enough to have been taken in by him. I should have known better that I was nothing more than just another woman to him, another conquest. This time I should have listened to Sara.

But, no matter how short-lived that relationship was and, to tell the truth, when we had become intimate, I had to struggle to enjoy myself. I'd tried so hard to feel the waves of pleasure I had with Geoff in the past. But nothing ever really happened.

Then there had to be Mick, but that relationship was a real fiasco, another story and memory that I would soon rather forget.

As my mind drifted back to what had happened earlier with Geoff, I had remembered how it use to be and was able to reach deep down inside, and give Geoff that part of me that was once so easily, and freely given. To once again experience that feeling of boundless happiness beyond my wildest dreams. But, lurking just around the corner, reality, and fear easily crept back in.

Geoff was an amazing person. He wanted to give me enough happiness to make up for all that lost time. There is really no comparison between having sex and making love. Anyone can have sex, but when one truly experiences the gift of making love, all else pales in comparison.

Yes, I still loved Geoff with all my heart. The physical contact between us earlier was so overpowering. Somehow though, I knew this was going to be our last intimate moment together. I was just wrong as to why.

For what took place the night before, I knew I was vulnerable. A part of me was saying if I saw him again, before I was to leave, I would have told him I wanted to stay and give us another chance. To tell him I was in love with him, he'd always be the one for me. I couldn't believe I was letting go. I knew he wanted to be with me every day for the rest of our lives.

If I had allowed that to happen, it just might have been me he had married. The time and children we might have had together would have been ours, not theirs. Grant it, I was nowhere near ready for children and perhaps would never be. Fear continued its stranglehold. Trust and commitment scared the *hell* out of me.

I fled, needing and wanting to escape completely from my old life and its associations. Where hope wouldn't alternate with despair, making that fresh start I had hoped for. There was a kind of safety I felt with closing the door on certain feelings or as I thought. I promised myself to never let myself fall in love again, love hurts. Betrayed and angered by Michel's so called friendship and now, marked by grim or bitter irony, Geoff's love for me, his wife-to-be was pregnant.

I knew I wouldn't be able to be in love with someone the same way as I was with Geoff, let alone make love with the same degree of passion, emotions, and intensity. What was perfect for us once was not anymore. All the good and joyous moments Geoff and I shared became entombed in the past.

There was nothing I would like better, in many ways, than to wipe the past from my mind, and start again. Wouldn't it be nice if whenever we messed up our life, we could simply press Ctrl-Alt-Delete, and start all over?

Leaving was the only way I thought I would have had any chance of changing, making a new life for myself, escaping from the past, from unhappy associations. Besides, by moving to a new place I didn't have to see Geoff with that other woman or remain afraid of running into Michel again. In reality, I truly believed that our love could not survive and overcome impossible adversity.

My bags were packed and I chose to leave, determined to make a new life for myself, and be free from emotional tangles.

I knew it didn't make any sense to my family and friends, especially giving up a great job as a civil servant that I worked so hard to get, for the unknown. But, it made perfect sense to me at the time. Though, not knowing my destination would turn out to be quite other than I expected.

For a while, I believed I carried nothing with me. But, when it came right down to it, all the unresolved past issues, resentments, coupled with a strong belief system that I didn't deserve anything good that I truly thought I could leave behind, was only going to follow me wherever I would go.

Chapter Eight

Alexis had stumbled across the velvet box as she slid her car seat back for some legroom. She didn't pay much attention to it at first, as she was making herself comfortable for the drive.

I didn't notice what Alexis had found or was holding on to. I was paying attention to my driving, trying to switch lanes for the turn off to the highway.

Once settled, Alexis looked the box over and opened it to find the ring.

"What a pretty ring, Liz. Where did you get it?"

"Oh no, I had forgotten about that. I mean I must have accidentally dropped it when I was rushing to pack the car this morning. It's a ring my, my mother had given me."

Being caught off guard and not knowing what to say exactly, I hoped my little white lie and answer was enough to tame Alexis' curiosity, and she wouldn't ask any more questions about the ring.

I had forgotten about the ring. It must have fallen from the dash at some point, from the night before, and rolled under the passenger seat.

"I'm glad you found it Alexis, would you mind putting it in the dash . . . thanks."

I couldn't tell Alexis the truth about the ring. She wasn't even aware of Geoff or what transpired the night before.

After taking the afternoon ferry, crossing from North Sydney, Nova Scotia to Port-aux-Basque, Newfoundland, it was late and dark when the ferry docked. Since Alexis was familiar with the roads, she drove. After a few hours of driving, we pulled up in the driveway of Alexis' mother's home, in Cape St. George.

Cape St. George is a headland and community of the same name, located at the southwestern tip of the Port-au-Port Peninsula of Newfoundland. The headland marks the northwestern limit of St. George's Bay. The Port-au-Port Peninsula is an arrow-shaped peninsula jutting out into the Gulf of the St. Lawrence from the west coast of the island. With its Roman Catholic traditions, Francophone culture, excellent music, and theatre festivals, the Port-au-Port region has made a name for itself – a full cultural experience, as well as spectacular, and breathtaking ocean views from immensely high sea cliffs being hit by large waves and rocky beaches. There are numerous opportunities for hiking, whale, and bird watching along Route de mon grand-pere – the lively French communities of De Grau, Cape St. George, and La Grand' Terre/Mainland area; descendants from French fisher folk, and Acadians. The peninsula is the only part of the island that is officially bilingual. But, visitors can expect most people they encounter to speak English. Just offshore in the La Grand' Terre/Mainland area is Red Island, which lives up to its name.

While not officially on the peninsula, the larger community of Stephenville is often associated with the peninsula as part of the Port-au-Port area. Stephenville and Stephenville Crossing are the points of entry on Routes 490, and 460, called The French Ancestors Route, when driving from the Trans-Canada Highway, Highway 1. From the Trans-Canada, it is about 40 kilometres to Stephenville, and then about six more kilometres to the isthmus, and Port-au-Port. There is no other option than to drive or take a chartered bus, but you'll frequently need to watch out for potholes, and heaved pavement [http://wikitravel.org/en/Port_au_Port_Penisula].

The inlet led to the port for boats and ships, and an Air Force Base was located on the edge of town. Under its Leased Bases Agreement with Britain, the United States had obtained rights to build the Stephenville Air Base in 1940. The air base was built near Stephenville to stage aircraft through the Maritime Provinces to eastern Newfoundland.

Although the base would eventually sprawl over 8,159 acres, it was a relatively small parcel of land consisting of 865 acres, and separated from the rest of Stephenville by Blanche Brook that was selected for the initial construction site in 1941.

Previously referred to as the Stephenville Air Base, the site was officially named Harmon Field on June 23, 1941 in honour of Capt. Ernest Emery Harmon, a pioneer in United States military aviation history who had served with the United States Air Corps during the First World War.

Although the base was not ready for use when the Americans declared war on Japan on December 7, 1941, it was ready early the following year to receive emergency landings. In August 1943, Harmon Field was finally opened for heavy air traffic with three concrete runways, measuring 150 feet wide, and between 5,000, and 6,000 feet in length.

Stephenville's landscape changed both dramatically and abruptly as hundreds of acres of this largely French-speaking farmland, many of which had been passed down through generations, gave way to the military airstrip, and its accompanying buildings. The largely French-speaking farming village quickly transformed into a booming, largely English-speaking garrison town. By May 1941, all of the affected families had been relocated. Originally, the Newfoundland government had planned to relocate the affected landowners to farmland in West Bay on the Port-au-Port Peninsula. However, the residents instead chose to receive monetary compensation for their land, and resettle in Stephenville.

Generated by the base's construction, the area's economy was simultaneously bolstered by the much needed and numerous employment opportunities, such as tinsmiths, sheet metal workers, construction labourers, and carpenters. Stephenville's population, reported to be about 1,000 in 1935, skyrocketed to more than 7,000 by 1942.

Stephenville's strategic location in the North Atlantic during the Second World War, coupled with its nearly ideal flying conditions, turned Harmon Field into a vital refueling stop for aircraft transporting personnel, and supplies to, and from Europe. The base also accommodated three B-17 bombers that were assigned to Harmon Field to patrol the Atlantic for German U-boat activity between 1942, and 1944. By mid-1943, 17 American military units and 4,000 soldiers were assigned to the base. In September of 1943, Air Transport Command took over Harmon Field from Newfoundland Base Command and assigned it the mission of servicing all aircraft moving troops, and equipment from North America to Europe. For the next 10 years, the base served as an important stopover point for transatlantic flights.

The end of the Second World War brought even more activity to Harmon Field as American troops poured back from Europe. While airfields at Argentia, Gander, and Goose Bay were used to help American, and Canadian aircraft return from Europe, Harmon Field's mission was to accommodate personnel, and supplies waiting for flights home.

The once obscure farming village of Stephenville had been transformed into a world-class airfield, which, at its peak, saw approximately 30,000 troops pass through each year.

The American Air Force continued to use Harmon Field as a site for the air defence of North America until it closed in 1966. When the Americans left the base, all of its facilities, including the approximately 400 buildings were converted to civilian use [http://www.heritage.nf.ca/law/stephenville_base.html. Article by Jenny Higgins. 2006, Newfoundland and Labrador Heritage Web Site – World War 11 Bibliography].

After spending Christmas with Alexis' mom, we rented a flat in Lourdes. A seasonal community, on the tip of a narrow strip of land with the Gulf of St. Lawrence on the west side, and the Port-au-Port on the east side.

For the first several months, everything seemed fine. The less conspicuous I was, the less the strain of maintaining the correct bright façade.

It wasn't long before we were the talk of the town though; I was the new girl on the block, subject of conversation and gossip. But I was making titanic strides when I would be faced with letting anyone get up close, and personal, too close. I had promised myself not to become emotionally attached to anyone again or intimate. To remain aloof, not to be beguiled by a man who could break a gullible girl's heart.

As time past, I heard through the grapevine that some people thought Alexis and I must be lesbians, and getting it on. I hated when someone didn't get the facts and made assumptions. Or, when people made it their business to know someone else's business. If they didn't get anything juicy to gossip about, then they felt the need to make something up to circulate around, whether it was the truth or not. In small communities, salacious gossip spreads faster than the speed of sound – people are invariably interested in hearing it, believing it, and passing it along.

Shallow minds making wrong assumptions or accusations. Damned if we do and damned if we didn't. Alexis found it amusing that some would think that way and it was easier for her to ignore it. She figured if that was all anyone had any time for, to talk about us then they were leaving someone else alone, and must not be too happy with their own life. Alexis didn't have the same hang-ups or issues as me. Besides, she had started dating again and was in the middle of a long-distance relationship.

I took things more to heart and wore it. Alexis didn't really give a damn what the gossips said, but something told her that I would. It's true, for some perverse way I did. Which was lesser of the two evils to choose from, being considered a lesbian or the lack there of in committing or wanting to have a monogamist relationship with a man? I knew I just had deep-rooted, psychological issues regarding intimate relationships. It was no one's business.

Alexis and Matthew new each other from previous years and somehow Matt found out Alexis was back in town. They had met again when Matt made a point of coming to town, using the excuse he was in town on business, to see if it was true, and if he could track Alexis down. The funny thing, he didn't have to look too far for this to happen. He was staying at the motel where Alexis was a bartender in the motel's lounge.

It wasn't long before they started dating. Matt would come to town on weekends or whenever he could. They kept their relationship under wraps. Growing up here, Alexis was well aware of the mindset of the community. I of course, had never lived in a small town. But I was finding out how intensely connected everyone was, how entwined their lives were. But Alexis knew. She had lived here too long to delude herself about the gossips. Once they found out that Matt was her lover, they would start.

I had to laugh whenever I heard Alexis say, "The townies would gossip the tread right off their lips." Anyway, once Alexis was finished with getting her education, we were planning on moving to the city of St. John's, where Matt was a successful businessman. Alexis wasn't sure if Matt was the man for her. They were only going to take it one day at a time. Besides, she was concentrating on her studies. Even with our big plans still in tack, Alexis and Matt would wait, and see if they could make a go of it, once we came to the city.

I was perhaps, and at the time, a tad jealous of Matt, in the sense he was putting a wrench in our big plans. Plans of moving to a place where higher paying jobs were more plentiful, like to Toronto or some other bigger city. There was nothing in our big plans for having one of us in a possible long-term relationship. But, on the other hand, I only wanted Alexis to be happy. Alexis would tell me though that she didn't really want to think about settling down again, we were foot loose and fancy-free.

Years before Alexis and I met, Alexis had already been married and had a child. They were divorced and her son lived with his father. Amazingly, her ex-husband and her had an amicable relationship and remained friends for their son's sake. They were better off as friends than being husband and wife. Alexis knew her son would have a more stable, healthy environment and great schooling, living with his father and grandparents.

Her ex-husband and son lived close to Chester, on the South Shore of Nova Scotia. The South Shore is located along the Atlantic coast, running southwest from Halifax Harbour to the western end of the peninsula at Yarmouth. When the British took control of the region in 1713, they initiated a program of importing colonists from continental

Europe, known as the Foreign Protestants, mostly from Germany and Switzerland. To this day, the South Shore retains many German place names and surnames as well as a distinct accent, compared to the New England settler's influence in the Annapolis Valley or the Highland Scot's influence in northeastern Nova Scotia and Cape Breton Island.

Christopher Rhodenizer, Alexis' ex-husband, grew up near Chester on the South Shore. He took over his father's quaint cottage and restaurant business when his father wasn't capable of keeping up with the pace of running either any longer, due to health issues.

Eventually, Christopher remarried. His new wife, Terri Lynn seemed to be a great person and everyone did his or her best working together to insure Nicholas was happy. Nicholas was smart as a whip and seemed to be happy. On several occasions, during school breaks, Nicholas had come to visit his mom and me on the island.

Dean Bannerman was Alexis' cousin. The gene fairy was in one hell of a great mood when he was born. Great looks must have been in Alexis' family gene pool. Alexis told me at one point or another that her cousin had a crush on me and she would like nothing better than for the two of us to get together. She thought we would make a cute couple. That explained why Dean always seemed to show up when I least expected it, pop-up out of nowhere.

Like the time Alexis forgot to mention to me that Dean was coming over for supper. She was off that day from school and had switched shifts with another bartender, deciding to invite Dean over, neglecting to inform me that she was doing so. She could have at least given me a call at work.

Alexis was out picking up a few groceries for supper when I got home early. I decided to take a bath and simply relax for the evening; it had been a busy week at work. Alexis returned unaware that I was home and taking a bath. She didn't expect me to arrive home until 5:30 or so. A co-worker gave me a lift home when we were able to get off work earlier than usual or expected for a Friday afternoon.

While I was bathing and Alexis was preparing supper, Dean arrived punctually at 5:00 p.m., as Alexis requested. What perfect timing. As I opened the bathroom door, I screamed in fright, startled and embarrassed. I was only wearing a bath towel. Point proven about his ubiquitousness. I sure wasn't expecting Dean to be at my bathroom door as I was coming out. I wasn't sure who had the look of surprise more, Dean or me.

Dean grinned, saying. "Oops, I didn't realize you were home Liz, sorry."

He scooted off, returning to the kitchen. I could hear Alexis laughing as she came knocking on my bedroom door.

"Hey Liz, Dean's our dinner guest tonight."

"Oh, that's nice to know, Alexis. Thanks for telling me."

Once I got dressed and joined them out in the kitchen, Alexis, and Dean were still laughing at what had just occurred. For as shy as Dean was, he gave me a quick look over, smiling, and couldn't resist in telling me he liked what I was wearing, but preferred the bath towel on me instead. I blushed, telling him that I was sure he did.

After supper, Alexis and Dean suggested that we should go out dancing and have some fun. We did go out, but I wasn't prepared to make this a regular thing with Dean. He wanted something more. A relationship. Just the mere word made my skin crawl. What neither of them realized was I didn't want a relationship. There was that commitment thing again. I kept telling myself it wouldn't work, anyway. However, Dean sure made it difficult for me to resist his advances and Alexis was incorrigible.

Eventually, this pressure would bring out the worse in me. Alexis and I would have our little spats over Dean. She just didn't understand why I was being this way and I didn't want to talk about it. I felt Dean needed to find someone he could share common interests and beliefs with; so together they could build a healthy relationship.

There was a slight resemblance between Dean and Geoff's good looks, sharp wit, but most of all, Dean's perseverance when hoping for more or at least to go out on a date alone. I didn't know Dean like I knew Geoff. The only difference I saw in their personalities was that Dean seemed to be more on the shy side. Geoff was far from being shy. I didn't want to compare Dean to Geoff, but the similarities were uncanny. That set me back on my heels a bit and I would put my guard up a little more whenever Dean was around.

I didn't recognize the kind of hate on I had for myself or portrayed. I was good at making things complicated for myself. At first, I started binge drinking, but it wasn't long before I abused myself more with drinking heavily, dulling all or any of my senses. Of course, then I had to dabble in using marijuana. It was easy to get, if anyone wanted it.

The only way it would ever be possible for me to be intimate or have sex again was when I was drinking alcohol, using marijuana, but not limited to, and having a smoke, all a great combination for impairment or interfering with my thinking and judgment. Otherwise, I found sex to be repulsive and hard to fake. The booze and drugs allowed me to be physical when it came to sex, inspired by lust perhaps. Just go through the motions, no emotions, bare bones, fundamental, and unromantic.

However, I ended up going from one extreme to another. Swearing off men, having nothing to do with sex, to going hog wild, and out of control with futile one-night stands; thanks to the booze and drugs. Lascivious, promiscuous behaviors, then quickly deserting them. Besides, I doubted men's sincerity, and their reliability. Dean seemed to keep tabs on my whereabouts and me. I couldn't date him or be intimate with him. I knew he was looking for more from a woman.

Somehow, I was able to keep enough wits or sanity about me when I indulged, struggling not to let it interfere with work. I am sure there were a few days when I wasn't at my best, but I managed to pull it off somehow. I did a better job at holding hard liquor than having a few beers. If I drank beer, it wouldn't take long for me to become *'three sheets to the wind, and under the table,* 'literally. Drinking was a favourite pass time for many. Looking back, it must have had something to do with my age, still being youthful enough I guess.

Drinking and using seemed to become a routine and heavily. Of course, the more I used, the more I needed. I would wake up thinking someone was playing the drums, what drums? Only to find out it was the pounding going on in my head. As soon as I could focus my eyes and get my bearings, it didn't take long for me to realize I wasn't where I should be, home, and in my own bed, wondering whose bed was I in?

Vodka was my choice of poison. Even earned the title *'The Vodka Lady,'* either straight up or on the rocks. My drink would be waiting for me as I approached the bar or the waitress, waiter would see that my glass was empty or pretty close to it, wasting no time in bringing me another. Otherwise, if picked up at the bar, whoever he would be, took care of ordering the drinks.

Getting to know all the single men around, besides Dean, wasn't too difficult, even though the majority still seemed to be related to Alexis in one way or another. However, there were plenty of other men not related.

The ratios, men to women were great. So many men compared to the number of women. Women really didn't have to worry about any competition. There were plenty of men to go around. It seemed easy enough to get picked up at the bar. The guys I met were not looking for anything permanent, one-night stands or the occasional *'romp in the hay.'* As long as I was under the influence, high or both that was fine by me.

However, once a girl's reputation goes bad it only gets worse. There are consequences with this type of lifestyle. It didn't help when guys who managed to pick me up at the bar couldn't wait to give a detailed description of their night spent with me, whenever they got together. Whatever happened to *"What went on behind closed doors should remain behind closed doors"?* The rumour mills were a buzzing. I am sure most of the stories were embellished. Facetiously, I would think to myself, I was glad I could put a smile on someone's face, at least someone was happy. I never remembered much, due to the amount of liquor I had consumed and/or the drugs I had used, reeling the morning after with a hangover. Guys will be guys with inflated egos, another notch in their bedposts. It definitely squashed the rumours about my sexual preference.

We did manage to develop some friendships. I was aware though that I could be both cynical and contemptuous at times. Doubting the sincerity and goodness of others and be deserving of contempt or scorn, feeling worthless. There were times when I would sulk and cry about what I thought someone was doing or had done to me. It tended to bring the satire humor out of me.

But, there were always those women who didn't seem to be overly impressed or jump for joy with our presence. Green with envy perhaps, a tad on the side of jealousy? We seemed to have moved in on their turf. I guess the playing field wasn't large enough as far as they were concerned. They definitely didn't want us breathing in the same air as they breathed. I am sure they would have helped us with packing our bags, if it meant we could have been gone sooner than later. We livened or spiced things up, we were hurt to think that they didn't feel the same way, *NOT!* Anyway, they seemed to have survived our stay for the next year or so.

The two local cabarets, country or rock were the epicentres of this small community, usually with live entertainment. There were a few other drinking holes around Stephenville, a pub or the two lounges. The pub was located in the shopping mall and the lounges were part of the hotel or motel. The hotel was in the centre of town, while the motel was on the outskirts of the town, just off the highway. The two motel owners were a couple friends of Alexis.

By day, Alexis was attending the community college to finish her education, while at night, Wednesday through Saturday she was bartending. I was working in the office of a popular local tourist attraction, *'The Festival Of The Art's Theatre.'* It would provide performers with a place to learn about the theatre, to work with professionals, and practice their craft. Some internationally and nationally known performers graced the stage, attracting theatre buffs from all over. Its plays ranged from original works to professional quality productions of Broadway hits.

The community thrived on the tourist industry. It was a busy place throughout the year, but especially during July and early August. Somehow, I was given the dubious task of keeping the performers entertained occasionally, during any free time they had. The nightlife was booming, drinking, and dancing was routine.

One night, a few of us from work, some of the performers, and the troupe's manager, Patrick, went to the lounge, where Alexis was bartending. We had planned to grab a bite to eat before heading to one of the cabarets. Alexis was known for her many wild intoxicating concoctions. They sure went down smoothly, but once they hit bottom it was a different story. Most people who came to the Island were game for the tradition of getting *'Screeched-In.'* The Island people are known for their friendliness and hospitality, and a Screeched-In ceremony is a testament of this, an experience one could never forget. Brad, one of the motel owners was in the lounge that evening.

"Hey, Brad." I shouted, trying to get his attention. Brad glanced over in my direction, waving back. "Come on over when you get a chance and tell our visitors how Screech-In came about. You tell the story so well." Brad was a character who loved to tell stories. He was so full of humor and drama. "Sure thing, Liz, give me a few and I'll be right over." Brad ordered a round of Screech for our table. You can't tell the story without everyone having a shot Brad figured.

Brad came over, ready to tell the story. Introductions were made around the table. "Okay, everybody here goes. Long before any liquor board was created, to take alcohol under its kindly wing, Demerara rum was a mainstay of the our Islander's diet, with salt fish traded to the West Indies, in exchange for rum. When the Government took control of the traditional liquor business in the early 20th century, it began selling the rum in an unlabelled bottle. The product might have remained forever nameless, except for the steady flow of American servicemen to the Island during the Second World War. As the legend goes, the commanding officer of the original detachment was having his first taste of the Island's hospitality and, imitating the custom of his host, downed his drink in one gulp. The American's blood-curdling howl, when he regained his breath, brought the sympathetic and curious from miles around, rushing to the house to find out what was going on." Brad continued with his dramatics, playing it up to the hilt.

"The first to arrive was a garrulous old American sergeant, who pounded on the door and demanded. *'What the cripes was that ungodly screech?'* The Newfoundlander, who had a habit of keeping silent, answered the door, and replied simply. *'The Screech! 'Tis the rum, me son.'* Thus was born a legend. As word of the incident spread, the soldiers, determined to try this mysterious Screech, and finding its effects as devastating as the name implies, adopted it as their favorite. Our liquor board knew they had a good thing and pounced on the name, and reputation. It began labeling Newfoundland Screech, the most popular brand on the Island, even today, but nowadays we use Jamaican rum. It brings a creative perspective to our unique and beloved culture, and making many people, who come from away, honourary Newfoundlanders."

One of the performers overindulged in Alexis' concoctions, made with Screech, and became rather intoxicated. She was definitely *Screeched-In* and now a honourary Newfie. When we arrived at the cabaret we lost her, loosing sight of her somewhere in the crowd. It wasn't until the following morning when my phone rang. Meredith was whispering when I answered.

"Liz, I don't have a clue where I am. But I guess I spent the night at some guy's house. Jack I think he said his name was. He's making something for breakfast, as we speak." The Jack, Meredith was referring to, was a local resident, carpenter by trade, who Meredith had met at the cabaret.

"Jack!" I exclaimed. "Well, he is harmless, I know Jack." "Here he is now, Liz, I'll let you speak with him." As she handed the receiver to Jack, I could hear Meredith giggling and thanking Jack for serving her breakfast in bed.

"Good morn'n, Liz, excuse me for a moment please, Liz, my mouth is full with a piece of toast."

"Sure Jack." Jack quickly finished chewing and swallowed the piece of toast, clearing his throat before answering again.

"Okay, there! That is better, good morn'n, Liz."

"Good morning, Jack. We were worried and frantically looking for Meredith. We even have the RCMP looking for her."

"What, she is fine. She was so drunk she ended up spending the night here Liz, and don't worry." Jack quickly added. "Nothing happened, Liz."

"Jack, please bring her back to the hotel."

"Sure Liz, but I think she should have her coffee and breakfast first. She must have had one too many of Alexis' concoctions last night before arriving at the Cabaret."

"Yeah, I guess you can say, *'Twas the rum, me son.'* She definitely has been Screeched-in, Jack. Let me speak with Meredith again, please Jack, and thanks."

"Sure thing, Liz. Bye for now." As he handed the phone back to Meredith, I could hear him say, "Here, Liz would like to speak to you again, Meredith."

"Hi Liz, sorry for chomping in your ear, but Jack has prepared me a feast fit for a Queen. How's that saying go, oh yeah, a way to a man's heart is through his stomach, well I think that can go both ways Liz. I must say though Liz, isn't it just my luck that I got drunk, don't remember squat, and here I am in a gorgeous man's bed, being served a wonderful breakfast to boot, and nothing happened."

"Meredith, Jack is a nice guy, one could say a real gentleman, and he wouldn't have taken advantage of you, especially when you were rather looped. You're lucky. Anyway, I'm glad you're okay Meredith and Jack said he would bring you back to the hotel, when you're ready. Patrick will be glad to know you were found safe and sound. We can all breathe a sigh of relief. Don't forget Meredith, you have a show in a few hours."

"Oh yeah, right and the show must go on, I guess. Okay, tell Patrick not to get his knickers-in-a-knot. I'll be there shortly, once I have some coffee, finish my breakfast, and get myself together, as best as I can Liz."

"Alright then, Meredith. I'd better notify our fine constabulary to call off the search, too." Meredith laughed.

"Yeah, I guess so. Screech sure is devastating as its name implies, Liz. See you soon."

"Bye Meredith."

CHAPTER NINE

When the following Saturday rolled around, Alexis and I decided that just the two of us would go out on the town, after she finished work. Matt wasn't going to be around this weekend, due to a work conference he was attending.

I came to the lounge mid evening and sat at the bar, waiting for Alexis to get off work. I perched myself on one of the swiveled bar stools and sipped on a few cocktails Alexis would make, minus the Screech.

A dart tournament was going on, which I spent most of the time watching. They were amazing to watch. I also chatted to some local patrons, who were also sitting up at the bar.

There was a young woman who came into the lounge around 10:00 p.m. She was by herself. She too ended up joining us at the bar. We all were having a friendly conversation. It was apparent that she wasn't from here. Some time had passed and she all of a sudden looked at me, and said. "Now I know where I know you from." I didn't realize she was trying to figure out if she knew me or not. I didn't recognize her.

"Pardon me?"

"Yes, Yes, I recognize you now and know who you are, what a small world it is."

I was at a disadvantage, curious as to how she knew me or from where. She started to ask questions.

"You are from Dartmouth right, the north end, your last name is Sulis right or are you married?"

"Yes, it's Sulis and no I am not married."

"Well, I'm Cathy Donaldson's younger sister, Jessica. You were friends and went to school with my sister; we lived down the street from you."

I almost had fallen off the barstool, replying. "Jessy! Oh my God! It has been quite some time since I saw you last. I would never have recognized you. You sure have grown up."

"So, tell me Liz, do you live here now? How did you ever end up here?"

She was full of questions, inquisitive. But, before I had a chance to respond to any of her bombardment of questions, she then asked me. "Hey whatever happened between you and Geoff O'Donnell?"

I was about to answer her, before she brought up Geoff. I remembered they lived across the street from each other. That threw me for a loop.

"I don't mean to pry, Liz, but we all thought you and Geoff would be heading to the alter, not marrying the girl that he knocked up."

Alexis had heard our conversation and when I looked up at her, requesting another cocktail, a stiffer one, she gave me a puzzled look. "Who's Geoff, Liz?"

They both were staring at me, waiting for my reply. I looked at Jessy. "Geoff and I were through our relationship long before Geoff met what's her name." Jessy looked at Alexis, shrugged her shoulders, saying. "Now, there was a love story if there ever was one."

I looked at Jessy with disbelief, as to what she just said, and now I was curious as to what she meant by that comment. But I didn't want this particular topic of conversation to continue. Alexis however, was more curious than ever. Alexis and Jessy started talking, as if I wasn't there. I couldn't believe this was happening. Jessy was more than happy to shed some light on the topic of Geoff and me. Giving her version, as she knew it, Alexis was being all ears.

I didn't want to hear it, so I excused myself and went to the ladies room to splash some water on my face. Just my luck that this would happen, I guess sometimes the world is a small place or not big enough.

When I returned, Alexis and Jessy were still chatting about Geoff, trying to see if I would shed any light on the subject. I continued to be evasive. Jessy told me that Geoff had a son and she was pregnant with their second child. I tried to be pleasant, but wasn't really interested in what Jessy had to say about Geoff. I didn't want to know.

Trying to change the topic, I asked Jessy what brought her here. She said she was with a group from home working. "Working?" I asked. "Yes." She then began to tell me that she was an exotic dancer and they would be in town performing shows for the next week, the first show being tonight, at the country cabaret, and then asked me if we would be interested in taking in a show.

I was quite surprised that was the farthest thing I would imagine Jessy would have picked as a career. I figured she would have gone on to university for some sort of formal education, becoming a teacher or a doctor. Everyone in her family either became a teacher or a doctor as I recall.

"What has Cathy been up to these days, Jessy?"

"Oh, she's been teaching at one of the elementary schools, married for three years to a surgeon, and has twin little girls." I chuckled saying. "So, Cathy became a teacher and married a surgeon, keeping it in the family eh?"

"Yeah, I'm, I guess, what you would call the black sheep of the family. I was always the rebellious one. I didn't see the need to go to university when I could make more money doing exotic dancing. It's not really a bad career choice, Liz."

I raised my eyebrow, grinning. "I guess not, if that's what makes you happy, Jessy." Of course, it helps when one has the looks and figure, Jessy certainly had both of those areas covered.

"Well, it sure pays the bills, Liz. Grant it, we tend to live out of a suitcase most of the time. Actually, we are well taken care of and the shows are done in taste. There's a limit on what we do and if any guy gets out of hand, tries anything to any of us, while we are performing, our bodyguards handle the situation, they keep things under control."

"Well that's good, Jessy." What else could I say? "Why don't you and Alexis, anyone for that matter, come over tonight and take in a show? We start at midnight." I gave Alexis a quick stare, unsure what to say, hoping for her to give some sort of a response. Alexis acknowledged Jessy's offer with a, "We'll see."

"Well then, I better get going. It was great to see you again, Liz, and nice to meet you too, Alexis."

"Nice to see you, Jessy." Alexis quickly added, "Likewise, Jessy." Jessy gave Alexis a nod and asked her if she would mind phoning her a cab. It must have been sitting in the parking lot as it was already waiting for her outside.

"Gesh that was fast. Well, hope to see you all later."

"Later perhaps."

"I hope so, Liz. Okay bye." I gave Jessy a quick wave goodbye as she left the lounge.

It was last call. A few patrons, who were still hanging around, ordered a nightcap. As Alexis was reaching up and hanging the glasses above the bar, she glanced down at me. "Jessy, seems nice; different, but nice, Liz."

"Yeah, I'm a little surprised though that Jessy has become a stripper. To each his own, I guess. I know we wanted to do something tonight, Alexis. I just didn't think it would be taking in a strip tease show."

"Ah, it's exotic dancing, Liz."

"Same thing isn't it, Alexis?"

"Oh, come on now, Liz. I think it would be a great show," Mackenzie quipped as he passed Alexis his empty beer bottle.

"You think so, Mac? I don't think taking in a show of exotic dancing was quite what Alexis and I had in mind tonight, unless of course, it's going to be guys doing the performing, like Chip-n-dales."

"Well girls, why don't we all go together, you wouldn't want to let your friend down, would you Liz?" I rolled my eyes, looking at Mac. "I'm sure you don't need to watch girls stripping, correction, performing exotic dancing, what would your wife say Mac?"

"Well Liz, if I do, then Anne might reap the benefits after." I couldn't help but laugh. "T-M-I Mac, just way too much information. Alexis I think Mac wants to go, I'm not sure if he will be able to keep his libido in check." "I'm sure the bodyguards will keep things under control Liz, even Mac."

"Mac, where's Anne?" Alexis inquired. He glanced over his shoulder, pointing in the direction to a table in the corner, at the back of the lounge. "Over there chatting to her dart friends."

"Why not ask Anne if she wants to go, if it will be safe for you or too hard on your old ticker?" "As I said, Anne might surprise you both and she will be a happy girl later."

As Mac moseyed on over to his wife, Alexis leaned over the bar to me. "Don't think you are getting off that easy, Liz."

"Huh, what do you mean Alexis?"

"I want to know more about this guy Geoff, who Jessy was talking about earlier."

"What's to know, Alexis? He was a guy I dated, end of story!"

"Oh no, you don't. Apparently, there's more to this story than what you are telling me, Liz."

"No, not really."

"Well, curious minds want to know and I want to know Liz."

"Alexis, please drop it."

"You got to be kidding me Liz, Jessy said she isn't alone in wondering whatever happened between you two, and I want to know if he's the reason you won't date."

"Won't date, what do you mean? I date."

"Not really Liz, I worry about you sometimes, not allowing yourself."

I cut Alexis off. "Not allowing myself to what Alexis, to get serious with anyone, such as Dean perhaps?"

"Dean is a great guy Liz." Alexis stated venomously. "That's what you keep telling me."

"Well he is and he will treat you right, Liz."

"This is making me uncomfortable, Alexis. Can we just drop this conversation, *please?*"

"Well, girls, are you ready?" It was a welcomed interruption by Mac. "Just give me a few to finish up here, Mac."

"Should I call for a cab, Alexis?"

"Sure Mac."

Alexis turned back to me and said. "For now Liz, I will drop the questioning."

"Gesh thanks Alexis, your all heart." We sat awhile in silence, waiting for the cab; business must have picked-up.

~

The cabaret was packed. Dean was sitting at a table, close to the bar, motioning to us to join him. Of all people, it had to be Dean. When we sat at the table, Dean ordered a round, but he wasn't drinking. The show went on. I didn't pay attention to it. I sat aloof for most of the time.

Alexis and Dean were both so secretive, looking at me when they talked. I couldn't make out what they were talking about and I let my suspicions, paranoia, get to the best of me. I didn't even realize how much I had been drinking.

I excused myself, pulling Alexis aside, telling her I was going to grab a cab and go home. I told her to stay and have some fun. Alexis responded by telling me she would get Dean to drive me home. My reaction to her offer was quick. "*No!* There's no need Alexis, I can manage on my own thank-you." I headed towards the door to leave.

The heavens opened and rain was now coming down in sheets. I figured there should be a cab outside, saving me having to phone for one. It was late and cabbies usually started to line up outside waiting for patrons as they left the cabaret looking for a ride.

As I went to open the door, Dean reached around me to open it. I stepped outside under the overhang, looking up at him. I decided on a defence of the most formal politeness I could muster.

"It's okay, Dean. You don't have to worry as I can get home on my own, thanks."

"You've been drinking, Liz. At least, let me make sure you make it home safe." Dean insisted.

An inarticulate mutter or groan came from me. He must be very obtuse if he can't see that I preferred my own company and getting myself home.

"It's okay, really. I can take a cab, Dean!" I turned, taking a few steps to see if there was a cab in sight, easily getting wet by the pouring rain.

Dean shouted out. "This is ridiculous, Liz." Reaching for me, he grabbed my arm, catching me off guard, and spinning me around. I was barely able to stand, losing my balance, reeling; Dean caught me, hugging me hard against his body. His blue eyes grew baffled as he looked into mine. His face receded, then rushed closer, but only his face as though the rest of him had ceased to exist.

He raised his jacket above us, a shield from the rain. It was breezy and the rain was coming down relentlessly. We were quite wet. Dazed, I couldn't move a muscle. I hardly dared to breathe. I was carried away strangely, but only for an instant. Then I came to my senses.

"What are you doing, Dean?"

"My van is parked right over there. There's no point in discussing it any further in the rain, so let me take you home, Liz?" Shivering from a chill, I knew I was doomed to be the loser in this argument.

Without further ado, he grabbed my hand while he wrestled with keeping his jacket above us with his other hand. We sprinted and dodged the puddles that were forming underneath us with every step we took.

We looked like a couple of drowned rats once we had reached shelter inside his van. Dean shared with me a few napkins he had on his dashboard. At least we could wipe our face and hands for now.

He glanced at me quickly, looking at me with a quizzical smile, as though sensing the tension, which was building up in me, but said nothing.

I felt my heart racing; my hands were clenched on my lap. I had decided that my qualms about being driven home by Dean must be stifled, but I was startled by the way he could disturb my defences. I remained silent as he drove me home.

I was glad when we finally arrived, pulling up into the driveway.

"Who is this O'Donnell guy, Liz?"

I turned to him then, blazing."Heaven give me patience!" It shouldn't have surprised me that Alexis would have said something to him. My suspicions and paranoia earlier were right.

"Sorry, I don't mean to be so impudent or abrasive, Liz, but doesn't it occur to you that we might discover a lot of common ground if you'd allow us to get to know each other?"

"There is nothing to tell, Dean, regarding Geoff. As for the other, you need a woman who's gentle and tractable, giving you her unstinting love and support in everything you do, unquestioning devotion, I'm not that woman." I quickly undid my seat belt, opening the door, and climbed out of the van.

"Liz, you've got to be kidding me, what on earth makes you think you know what I want?"

"Just forget it Dean, thanks for the drive home."

"Wait! What if I want an independent, spirited, and self-willed woman like you?" Painstakingly ignoring him, I closed the passenger door and ran towards the stairs.

Dean quickly jumped out of the driver's side of the van and followed me up the flight of stairs to the landing, and door. Torrents of rain continued. As I fumbled and dropped the keys, his reflexes were quick, snatching the keys before they would have hit the landing.

"Here, let me get the door." Once he unlocked and opened the inside door, he held the screen door open, motioning for me to go in. I ducked under his arm and slipped past him.

I didn't realize how close he was behind me, until I turned around; he was dangling my keys in front of me. As I reached out to retrieve my keys, I told him. "There, as you can see, I made it home. I'll be fine and thanks again for the drive."

His face assumed a pugnacious expression, but he wasn't eager to push things too much further, especially to end up fighting.

"What is wrong, Liz?" "Nothing is wrong." "Do I scare you or something, Liz?"

"Scare me?"

"Apparently I have done something to make you uncomfortable when I am around you. This O'Donnell guy isn't any of my business Liz and you don't have to tell me anything, I'll drop it."

"Thanks and tell that to your cousin too, please. Perhaps you should return to the bar, Alexis might need a drive home?"

Dean shrugged his shoulders. "Okay, Liz, good night." The screen door slammed behind him as he left. I stood there, damp, wet, cold, and miserable, staring at the door. A few moments had passed and Dean was back.

"Can I please use your phone to call a cab? My van won't start; it must be wet. I should have known better than to drive that wretched thing tonight. She's temperamental, especially when it rains."

"Do you always refer to your van as a she?"

"Only when 'she's temperamental, Liz."

I couldn't help but to stare at him for a few moments. His wet tee shirt and jean jacket moulded to his torso, while his jeans were clinging to his legs. I only had to see him to feel my nerves tightening; my awareness of his every move warned me of the potential power of his physical attraction over me. Both of us were dripping wet, soaked clean through. Realizing I was staring, my demeanor softened.

"I need to change and dry off. And so do you, Dean, before we both catch a cold or something. Let me get you something to change into, so you can put your wet things in the dryer. Perhaps the rain will let up some, then I'll phone for a cab."

"What do you suggest for me to change into, Liz?"

"I don't know. I can give you a bathrobe, until your clothes dry at least."

"What, yours or Alexis' bathrobe? That should be cute!" Chuckling at the thought.

"No, Matt stays with us when he is in town. This should do the trick, Dean." Passing him Matt's bathrobe. "You know where the bathroom is." Dean sheepishly grinned. "How could I forget, Liz?"

As he turned and started walking down the hallway to the bathroom, my hormones cranked to life, making me feel edgy and weird. Appreciating Dean's cute butt was one thing, but feeling the live wire stirrings of desire was another. The former was fun, the latter unsettling.

I went to my room to change, putting on a tee shirt and a pair of sweat pants. As I came out of my room, towel in hand, and drying my hair, Dean was sitting at the kitchen table in Matt's bathrobe.

"Do you want me to put your wet clothes into the dryer along with mine, Liz?"

"No, that is okay. I have my things hanging up to dry; I'll be doing laundry sometime tomorrow."

Dean started the dryer. As he walked back to the kitchen, I noticed how great he looked in the bathrobe, realizing he no doubt had nothing on underneath of it. Somewhere, I'd lost the thread of thought.

"The bathrobe fits you well; here are Matt's slippers, too."

"Thanks, I can't believe how wet we got. It might take a bit for my clothes to dry, and I'll have to deal with my van tomorrow. It may need to be towed."

I walked over to the counter to pick up the kettle. "I'm going to make some tea. Would you like to have some, Dean?"

"Sure, tea would be fine. Thank you, Liz."

The rain still hadn't let up, as Alexis came through the door. "Wow, it sure is raining." Alexis began to laugh as she looked at the two of us.

"What is it that you find so amusing, Alexis?"

"Well, I see Dean sitting in Matt's bathrobe at our kitchen table."

"What's so funny about that Alexis? We both got caught in the pouring rain. His clothes are in the dryer, and his van wouldn't start."

"I see. Am I interrupting anything guys?"

"*No!* You're not interrupting anything, Alexis."

"Oh, too bad!" Alexis shouted back as she was heading to her bedroom to change.

"Geshh, she never gives up." Dean didn't utter a response. The quiet moments that past between us seemed like an eternity, until Alexis returned to the kitchen. "Is there any tea left, Liz?"

"The pot's on the stove help yourself." Alexis prepared herself some tea and joined us at the table.

"Hey Dean, thanks for bringing Liz home."

"No problem."

"You know Alexis, I am pretty resourceful, and I could have gotten a cab."

"Dean didn't mind bringing you home Liz, did you, Dean?"

"No, not at all."

"You know, Liz. You two would make a cute couple."

"Give it a rest, Alexis."

"By the way Liz, so what's up with this Geoff guy?"

"Alexis, what am I going to do with you? There is simply nothing to tell."

"I don't believe it, Liz."

"Alexis, I'm going to my room, while you two sit here and discuss whatever it is you want to talk about, besides me."

"What else is there to talk about Liz, but you?"

"Alexis can wait with you Dean, I'm sure, while your things dry, then she can phone for a cab. Thanks again for the drive Dean and good night."

As I got up from the table to leave I nodded to Alexis, giving her a stern frown, and catching her nudging Dean under the table.

"Wait, Liz!"

"What now, Dean?"

"Can I talk to you for a few moments, alone, Liz?"

Glancing at Alexis as he asked me, Alexis jumped to her feet. "Sure, I will make myself scarce and go to my bedroom, so the two of you can be alone."

It suddenly dawned on me. It wasn't a coincidence that Dean was at the Cabaret. Alexis and Dean schemed together. So much for us going out by ourselves, the only thing none of us were aware of, until earlier with Jessy was the entertainment.

Alexis scampered off to her bedroom. "Dean, I am pretty tired, I need some sleep."

"That is fine, it won't take long for what I want to say, Liz. I just want you to know that I like you. I only ask if somehow you could let go of whatever it is that's troubling you about me or tell me what it is or at least consider giving me a chance."

"Dean, I think you are a great guy. I just don't think it would work."

"How do you know Liz, unless you give us a try?"

"I just know."

"At least give me some sort of inkling to your reasoning, Liz."

"There's no point in discussing it, Dean."

"Yes, there is," Dean said tersely. "You don't think I'll understand, is that it, Liz? How can I, unless you tell me?"

Oh my God, this was dejá vu, present and past brought together. Like Geoff, Dean was insistently drilling me for answers? It scared me to the point that I couldn't allow myself to think. What was I going to say?

Suddenly, Dean placed his hands on my shoulders. "Please, Liz, I don't want to hurt you. I only want to spend some quality time with you, alone, so I can get to know you better. I need to know what I am up against?"

I was at a loss for words. I couldn't hear my own thoughts over my heart racing so, echoing his words in my head. As I looked into his mesmerizing eyes, those baby blues had me in a trance. I was sure they saw through me and he was able to read my mind at that particular moment.

Next thing I knew, he was holding me in his arms. I was trembling. "Are you okay, Liz?" I struggled to respond.

"Ah, yes, I, ah, guess I'm still chilled from getting wet, I hadn't warmed up enough, I guess."

It actually had nothing to do with getting a chill from being wet. It was in the way he was holding me, a cocoon-like embrace. He tightened his grip as he rested his lips against the crown on my forehead, and whispered.

"We can make this work, Liz. I know we can. You just have to give it a chance."

With my eyes closed, I couldn't help but sense his passion and how well the cologne he was wearing matched his body chemistry. Remembering quickly that all he had on at the time was the bathrobe.

The few unsteady steps I took backwards were sedate, but only out of necessity. I didn't want Alexis to hear us. I told him to follow me into the living room, so we would be out of earshot range.

Once in the living room and as I turned around to face him again, he took hold of my face in his hands as he leaned down to kiss me. I didn't resist, his kiss was so soft and tender. We continued to kiss passionately for a few moments longer.

As we kissed, thoughts raced through my mind. Why do I struggle so with desire, reality, and expectation, what one wants, and what one gets?

Struggling to comprehend why they are always different my sensitive responses to the problem of being alive, and mortal.

Our lips parted briefly, both catching a breath. "I better stop now, before it's too late, and go check on my clothes." As he went to move, I stopped him. At that particular moment, I wanted him. So impulsive, I know. I reached out grabbing hold of his arm. "Your clothes can wait."

I knew I caught Dean by surprise. I caught myself by surprise. It was a dizzying fact to comprehend, but my libido had come alive in Dean's arms a moment or so earlier, and that kiss, well, I sat down on the couch, reaching up to Dean, pulling him down beside me.

Dean hesitated and then asked. "Are you sure? If I . . ." Cutting him off, from what he was about to say. "Stop talking and asking me questions, Dean." As I drew his mouth to mine, I told him to kiss me. Kissing me wasn't something I had to ask Dean twice. A kiss that would turn into something else, how it was even possible I felt tempted?

If I couldn't make my life right, completely right, I had no interest in playing the game. Maybe loneliness was part of the insanity I felt at that particular moment or my need for him. Those soft, deep kisses kidnapped my emotions. I tried to doubt this could be real.

However, my cold, tough exterior was crumbling. It wasn't anything to take lightly. All of Dean's charms conspired to make him irresistible. A special connection with a man, I'd never felt would be possible again before now I wouldn't let it be possible. Yeah, I'll have this night and enjoy it to the fullest. Besides, wasn't I giving him what he really wanted?

Taking his hands I pulled Dean, propelling him to move with me, leading him down the hallway to my bedroom. A step or two inside my bedroom, I closed the door to rid him of the bathrobe.

The draw tie was holding the bathrobe closed. It just took a little tug, there, I slipped the robe from his shoulders, and it dropped to the floor. What a magnificent man. My nimble, quick fingers reached for his, I inched walking backwards, until the back of my legs touched the bed.

He reached up threading his fingers in my long hair and then, taking hold of my head, and keeping it still, he began to kiss me again. I had to concentrate, as he was naked. I did my best to pour all of myself into that kiss, a reassuring kiss, giving, and taking. It wasn't going to be easy, to get real, real emotionally naked. Just then, he took a moment to assure me he had protection. "I'll return momentarily, don't move."

I watched him reach for the bathrobe, slipping into it again, and then darted out of the room. I undressed and crawled in under the sheets.

Chapter Ten

"Sorry, I had to find my wallet. Now, where were we?" I pulled the bed sheets back. "Come here and I'll remind you." The heat of his powerful body warmed me as he hugged me close. I inhaled deeply. When he rolled me beneath him, he said, "No matter what, Liz, from this moment on I want to prove to you that you can trust me." The way he looked at me, I trusted what I saw in his eyes. I kissed him, I wasn't going to lie about what I was feeling, what I wanted or needed. We complemented each other in every way, physically, and emotionally.

Lying stolid, I could hear Dean's easy, rhythmic breathing, it was too soon to be awake. I was weary and lazy from our early morning 'bout of passion. I hadn't had enough sleep. I must have dozed again.

When I eventually awoke, I opened my eyes, and to my surprise, Dean was lying next to me on his side, looking down at me. He reached over to move tendrils of hair curling, covering my eyes.

"Good morning, beautiful."

"Oh yeah, I'm sure I'm a sight for sore eyes. What time is it Dean, did you sleep at all?" He glanced at the alarm clock on my nightstand.

"It's almost 8:00 and yes, I got some sleep. I've just been watching you sleep, bewitched by you, and what we'd brought to each other earlier. I didn't want to disturb your slumber, you looked so peaceful, and snoring"

To my chagrin, I hit him in his arm, emphatically denying that I snore. Dean laughed, rubbing his arm where I hit him. "Ouch, okay you don't snore."

Stretching and yawning, I uttered a moan saying, "Almost 8:00, it's way too early, hard to believe it's morning, I need more sleep."

Dean leaned over and hit me with a pillow. "How could you need more sleep, you already got plenty of sleep. Me, on the other hand." Smiling sheepishly as he said it. I shot the pillow back at him and a pillow fight ensued. Next thing I knew, Dean grabbed me and held me down in the bed, laughing as he asked me. "Do you want to give up yet?"

For one brief moment, I became tense, feeling uncomfortable in the way he was holding me down. There wasn't much distance between our faces, especially our mouths. If I had the chance to answer him, I know I would have said yes, I give up. But, he kissed me. A few moments had past, I couldn't catch my breath. "Dean, I need to come up for some air?" Sitting up, I drew my knees into myself, rocking, with only the bed sheet covering me.

"I have come to care about you deeply, Liz. All I'm really asking for is a chance to just make you happy. I don't want to see anything happen to you or you get hurt. I could treat you right. I see you as a woman who is wild and shy, practical, and impulsive. Intriguing contradictory qualities you possess, definitely a paradox."

Was this more than an infatuation he felt towards me? Something was welling up in me. I tightened my arms around my legs resting my head on my knees, in an unconscious self-protection. I had been struggling for so long and so hard, to put my past aside. I wasn't searching to end this hurting. But out of nowhere, he made me feel. This was a time I could no longer deny how badly hurt I was. Emotionally, I felt that there was something missing in me, a gaping hole that had never really been filled. Not something wrong in my life, but an absence of something right. It was apparent that Dean genuinely liked me.

I knew I liked Dean, but was unwilling to take him into my confidence. Even after a blissful night, I had some distaste for talking about my personal matters. How I ever got saddled with Dean, when all I ever wanted was to be left alone, it was beyond me.

"What's going on inside Liz, what's with that cover that you keep your heart under? Something so bad has brought you so much sadness or grief. It's as if you learned to pretend that it no longer had the power to hurt." His gaze was fixed on my reaction. I blinked my eyes in disbelief, rigid set to my shoulders. I was numb, I didn't answer.

"God, yes, that's it." His instinct told him I was hiding from something terrible that hurt me or from someone. At that instant, he knew he was right that something happened or more like it, someone had really done a job on me, but who, and how exactly? He knew so little but said so much. The words spoken aloud in his voice hammered through my heart.

Dean was someone to be reckoned with, a man of both outer and inner strength. "Why do I get the feeling, Dean, that you think you got me all figured out?"

"Do I, Liz? Do you want to tell me about it?"

"No!" I said flippantly.

"You can't spend your life hiding from the sensual woman you are, Liz. What are you running from?" I fidgeted. "At times Liz, you're more like an observer of life, rather than a participant. Maybe there are things you don't want to remember. I realize, it's none of my business, and I don't want to push, but . . ." He stopped short.

My thoughts were a mish mash. I covered my eyes with my hands and began to cry.

"It's this guy Geoff, isn't it, Liz?"

"What?"

"Geoff hurt you?"

My despairing, tear-filled eyes met his. His blue eyes darkened, looking furious, reflecting the hatred that was going on in my soul, at that particular moment.

"No!" Burst out of my mouth, as I gasped for a breath. *"No,* it wasn't Geoff." Damn Dean, I thought to myself. What was he doing? Damn myself for letting him continue. Exasperated I said. "Will you stop being so damned all-knowing!" I felt exposed, as if Dean was seeing through me, with some sort of x-ray vision. No, there was no way I could tell Dean about this side of me. I felt powerless; at the same time I had a sickly feeling in my stomach. My heart was racing erratically. I looked the other way, hoping Dean wouldn't notice the tears that were continuing to trickle down my cheeks. Quickly I would brush them away.

"Liz, there is only one way to conquer fear and that is through love." Dean didn't know what else to say or do. Thinking to himself, if he could pleasure my body, and seduce my mind, then perhaps he could eventually reach my heart.

I found myself taking in a sharp, indrawn breath. *"Love?"*

"Yes Liz, love."

I could only look at him and plead and try to make him see. I awkwardly continued. "Dean, listen, I have difficulty with relationships and admitting how I feel." I was feeling rather flushed.

Dean was silent for a moment and then he asked. "How do you feel, Liz?"

My colour of my cheeks deepened. "I, uh, I am attracted to you, I will admit that. Last night, last night was wonderful, but I realize I'm still afraid. I was trying to find the words before, I was trying to find the right thing to say." I paused. "I'm scared."

"What are you scared of, Liz?" Dean implored. I looked into his eyes. "I'm scared of heartache and humiliation. I don't know if I can love or if I could ever fall in love again, it's, it's so, I just don't know." I lowered my eyes for a moment, as I scrambled to find words to continue.

"I don't have a good track record, Dean, when it comes to guys. I was hurt a very long time ago, early on in the relationship I had with Geoff. There was a time, Geoff was the one I could trust, with my hopes, and dreams, and give my heart to. But, I sabotaged that relationship and then things got too complicated. I deliberately became involved with men who were either unavailable or completely wrong for me. Like, Mick for instance. Unbeknownst to me at the time, he was an alcoholic, with a rap sheet longer than his arms and legs put together. The police caught him after one of his drinking binges." I paused again for a moment, asking Dean to pass me a tissue that was on the nightstand, patting beneath my eyes with the back of my hand. I thanked him as he passed me the box.

"You're welcome, Liz."

"Anyway Dean, as I was telling you. He had borrowed my car and got road rage after a guy had cut him off. He drove after the guy furiously, eventually causing the guy to go into a ditch, pulled the guy out of his car, and started to beat him. Mick was arrested. Luckily, the man he beat pulled through. To make a long story short, he made threats towards my family and me. He ended up spending more time in prison. My lawyer notified my parents and I when he was getting out. We had to get a restraining order against him. I was so fearful that he was capable of so much more, what was a restraining order going to do? The threat and living in more fear was traumatizing."

Dean sighed, settling himself cross-legged on the foot of my bed. I had a habit of combing my fingers through my hair, I wasn't conscious of doing it though, as I spoke. But, Dean was conscious of it because he liked watching my hair sift through my fingers, falling back onto my shoulders.

"You're staring at me Dean."

"I'm staring, trying to get my fill of you, looking at you, because I feel you are about to tell me that I can't be apart of your life. Am I right, Liz?"

I shrugged my shoulders, nodding my head in a slow, up and down motion, indicating a yes.

"What's the statute of limitations on self-chastisement, Liz?"

"Pardon, what do you mean?"

"You don't live life Liz, you defy it. Self-sufficient, Liz. Those invisible walls you erect every time I try to get up-close and personal."

"That's not fair."

"Oh, it's not?"

"No!" I exclaimed.

"Don't run from me or be afraid of me then, Liz. Let me be a part of your life and give my love a chance, because if you were mine, I would give you the world. There'd be no reason for you to keep hiding." He reached out with the back of his fingers, gently stroking my cheeks as he continued to speak. "I'm going to kiss you now." Dean dipped his head, lightly brushing his lips over mine, before our mouths actually joined.

No matter what, he wanted to prove to me that I could trust him that he'd be there and he wouldn't hurt me.

I choked back a sudden uneasy gulp of air as our lips parted; my face turned a crimson rose. I gazed into his deep, baby blues. There was something hypnotic about the way his eyes were transfixed on mine, a piercing stare. We both remained motionless for a few moments.

I thought to myself, in such a short time, how did I get so far from my humdrum life? My emotions were stirring. Dean's poignant, pointed questions clued him closer, as he tried to hone in to my past; but there was something more ominous for which I stayed elusive, closemouthed, and unwavering, not to divulge anything more.

My old instincts were kicking in. Fear had haunted me. Anything good wouldn't last. Besides, I would only end up being hurt again or I would be the one doing the hurting or disappointing anyone I got too close to. There was just too much baggage.

I didn't know any better. I had become harden to having any sort of a loving relationship, due in most part to the ghost of the past. Love had become my greatest intangible, an imponderable force. Love was full of too many inconsistencies and contradictions. It was a disabling emotion to me, not easily being able to clearly express it, define it or grasp it in my own mind, let alone to anyone else.

I was not looking for love. Not having to worry about losing love or being hurt by love. In short, I was not going to be charmed, troubled, and lead astray by love. Sure, love starts out with so much excitement and hope, but nothing fails as often as love.

"I think you're falling in love with me, Liz. You just don't know it yet." Dean remarked contentiously.

"I recognize the symptoms, because I've been suffering from the same symptoms. I know I'm in love with you, Liz. There, I said it. But, I also know that love is a touchy subject for you."

"You're saying that you think you're in love with me, Dean?"

"No, I didn't say I think I'm in love with you, Liz. I said I know I'm in love with you. Thinking and knowing are two different things. I wanted some time to romance you, get to know you better. But, you don't make asking you out on a date easy. You keep rejecting me. This was not a one-night type of thing for me, Liz. I want you to know. The old fuddy duddy that I am, I favour the one-man, one-woman for life concept. I don't want just casual sex with no feelings, no strings, and no expectations between us. I feel in my heart, there would never be another woman like you, Liz, for me. But, I have a suspicious feeling that you're about to tell me that there will never be a chance in hell of us to at least date. That there will never be another night like this. That there will never be an experience we just shared of making love, like the way we made love earlier this morning Liz, will there?"

"Wow! Dean, I don't know what to say, really. I don't have a crystal ball and we don't really know each other. Don't you think you or we are perhaps rushing things a little?" Dean stiffened, tightening his embrace. "Well, it sure isn't due to the lack of me trying to get to know you, Liz."

I reached up, brushing the hair from his brow. "Why is it that being with you makes me dizzy and weak in the knees, Dean? I've never had a problem walking away from anyone. I promised myself not to get attached or emotionally involved with anyone again. I was doing so well. You're right, you said I don't live life; I defy it, self-sufficient, Liz. I don't as a rule put myself on the line for anyone. There is a purpose for those invisible walls I erect every time someone gets too close to me. I'm not afraid of being alone. I haven't been in a very long time, until . . ." I paused.

"Until what Liz?"

"Until, until you, Dean." Dean saw my feelings in my eyes. "Alexis told me that fate has a way of bringing the right people together in odd ways, and at odd times. Just when you least expect it."

Smiling, Dean inquired. "Oh and what else does Alexis say?"

"If she were me, she wouldn't fight it and all the other clichés."

"Well, I got to say I agree Liz."

"I'm nothing like Alexis, Dean."

Yes, we dated. Was it Dean's uncanny, striking similarities he had with Geoff? No, it couldn't be or could it? Besides, I couldn't still be in love with Geoff? Or could I be? That would be ludicrous.

Dean tried his best to romance me. Dean's spontaneity was part and parcel of the many qualities and virtues I liked about him. Okay, loved about him. *No*, wait. Oh, I don't know. I was so confused, okay messed-up. I also loved, liked, the many fun times we had shared together, but I guess it just wasn't meant to be.

Disappointing him, failing him physically, was just as worrisome as failing him on the inside as a woman, as a mate. I knew he wanted more. He had made the comment to me that soon he was hoping we might get married and start a family perhaps. Not that that was a proposal, he just wanted to put the bug-in-my-ear as to his hopes and dreams.

I couldn't bring myself to get any deeper involved with Dean, unable to promise or make some sort of commitment to him. He wanted me to make myself vulnerable to him, more vulnerable than I already had been, and I just couldn't. But, he had brought a part of me to life that I hadn't expected, hadn't dreamed of. But still, I couldn't go all the way and make that type of promise or commitment . . . or use that *L-word*.

Marriage is a big deal and a possible proposal should be given respect, even if I couldn't see myself going through with it. It wasn't fair to Dean. Something was still holding me back? Had I come all this way only to fail? Would love continue to be my greatest intangible, an imponderable force?

Dean's last words to me were itched in my mind. "I can't afford to get in any deeper, Liz. I have real, legit feelings for you. I'm no longer sure what I am doing here with you? I just can't take it any further, to remain in a relationship with a woman who can't commit, and tell me that she loves me. If you could, it might change everything. You'll never find a peace of mind until you listen to your heart, Liz."

I didn't know how much I needed Dean until the night I watched him walk away. I felt something inside of me tear away when the door had closed at Dean's back, and I knew I should have stopped him, but I didn't. I did love Dean. I just couldn't say for sure that I was in love with him. I couldn't handle it, because I'd given up on *happily-ever-after*.

Haunted by a sense of loss grew until it was a permanent underlying ache, which I carried around with me. I had alienated Dean and lost the chance of something, which he had thought worthwhile, and which I knew now, could have transformed my life. He had asked me not to run away from it, to give it a chance to grow, and I had done the reverse.

Okay, was I out of my *cotton picking mind*? What was I thinking? Or was I simply just cursed? Any woman in her right mind would have given their eyeteeth to be with Dean. I was unmercifully hard on myself and definitely not in my right mind, commitment phobic, and love phobic. Most men seem to pass through my life.

Chapter Eleven

Alexis had graduated and we had moved to the city, the other tip of the Rock as it was called, the other side of the island. A vast contrast from the small west coast community we had been living in. Small to me anyway, I could have thrown a rock from one end to the other.

Mountains and cliffs enveloped us in the city with a neighbouring town that shared a busy harbour, so serene, tranquil, and picturesque, sitting bowl like. The Puffin, being the provincial bird made its home in the cliffs. The narrows provided the means of passage for ships entering or leaving the harbour. Soon the town of Mt. Pearl's population grew in stature and status, becoming a city, a twin city with St. John's – the capital of the province. Almost identical from the twin cities I was from.

The only differences between these four cities, two were joined by land and shared a harbour, while the other two cities were separated by a harbour, which they shared, but were joined by the two bridges. Sure one could get from one city to another by land, but had to drive around the basin through another town. So the bridges provided a link, an easier thoroughfare between these two cities. On the outskirts of the four cities were other towns, villages, and communities.

I got a job Monday through Friday as a secretary in the Town Hall of Mount Pearl, before the town was deemed a city. Alexis worked nights in a local restaurant as a bartender, searching for a job in her chosen field, a court stenographer.

I ended up continuing to drink and drank frequently, whenever I could. Alcohol became my so-called best friend. I lived a double life, somehow working by day and drinking by night, on a regular basis. I didn't slow down any on the weekends.

I was unaware if Alexis had any clue what was going on. Our work schedule didn't let us see much of each other and other times Alexis spent with Matt. It seemed the only way we got together was when we took out our calendars, so we could set some time aside.

Alexis never understood whatever really happened between her cousin Dean and I, and I know she was disappointed, but she wouldn't make mention of it or ask me any questions. We were becoming somewhat distant. This path of destruction I was following continued for some time, causing me to crash and burn. Such an outcome is inevitable.

One August Friday night, in '86, I was alone with my 40 oz., bottle of Vodka. I drank myself into one hell of a stupor. Definitely lessening my ability to feel, mental numbness. I must have blanked out. When I came to, I was slumped down, with my back against the wall, between the kitchen, and living room. It was beginning to get dark; no lights were on. Didn't matter, I couldn't see, I wasn't wearing my glasses. I could care less. Everything was just a blur anyway.

Unable to comprehend the impact of the mess I had gotten myself in, I reached for the bottle. It was bone dry. But the knife was still in my hand, blood all over me.

At first, it didn't register what I had done to myself; I was oblivious to everything. All I wanted at that moment was another bottle, another drink. My movements were pretty slow and clumsy as I crawled, dragging my *butt* over to the kitchen cupboard. It seemed like it took an eternity before I could position myself enough to unscrew the cap from the bottle and take another swig. Somehow, with the bottle in hand, I crawled back to where I had been slouching. The end table was close with the phone.

The depressive state I was in, coupled with my heavy drinking, had its grip on me. Aloneness, loneliness, sadness, and hopelessness were overwhelming, an angry, frightening place to be in. I had reached a point of suffering, where tears no longer flowed, and all hope had been abandoned. Drinking had taken its toll on me; one could only live like this without the bottom petering out, it had to catch up with me at some point. I guess some of us would rather leave this world than change.

Hell, I couldn't even do that right; one would think with all the alcohol I had consumed I would have had blood alcohol poisoning. I couldn't imagine why not.

I managed to light a cigarette, then reached up to grab the phone, trying to rest my head while I dialed. I don't know what compelled me to call. I almost put the phone back in its cradle as I listened to the phone ringing on the other end.

Perhaps my parents weren't home. If I was to tell my mother, was I ready to bare the brunt of all the things I didn't want to hear, all the, I told you so's or it was only a matter of time. Would I hear all of my mother's disappointments in her voice? The disappointments that come along with having a daughter that turned out to be such a failure, a black sheep, a rebel, and a disgrace. I wasn't the smart one, I wasn't the one who would or could amount to anything, that constant nagging, a thorn in their side. The last thing I wanted to do was complicate things further or to continue being an embarrassment, and burden to my family.

To my vague recollection, piecing together the bits of our conversation, my mother said something about time, it finally happened. Was it a mother's intuition or a *Divine Intervention*? It was as if she was expecting this day to come and had prepared herself. I hadn't said much, but she knew. I had created drama and panic, the need to be rescued. That was going to be difficult, since she was so far away. My Mom didn't know anyone here except Alexis she had never been here.

Alexis was working and wasn't planning on coming home, until sometime the next day or Sunday. But somehow, my mother was able to talk me into making a verbal agreement with her, not to do anything until she was able to figure something out, and call me back. She told me she didn't want to hang up, but she had to make a phone call. I was not up to arguing with my mother, but I was worried about what my mother was going to do or whom she was going to call.

I don't really remember saying good-bye, hanging up the phone or how much time had elapsed when I heard the phone ringing. I hadn't moved from the spot on the floor where I had been sitting.

Arrangements were made. When I asked my mother what she did, she told me she had contacted Kenny, her friend's nephew in New Brunswick, who had contacts with people over here.

Oh great, Kenny was a minister, so that meant the people over here were involved with a church no doubt. That's all I needed now, someone getting spiritual with me. I was not in any frame of mind for company, let alone to discuss God or whatever. I had to figure out how I was going to bandage my wrists before they came and find a long sleeve shirt to wear to cover up the bandages. Of course it had to be August, not the type of weather one would wear a long sleeve shirt in. My mother remained on the line until I returned. Someone was downstairs . . . they were fast.

It wasn't that they were an older couple, a husband, and wife, strangers sitting in my living room; but they were from the suicide prevention organization, *Turning Point*. The events of the next 24 hours were going to be emotionally draining. I was petrified, uncomfortable sitting in my own skin, not to mention sitting in my own home. What an embarrassing, awkward time. So much pain, shame, anger, and fear, emotions were heightened, and mixed. Strangers knowing my business, it was humiliating. I was only hanging on by a thread to whatever dignity I had left, if any.

They actually were a soft-spoken couple, gentle, caring individuals, posing no threat, no pressure. I eventually was able to relax a little in their presence. I knew I needed help, but at this point I didn't want anyone getting into my head. I was of the opinion that talk was over-rated. It was protocol however, for anyone who attempted suicide to have a psychiatric evaluation. Luckily for me, the psychiatrist made house calls. I wasn't aware that psychiatrists made house calls, but he was part of Turning Point.

For some reason the psychiatrist agreed not to report my suicide attempt, if I promised to work with one of the volunteer Turning Point counsellors. He was concerned about my wrists. But I didn't want anyone to see them. I figured since I was still alive it was apparent that I didn't do enough damage to warrant going to the hospital. I didn't want to go to the hospital, unless I was in a body bag.

The psychiatrist managed to convince me to at least let him check my wrists. They were a mess, but they would heal. He said I was a lucky girl. I didn't feel that way. I forgot that a psychiatrist was actually a medical doctor before they specialized. I was paired with Emma Bambury, who took me under her wing.

When I was at my lowest point in my life, God sent an angel to watch over me. That angel was Emma.

My Mother's flight had arrived that afternoon. She was on a mission; she wanted me to come home. I wasn't ready for that. She stayed with me for a few days, making sure I was going to be all right. It surprised Alexis to find my mother here, when she came home the following night.

Life got in the way of our big plans and seeking happiness somewhere else. Alexis and I would end up going our separate ways, but remained as friends. I stayed in the city, while Alexis returned to the west coast of the island, where I visited her once, a few years later. She had remarried, not to Matt, but a man she had met while working as a court stenographer. I was happy for Alexis, she found happiness with her new husband and a baby was on the way. But, we ended up loosing touch over the years.

Religious beliefs often go hand-in-hand with guilt. I still was missing it or not understanding it clearly and I couldn't shake the humiliation, and guilt. I simply continued to bury it. Hiding the garbage still inside me. I hadn't yet realized that my thinking, feeling patterns I had learned early in life had brought this abuse upon me. I learned early about abuse and fear and continued to recreate those experiences. Being so closemouthed at times has its disadvantages.

Perhaps, with time, the new people in my life and my spiritual awakening of sorts would soften me from being so unmercifully hard on myself. I was hoping to be able to recapture something of the old carefree happiness. I had remained long enough in my own little corner of the world, but now I had to come to grips with earning a living again. Jobs were not all that plentiful. To find a good paying job, on top of everything else, seemed just too much, but I was trying to remain optimistic, something would eventually come along.

Prospects seemed hopeless, until I got an interview from a newspaper add I had responded to a few weeks previously. Remembering I had hand delivered my resume to the address and person mentioned in the advertisement.

At first, I thought the pay was too little to live on, but decided to take the position when it was offered to me; at least it would get my foot in a door. It was a secretarial position with the head office of a sheltered workshop for adults with intellectual disabilities.

A few months had passed as I was settling in. It was during this time that I became a volunteer advocate, representing, and acting on the behalf of those who needed a voice. I quickly became involved in, and touched by, the triumphs and disasters of others. Beckoning me to further my education, a complete career change.

Once getting specific training I worked with adults with intellectual disabilities, and Mental Health Consumers through the Department of Social Services. Facing the many challenges lying before me, a learning grid of what would come, both personally, and professionally.

I also learned some Sign Language along the way, so I could communicate effectively to the deaf, and pioneered an after school program for troubled teenagers. Limited resources or shoestring budgets limited things, but with the help from local churches, the Department of Social Services, and the many volunteers, we were able to help many struggling teenagers find new direction in his or her life.

My days and nights were kept busy. Taking all the ups and downs, scrapes, bumps, and bruises; in a way that one soon learns is the nature of the job. Oh and yes, not to forget the many whimsical pitfalls or shortcomings politics plays.

Chapter Twelve

Winter was drawing near. A friend of mine, Leslie, had asked me if I would consider moving-in-to one of her neighbour's home for the winter, to look after it. An elderly man, whose mobile home trailer was so beautifully cradled deep within the woods, on a pond, on the outskirts of the city.

The elderly man's wife had recently passed away and his health was of great concern for his daughter and her family who lived on the Gulf of Florida. He wasn't willing to sell his home yet, but considered spending the winter months with them in Florida, if he could get someone to stay, and take care of his home, and dog from November until April.

I had gotten to know Leslie through the after school program at the church. She too was one of the dedicated volunteers. Leslie and her husband Tom couldn't have any children of their own. She was in a serious car accident a couple years back and the injuries she sustained would prevent her from ever having children. But she loved children, a born natural. Every year, moose collisions are all too prevalent on the Newfoundland highways. Colliding with these animals is potentially fatal for the humans and at the very least, is likely to cause a lot of damage to a car, let alone to the animal. The car she was a passenger in was totaled and somehow the moose got up and walked away.

Leslie had a generous heart and genuine concern for just about everyone. Her day would start with an early rise to get all her daily baking in; which consisted of, homemade baked breads, sweet breads, biscuits, cookies, squares, jams, jellies, and stews, etc. Making large enough batches or quantities that could feed any army or at least the small close-knit neighbours.

She was like little Red-Riding Hood, making her rounds to distribute and drop-in, bearing her gifts of scrumptiously baked goodies. Taking time out along the way to sit and visit with her elderly neighbour, sharing a pot of tea with a sweet or two.

One morning, Leslie took me along to visit with her elderly neighbour. It actually would work out great for the both of us. I was in the process of looking for another place. Presently, I had been staying with friends in the city, another couple, Karen, and Bill. Not wanting to wear out the welcome mat and the fact I usually didn't like to stay in one place for any length of time, this would be a great opportunity for me to have a place of my own, even if it was temporary. Time was drawing near for the elderly man to leave for Florida, but hadn't found anyone, until I showed up on his doorstep with Leslie.

Winters were usually harsh enough in the city, but to live on the outskirts of the city, in the woods, on a pond, would perhaps prove to be even more of a challenge. It was really the only downside to this living arrangement. But I figured I could adapt and make it through the next six months. If there were any problems it would be great having Leslie and Tom close by. Perhaps Leslie would consider keeping me supplied with her many varieties of baked goodies too. Homemade baked goods always tasted better than any store bought, especially if they came from Leslie.

The elderly man's spunky, adorable, and lovable two-year-old Golden Retriever named Goldie would make a great companion for those long, cold winter nights. She probably would have licked to death any unwanted strangers though, as opposed to guarding, and protecting me. When outside playing, Goldie usually romped around with her two buddies, a Black, and Chocolate Labrador Retriever. It was obvious how they got their names, Blackie and Chocolate. Both of which belonged to Leslie and Tom.

I decided to take up the offer. Besides, it would be a great reason for cross-country skiing; an easy way to get around in the area, and a great way to get some exercise. A quiet and restful place where I could be alone when I wanted to be, away from the hustle and bustle of the city.

Arrangements were also made with a local contractor, for any snow removal and I had a pretty good reliable four-wheel drive vehicle to help me maneuver through any of the tricky winter road conditions. On a good day it would only take about 20 minutes to drive into the city. Of course that was on a good day.

I was starting to get to know a few of the other friendly, close-by neighbours. In particular, AJ, rather a distinguished, handsome, tall, and rugged man, with a touch of premature greying in his well-groomed hair, and beard. A recent divorcee, who if I were to guess his age, I figured it was safe to say he was somewhere in his early thirties. Leslie had introduced AJ to me. Our paths had crossed on one brisk Saturday afternoon. Leslie and I were out 'n' about, cross-country skiing with our dogs frolicking along side us.

AJ was about to ski by, when Leslie greeted him. "Howdy AJ, beautiful day isn't it?" "Oh Hi Leslie and yes, it's a fabulous, beautiful day for being outside." A response he gave as he skied over to get closer to us. Realizing he didn't recognize me, he asked for an introduction. "Leslie and who do we have here?" "AJ, I'm sorry, I guess you and Liz haven't actually met?" "You've guessed right Leslie." AJ chuckled. I nodded my head in agreement. "Well then, let me make the formal introductions. AJ, this is Liz Sulis, Liz this is AJ Giovanni. Liz is the one taking care of Mr. Bryson's home, while he's in Florida for the winter." AJ gave me a quick look-over.

"Oh, so you're the lady whose staying at old-man Bryson's trailer?" "Ah huh." "Well, it's nice to meet you Liz, if there's anything you need or if there's anything you need help with, just holler. I'm only two-doors down from you." "Thanks and it's nice to meet you too." "Well girls, enjoy the rest of your afternoon skiing. Sorry I can't stay to chat or join you in some skiing, but I have to get back, got some work to do." AJ gave me a smile. "Remember Liz, if there's anything, just holler, and it was nice meeting you." "Thanks and likewise."

"Well, ciao for now ladies." Before we continued on with our skiing, I glanced back over my shoulder. I caught sight of AJ as he quickly disappeared through the gorge we had just skied through a short distance back.

"Liz, AJ is a nice fellow. You both should get to know each other." A tad beleaguered. "Oh, you think so eh Leslie?" "Yes! I do." Leslie gave me a quizzical smile, a teasing nudge, then sprinted off telling me to hurry or she would leave me in her tracks.

AJ was a Conservationist with the Parks and Natural Areas Division of the Provincial Department of Environment and Conservation. How fitting, he made a great partner for cross-country skiing and certainly knew his way around the area.

It was becoming abundantly clear to me though that Leslie was purposely reneging or making excuses not to come skiing whenever AJ would be joining us. Whatever her excuse or reason, she would tell the two of us to carry on without her, go, and enjoy ourselves together. This must have been Leslie's way of trying to be a matchmaker?

Not only was he a great cross-country skiing partner, but he also made an expert nature guide in a wildlife oasis. Especially, when he took me off the beaten track, no trail markers, no public buildings, and no roads. One could only get around on cross-country skis or by snowshoes to keep from sinking in the deep, soft snow. All-terrain vehicles, ski-doos or snowmobiles were prohibited in these areas.

These pristine, but accessible treks were so picturesque, a placid serenity. Much like most places in the province. They allowed you to capture glimpses of a critical habitat for a variety of endangered or threatened plants, and animals, in an area of superb natural beauty.

AJ shared with me how many creatures could only survive in very particular habitats. For instance, the Newfoundland Pine Marten depended on the old-growth forests, full of fallen logs, rotting leaves, and stumps. Cleared woods and new forests replanted after logging failed to serve the needs of this species. Nearly 70 percent of this Marten's habitat had already been lost through logging. I could truly understand and feel for how this situation exasperated him. Although other Canadian provinces and territories have Pine Martens, the Newfoundland species was not found anywhere else in the world. Now at least, a recovery team was developing a plan to make sure the Newfoundland Pine Marten would never disappear.

AJ led me on so many adventures, to places where nature, in our own back yard is to reign supreme. He was a great teacher. I learned so much about the many species that flap, leap, howl, squeak, and flower there. Every adventure was a new and breathtaking experience, in an ecosystem that interlinks and interlocks with the many rivers, brooks, streams, wildlife, and vegetation. When we had the time, this was a great way to unwind and release everyday stressors, in an almost effortless, but enjoyable way to get exercise.

It was easy for AJ to show his conservation stripe, a great advocate and it wasn't difficult to share in his interests. AJ worked at warning others of how important it is to take care of these forests and instilled in me a greater appreciation, and awareness of just how fragile our ecosystem was becoming, and what we can all do to help protect it. He would make sure we left nothing out of place or disturbed during any one of our many treks we took together.

AJ would also lend-a-hand whenever I needed help with replenishing the wood, for the wood stove. Together, we would haul wood from the woodpile stored inside the backyard woodshed and carry it into the trailer. At first, I was a little leery in having to use a wood stove. Growing up in a city I was spoiled with having the luxury of electricity to heat the home and electric stoves to cook on, unless of course, there was a power-outage, especially during the winter. Then things could become rather primitive I suppose, depending on how long the power-outage would last. However, it was a luxury I was accustom to, but I was getting pretty good at starting and stoking the fires.

Before Leaving for Florida, Mr. Bryson made sure that I knew how to properly use the woodstove and left me with easy instructions. I was gaining woodstove wisdom, in its day-to-day operation, especially with setting a fire to hold overnight. I didn't realize there was so much to learn, in using woodstoves and using them properly, and safely. I did however, have to use the whiskbroom on a regular basis to sweep-up any spilled ashes and bits of bark or wood that landed on the floor. Otherwise, AJ attended to the woodstove, keeping the fires burning whenever he was over.

Actually, AJ and I were spending quite a bit of time together it seemed these days, outside of our busy work schedules. Not that I minded, he was a great handyman to have around, as well as a great neighbour, cross-country skiing partner, and nature guide. A teasing, casual friendship was all that had evolved. I suppose it could have been rather boring at times, even though Goldie made a good companion. She just didn't talk much. On the other hand, AJ was a great conversationalist. I guess I could also say he was becoming a great dinner companion too. Neither of us really preferred to eat alone. Besides, I loved to cook and he loved to eat. Working as he did, especially in our great outdoors, I'm sure contributed to his great appetite. Later in the evenings, AJ didn't like the idea of me walking Goldie alone at night, so he would join me on her nightly walks.

We started spending our Saturday evenings together with Leslie and Tom. Alternating the Saturday's, taking turns with cooking. After supper we would team-up, girls pitted against the guys, and enjoy a game of crokinole or cards. This Saturday night was our turn to be the hosts. AJ and I decided to have supper Tuesday night so we could plan on what we were going to serve on Saturday.

~

Tuesday's usually were a busy day for me at work, never getting home until sometime around 7:00 p.m. or shortly thereafter. AJ told me not to worry about tonight's supper; he was taking care of it. He phoned me when I arrived home at a quarter to 7:00.

"Tonight! Me pretty lady, I'm taking you out to a very fine and elegant dining establishment to wine and dine you. I know the chef personally and he is in the throws of preparing us one of his finest gourmet feasts. So get your dancing-shoes on me pretty lady and I'll be over at a quarter pass 8:00 to pick you up."

I began to laugh. "I didn't know or realized you danced AJ? So tell me, where are you taking me and what should I wear?" "Ah, it's a truly excellent restaurant, with elegant décor, a wonderful ambience, and the food is 'par none. So, I would venture to say, a semi-formal attire would be appropriate for this night." "Well then AJ, I just got home from work and I think I better take a shower, and slip into something more appropriate than what I am wearing now." "Fine, me pretty lady. Your escort will swing by to pick you up at a quarter pass 8:00." "AJ, you surprise me. I would never have guessed you for a type of guy who would want to wine and dine in an elegant establishment, and to think this evening might include dancing." "Well, me pretty lady, tonight I might just surprise you. Now! Go, scoot, and get ready." "Okay AJ, bye."

I sat for a moment, shaking my head in wonderment. "Wow, I haven't seen this side of AJ yet Goldie." Wondering what AJ was really up-to. Looking down at my wristwatch I saw it was nearing 7:15 p.m. "Oh Lord, I have only an hour to get showered and dressed. I better get a move on then and get my butt in gear, huh Goldie?"

Goldie followed me down the hall and into the bedroom. I opened the closet bedroom door to see what I could find. I took from the closet a stunning, elegant black evening dress that I hoped would still hug me in all the right places. I held the dress up against the front of me as I looked in the full-length mirror. It definitely wasn't the little silhouette black dress Audrey Hepburn wore in the movie 'Breakfast at Tiffany's.' Typically, only two out of every 10 woman are able to wear that. But I figured this dress should put a little rumba in my saunter when I slipped into it and sure to please on any dance floor.

Now, I had to find the black, patent leather, and wing tip, four-inch shoes that I had originally bought to go with the dress. When I located them and removed them from the shoe rack, I glanced down at Goldie. "What do you think Goldie? Oops, on second thought, I guess you're not the one I should be asking. I'm sure you are eager to play with them or chew them." I gave a quick look around. "Your slippers are in the hallway girl." I motioned, pointing in the direction of the hallway. "Go get your slippers girl." Goldie remained sitting, eyeing the shoes in my hand and licking her chops. "Oh no you don't Goldie. I know what you are thinking. I'll put them back in the closet for now, so you won't be tempted."

I shaved my legs while in the shower, killing two birds with one stone. Once showered, I then put my make-up on, using the bathroom mirror. The lighting in the bathroom and over the mirror was the best light I had for this delicate operation. I never had any real reason or opportunity to get dressed-up or wear much make-up as of late. The last time I remember wearing this dress and shoes was when I flew back home for a weekend to play the piano for Sara and Jason's wedding, and reception in April. That was certainly a brief trip, but I was glad to see Sara again. She sure made a beautiful bride. She had asked me to be the pianist at her wedding when she had called me, excitedly telling me she was engaged. I'd rather play the piano, than be asked to be a bridesmaid for any of my friends' weddings. Besides, it saved me from ever being stereotypically cast as 'always a bridesmaid never a bride.'

Of course, the kind of work I was doing now, didn't really call for any dressy attire or make-up. Besides, I didn't really have the time to fuss with makeup and fancy hairdos, so I got away from doing it. But, as I stood there, in the bathroom, putting on the eyeliner, and mascara, with a touch of apricot eye shadow, I noticed how it all enhanced the tiny green flecks in my hazel eyes.

Returning to my bedroom I picked out some jewellery. A pearl necklace with matching earrings my mother had given me for Christmas one year. I proceeded to finish dressing. I clothed my body in black lingerie with a strapless black bra and sheer black nylons. Then slipped into my dress and shoes. It didn't take me long to realize I hadn't worn these shoes in a while. I'd hoped they wouldn't kill my feet. Chuckling at the thought, I'd certainly do a great job of aerating the lawn with these. I considered bringing an ace bandage and an ice pack to treat my ankles. I must be crazy to wear these shoes, but oh well. They at least would help elongate my legs. On second thought, I figured I'd better wear my black boots and carry my shoes. It's winter after all and spiked-heels won't be a good thing in the snow and ice. Switching shoes for knee-high boots, I put my shoes in a shoe bag and placed them on my bed until I was ready to go.

I was almost ready, final touch of accessorizing with the pearl earrings and necklace. Everything seemed to have come together. I glanced over, squinting to see what the time was on my digital clock radio. It was 8:13 p.m. Wow! That's cutting it close, but I still have two minutes to spare.

I had decided to wear my hair up, due to the dress I was wearing. My ash blonde hair was a little more than shoulder-length. Once up, I was ready. Oh, I had almost forgot. I needed some perfume. I didn't want to spray too much on. Obsession was the perfume I chose for this occasion. Some perfumes are so overwhelming and overpowering that they cause some people to have sensitivities to some scents or perfumes. Of course some people must bathe in it too. To be on the safe side, I only sprayed a squirt or two behind each ear and on my wrists.

I hoped what I was wearing would be appropriate, but not overly dressy for the atmosphere AJ was about to take me to. Good thing I had given myself a manicure the night before, before going to bed. They would have to do. I had brushed on two clear coats of nail polish.

My long, black dress coat was hanging-up on the left-hand side of the bedroom closet. I took it off the hanger, slipped it on, with a stylish multi-coloured silk scarf, adding an instant glam factor. Reaching over to my dresser, I grabbed my black leather dress gloves, with cashmere lining, a small black elegant leather purse, and carrying-bag with my shoes, still lying on the bed.

"Ta-da! I'm ready Goldie." As I twirled around, showing myself off to Goldie, I looked myself over again in the mirror, from head to toe, to make sure everything was complete. "What do you think Goldie?" Goldie had been watching every step I had taken during my transformation from a 9:00 to 5:00 working girl, to an elegant, fashionable lady, who would make a fairy Godmother proud.

Chapter Thirteen

I heard AJ knocking at the door. "Hello, are you ready Liz?" He shouted, as he showed himself in. "Yes, I'm ready, come in, I'll be right there." "I'm already in Liz."

AJ was standing in the kitchen as I was walking down the hallway. "Wow! Liz, you look smashing, simply stunning, and gorgeous. I've never seen this side of you before." I blushed. "Thank-you AJ. Wow! You look rather dashing and Dapper Dan yourself." AJ was wearing an Italian-tailored Giorgio Armani midnight-blue suit.

"Well, thanks me pretty lady. But I must say Liz I've never seen you look so beautiful as you are tonight. I mean you're a beautiful lady anyway. You're just more radiant and stunningly beautiful tonight. You'll definitely be the centre of attention tonight Liz." "Thanks AJ, but stop, you are making me blush."

As I was able to get a better look, I noticed something different about AJ. "Oh My God! AJ! You shaved. Your beard, it's gone! You actually have lips. I mean, ah, um, I mean I can see what your face really looks like." AJ was laughing; he actually had a beautiful smile that revealed two dimples. He definitely had lips, luscious even. His grey eyes sparkled when he laughed, a very deep and masculine laugh.

"Yes Liz, I have lips, two to be exact." I was blushing again. AJ took a couple steps, which brought him in closer to me. He was now towering over me. It must have been that he was wearing a suit and his posture was better or something. I never realized just how tall AJ really was.

"Can you see my two lips now Liz?" He grinned, as he asked me. "I mean can you really see them?" AJ arched himself over me, lowering his head. Our lips were only inches apart. "Ah huh, now I can see them clearly, both to be exact." The intimate distance between us left me breathless.

AJ smiled. "Good, now me pretty lady, are you ready to go? Supper is waiting for us." I had to catch myself, to get my breath back. "Yes AJ, I am ready, let's go." He extended his right arm, bending it at the elbow for me to wrap my arm and hand around his forearm, as he escorted me out to his car.

The contractor had ploughed the driveway, but AJ had shovelled the snow from my door to the driveway earlier in the day. Figuring that by doing so, it would make it easier for him to help me out, and into his car for this evening. "Thanks AJ for shovelling." "Your welcome Liz." Once I was seated in the passenger side, he scurried around his car to get to the driver's door, opening it to let himself in. Once we were both buckled-up he turned the car on. I was so surprised at how this night was starting to unfold. I never realized just how gorgeous and handsome AJ really was. He looked so different without his beard.

Once AJ backed out from the driveway, he turned the car heading in the direction of his house. "I forgot something at the house Liz." As he pulled into his driveway and stopped, he turned off the car. "Well, since we are here, why don't you come in for a moment? It shouldn't take me long for what I have to do. No point in keeping the car idling and I wouldn't want you to get cold out here Liz."

A little puzzled, I agreed to go in. He escorted me into his house. "Wow! AJ, you have a lovely place here." "Thanks Liz, come on in." After all this time we had been spending together, I couldn't remember ever being inside his house. It always seemed we spent our time together outside or at the trailer. Except of course, when we spent time with Leslie and Tom.

I noticed a fire roaring in the fireplace. Somehow missing the smoke that was bellowing from the chimney outside. "You have a fire going AJ, if we are going out?" Suddenly, I noticed his table was set for an intimate dinner for two, leaving me awestruck, and speechless. Set out before me were two fine china place settings, an elegant, and striking centerpiece containing a gorgeous arrangement of six red roses, mixed carnations, accented with greenery, and airy baby's breath, festooned with ribbons in a silk-swathed vase. The allure and warm glow radiating from the two candles burning, and a bottle of red wine opened on the table to breathe, helped with the finishing touches of the romantic ambiance AJ had created.

"Hey, what's going on AJ?" Pleasant savory aromas were filling the air and my sense of smell. "Ah me pretty lady, welcome to my elegant dining establishment. Here let me take your coat." A little stunned, I unbuttoned it. After he helped me slip it from my shoulders, I removed the scarf from around my neck, passing it to him, to place both on a near-by coat rack. I removed my boots, reaching into my bag to get my shoes. Once my shoes were on he took me by the hand, leading me over to the table. Pulling the chair out from beneath the table he asked me to have a seat.

"Now for your listening pleasure, I hope you like classical, perhaps a little opera?" "Huh, um, yes, I like classical, opera." "Great, I'll play something fitting that I think will suit this type of atmosphere." "Sure." I was still awestruck and speechless; this must have taken him a lot of work, time, and energy to prepare for this evening.

As AJ was choosing the music, I realized this was something I would never have expected and wasn't expecting. I wasn't sure what to think. This was definitely a side of AJ I hadn't seen before. It wouldn't have even entered my mind to ever expect such a thing to happen. I was flattered though, just a little uncomfortable or embarrassed perhaps.

For one brief moment, I felt a little anxious, flushed with genuine trepidation. Was AJ expecting anything more than friendship? It had been a long time since I felt this vulnerable. Before I could continue with my thoughts he returned to the table.

"You've taken me by surprise AJ." "Oh, you like?" "Yes, how couldn't I? You're sneaky though." He cringed. "Sneaky, me pretty lady? I would say, a romantic at heart, not really sneaky." I could feel myself becoming red in the face again.

While some kitchen Casanovas viewed cooking for a woman solely as an element in the certain seduction arsenal, perhaps AJ was more interested in creating a romantic, memorable date than in wielding a spatula simply to score. However, I already knew he was capable and a talented producer of delicious meals.

As I could hear the music softly playing in the background, I recognized his choice? "Nice choice of music, its Luciano Pavarotti isn't it?" "Ah, you know your opera and yes it's Pavarotti. One of the greatest tenors ever, that when he sings a melody it bleeds romance. He has the greatest range of classical tenors and the best control of any singer I know."

"Yes, he's one of the three tenors, Placido Domingo, Jose Carreras, and Pavarotti, the world's most renowned tenors, and my mother's favourite singers." "Your mother has great taste in music Liz." "Yes, she knows her classical and operatic singers and it's because of her I was a music student. A piano student to be exact." "Ah, something new I just learned about you Liz. Do you still play the piano?" "Yes, I still play. Obviously I don't have a piano here. The only one I ever seem to get to play sometimes is the one at the Church. But I usually play when no one is around. I do try and take a little time to myself at the church before the kids show up." "Kids?" AJ curiously questioned. "Yes, I volunteer at a church with an after school program, to give kids something to do, keeping them off the streets, and hopefully out of trouble. Actually, that is how Leslie and I met, she is one of the other volunteers."

"Oh, but wherever do you get the time Liz?" "Oh, I don't know, I guess I just make the time. After all it's just another thing to juggle, to plan, and conquer. The program doesn't start-up again until after the Christmas holidays, around mid-January." "I believe this time we spend together tonight Liz will reveal the many other talents and virtues you have tucked away. Perhaps, someday you'll be able to play something for me on a piano?" "Well, perhaps someday AJ, but unless you have a piano kicking around somewhere, I doubt it. Besides, I just play for my own enjoyment when I can, and I'm a little rusty. It's kind of hard to keep up with playing when I don't have one here at my fingertips. My parents have my piano. It wasn't something I was going to carry around with me when I moved here. Besides, it wouldn't have fit in my car anyway." I smirked. "Other than that AJ, there isn't really much else to know about me." "I don't believe that for a second Liz. Everyone has many things to share. Life is full of interesting life experiences, good or bad, giving us all stories to tell or talk about." "Well, I suppose so AJ."

"Would you like some wine Liz, do you like wine?" As he asked, gesturing towards the open bottle of red wine sitting on the table. "Yes, I like wine." "Perfect, some of this wine will go with what we are having for supper." "That will be fine AJ." "Excuse me again Liz, while I check on how supper is coming along and pour us some of this then." I smiled, AJ picked up the bottle of wine and glasses as he headed to the kitchen.

"Here you go Liz." He extended his hand passing me one of the glasses he had just poured. "Thanks AJ. So tell me please, what are we having? What smells so delicious and has been tantalizing my senses, and will no doubt my taste palate too?"

"Ah, I took the liberty of preparing for us." I couldn't help myself from laughing, which interrupted him from finishing what he was going to say. "What's so funny Liz?" 'I'm sorry AJ for laughing, so you're the chef too? I guess this means we are not having any take-out or home-delivery? It also explains why you said you know the chef on a personal level."

AJ gave an amusing chuckle. "Chef Antonio Juliann Giovanni at your service, better known to you as, Chef AJ, and no, it isn't take-out or home-delivery."

It suddenly dawned on me that I never knew or asked him what AJ stood for. "So that's what AJ stands for, Antonio Juliann." "Yes, that's me." "Well it's nice to know what AJ stands for. Sorry, you were about to tell me AJ or should I say, Chef Antonio Juliann Giovanni what tonight's menu entails."

"Oh yes, right. Tonight's menu me pretty lady, consists of first, Insalata, lattuga con le mele, uva sultanina e dadi di pino, then for the main course, Arrosto di maiali rotolato, farcito con spinaci e mortadella e patata cotta, and last, but not least, for dessert, Torta italiana della crema del cioccolato della mia madre, con dopo il liquore italiano del sud del pranzo, Mandarino."

"AJ, it all sounds so delicious in Italian. However, my Italian's rather limited and I don't have the foggiest idea of anything you have just said. Would you mind translating?" "Nope, you'll just have to trust my culinary skills and eat when it's ready. It should be ready in about 30 minutes or so. That should be enough time I figure, for us to drink our glass of wine while we chat for a bit, and listen to the music."

I took a sip of the wine. "This has a fresh and lusciously berry taste and powerful floral aroma AJ, what is it?" "It's Costanti, Brunello di Montalcino red. It's one of the best of Italian red wines. Unparalleled elegance and complexity don't you think." "Oh, a wine from the Italian Tuscany region?" I took another sip. "Yes, it has remarkable structure and exquisite balance."

I noticed AJ was watching me intently, with a raised brow. "Oh, so you're a wine connoisseur too Liz?" I couldn't help from laughing. "*No*, far from it AJ. But, according to my Grandmother, who, like you is Italian, and sure loves her wines, has mentioned that the Tuscany reds are the most sought-after of the Italian wines. That's not to overlook the reds from Sangiovese, Piedmont, Umbria, and Southern Italy of course." "Of course not." AJ amusingly smiled as he took another sip. "Grant it, Nan would also say that Italy's wine industry is such a muddle. The home of the most disorganized wine industry in the world. That's next to Spain of course, whom, according to her, is trying desperately to grab this crown." Not to sound too disapproving of Italy's wine industry, I quickly added. "My grandmother would come to their defence though, by saying how amazing it is that thousands of Italy's wine producers manage to serve up some delicious vintages of wines out of their hundreds of obscure, indigenous grape varieties." "I'm impressed Liz, your mother has great taste in music and your grandmother sure is knowledgeable about Italian wines, they have taught you well."

I had to quickly try to stop the trickle of wine that managed to escape from the corner of my mouth as I was removing the wine glass from my lips. "Excuse me AJ." As I reached for my napkin that was lying next to me on the table, AJ quickly came to my aid, reaching over with his napkin to catch the wine I had missed.

"It's a shame to waste any of this. Thanks AJ, sorry, how embarrassing that was, not a smooth move on my part." I was relieved though that none happened to get on my dress. "It's ok Liz, relax, it's nothing to be embarrassed about." He had finished wiping my mouth and chin, pulling his hand, and napkin away.

"So Liz, tell me more about your grandmother." "More AJ? What do you want to know exactly?" "Well, for starters, where in Italy your grandmother is from, how she met your grandfather perhaps or what about other family?"

"Actually, she's my step-grandmother. I don't really know her that well and I didn't meet my grandfather until he was on his deathbed; I was 15 or 16 at the time. I don't think my father or his brother, my Uncle Bruce, were ever that close to him. Might have had something to do with my grandparent's divorce, some time before the Second World War. After their divorce, my grandfather, Wilfred, and his new wife, Alma, moved to New Hampshire, Massachusetts from Boston. Wilfred was a good friend of Alma's sister, who had been living in Boston at the time, and that's how they met. But, Alma's sister had moved to California to get away from the cold." I took a moment to take another sip of wine, managing not to spill any this time.

"Alma is from Venice, they had fallen-in love, she immigrated to the States, they got married, had a daughter, and a son, and the rest is history. But when my grandfather had died, my grandmother moved to California to be with her sister. Alma visited us a couple times when she was healthier and could tolerate the long flight from California to Halifax. She made the best lasagna I have ever had and she always wore a sweater, finding a chill in the air. Apparently, our summers were not warm enough for her."

"Is she still in California with her sister Liz?" "No, actually, her sister passed away unexpectedly, a couple years ago, so she moved in with my Dad's half-sister and her husband, who live on the Gulf of Florida. Other than that, there isn't much else to tell about my family, except I have two older brothers, Donald and James, who are both married, with children, and live in Dartmouth. Of course, that's where my parents live too. Anyway, enough about me, what about you Antonio Juliann Giovanni? Tell me about your family?"

AJ thought for a moment. "Um, well, my father, he died when I was a boy, I was 7. He perished in a fire." At that moment I could sense his emotions building inside. My heart went out to him.

"He was a fireman and was on the 3rd floor of a building trying to rescue someone when the roof collapsed." His voice softened and tapered off, while he tried to choke back his emotions, pulling away for a moment to gain his composure. I realized how sensitive he was; still filled with grief and passion of a father he never had a chance to get to know.

"I had to grow up quick. I was only a kid I know, but back then, knowing, and seeing how much his death crushed my mother, the love she had for him, I knew I had to be strong, for her sake. So, I tried to be the man of the house. Each night, before she went to bed, I would sneak down-stairs, and see my mother hugging my dad's picture so tight, resting her head on the frame, and cry, sobbing uncontrollably." AJ stopped for a moment, taking a deep breath, before he continued. "Anyway, my mother had Alzheimer's, she died a few months ago."

My words were laced with sorrow as I reached out my hand to cover his, in a comforting manner. "Oh AJ, I'm so sorry, I didn't know. But, you didn't tell me." "That's her picture over on the mantel piece of the fireplace. Would you like to see it Liz?" "I would love to AJ." He walked over to get the picture, as he handed me the picture he sat back down.

"I actually felt she had died five years ago, when I thought I had already mourned her death, in a way. You know you got to hold your parents dear Liz, because it's an awful world without them." "Oh! AJ." I wanted to say more, but I couldn't because of the sympathetic lump that was welling up in the back of my throat, and the fact my own eyes were already misty, and teary-eyed. I reached over again to touch his hand; covering it ever so softly, giving it a comforting squeeze.

He reached out with his other hand, brushing the back of it along my cheek. "Well, I definitely can see where you're good looks come from AJ. What a lovely picture. I'm sure your mother was as beautiful on the inside, as she was on the out." "Thank you Liz and yes she was so beautiful in so many ways. I loved my mother." "I can't even imagine what it would be like without my mother or father AJ. I'm so grateful that they are both well. It is so easy to take them for granted, I just." "It's okay, really Liz."

"AJ, tell me more." "Well my mother did remarry." "Oh, so you have a step-father? Is he still alive, if so, where is he?" "Yes, I have a step-father and yes he's still alive. My mother had married him a few years after my father's death. He adopted me, but when I got older I legally changed my name, taking back my father's name, Juliann Giovanni. Not to say that she didn't love him, I just think she married him so I would have a father figure or a male mentor. Money had become tight so I'm sure she had hoped he could provide for us both. That he did and in more ways than one. I'm sure you can well imagine I wasn't too keen on my mom getting married again; at least I wasn't at first. I thought I would lose my status of being the man of the house. But that wasn't the case; he's a great man and was a good husband to my mother. He treated us both well, all I ever really wanted was for my mom to be happy."

"I'm sure she was happy AJ. He wasn't your real father I realize that, and I know I don't know him. But I'm sure it's safe to say he knew he couldn't have nor expected to have filled your father's shoes. There's no substitution for a real father's love. But from what you are telling me, it sounds like he really loved your mother, and you. Wanting to take care of you both, the best way he could. And from what I can see, he did an excellent job?"

"Yes Liz that's all true. He's living in Grand Falls. Walter was never one for being a city slicker. He had worked for Hydro-Abitibi, until mom got sick and he had to retire. I know it was hard on him, to see her this way. He took care of her, until he no longer could, and we felt we had no choice but to put her in a nursing home. That didn't stop him from being by her side, every step of the way, even when she succumbed to this horrific, debilitating disease. I hate to say it, but it really was a blessing in disguise. Now I feel she can rest in peace, she is with God, and enjoying being reunited with my father. I thank my stepfather Walter for all that he has been and done for my mother and me. We keep in touch and I visit him whenever I can."

AJ's story was so compelling, I almost forgot. "Oh AJ, what about telling me where in Italy you are from?" "Well, I'm from Marciana Marina, a small town on the north shore of Italy's Elba Island. Mom took me to Italy whenever she could to visit family and friends. She wanted to make sure I kept my Italian roots. Walter came along on a few of our trips, but his work kept him fairly busy. It's a great place to do some sea kayaking Liz, an extraordinary patchwork of natural landscapes, about 20 kilometres off the Tuscan shore."

"It sounds so beautiful AJ, I use to kayak, but never sea kayaking." "Well then, perhaps someday we should try it Liz?" AJ finished his last mouthful of wine and when placing the glass back down on the table he stood to his feet. Stepping behind me he took hold of the back of my chair.

"Would you like to dance me pretty lady? I did ask you to put on your dancing shoes." "Okay, sure AJ, but what about supper?" "We still have a few minutes Liz." AJ helped to move my chair out, as I went to stand. He took me by the hand and led me into the living room, stopping long enough to turn the volume up on the sound system. Then turned to me. "Would it be all right if we danced close?" "Yes AJ, otherwise I would suggest you play something a little more up tempo if we were not to dance close." "Oh, would you prefer to dance apart Liz, something a little more up beat?" AJ asked dryly.

I cleared my throat and smiled. *"No!"* Feeling a little apprehensive. "I just meant, how else would we dance to such romantic and soulful music, unless we danced close." AJ felt a tinge of nervousness. He was enjoying his few years of being a bachelor and celibacy, since his divorce from Tina, a time of emotional, and physical R and R.

As he took me in his arms, we both stood for a moment without moving, gazing into each other's eyes. "Your eyes Liz, are actually hazel, with deep flecks of green. They dance with amusement in a way I find absolutely adorable. You are so beautiful Liz. It's heavenly having you here with me tonight."

I could feel my face turning red again; realizing how much he was making me blush. He drew me in closer to his body and began to move, gliding me across the hardwood floor. I was trying to steady myself and keep in step with him. I started to feel a little light-headed, flushed with, could it be, romantic feelings. I was in the arms of a very attractive man that I was seeing in an entirely different light. I already saw him as a man who articulated with great intellect, a man of much character, and substance. Now, tonight, I could say, romantic, warm, and gracious, with many surprises, and spontaneity. And oh, could he dance, it was like I was dancing on air.

Who was this intriguing, mysterious man? It was as if we had just met and this was a first date. Not that we had ever really been on a date before. Sure we had been doing things together; cross-country skiing, taking Goldie for walks, getting together with Leslie and Tom on Saturday nights, even sharing suppers, but nothing ever like this. But I never saw any of that as a date, just neighbours getting together, doing things as friends.

The music stopped, I gave an incredulous gasp. I told myself with would-be airiness that the music had to be the most evocative thing there is. "Liz, can we continue this after we eat, supper is ready?" I had forgotten about supper. "What, oh sure, eat, yes, right you are." Pull yourself together Liz and fast. Tonight I felt I was so out of my league with AJ. Before he was willing to let me go out of his embrace, he moved his right hand gingerly, touching my chin with his index finger, tilting my head so he could look into my eyes once again.

"I hope you don't mind, but." He lowered his head, until his lips covered mine, kissing me gently at first, my eyelids closed as I could feel my heart begin to race. I was soaring off into space, seeing stars, a rather euphoric feeling. Warm and fuzzy all over as though I was beginning to spin out of control, way out of control.

Could this really be happening? His kiss deepened, with increasing intensity. He tasted so good; his lips were so sweet, moist, and tender. I was loosing myself even further in this invigorating kiss. All of a sudden, our lips parted, not that I wanted them to part. But he was the one who stopped the kiss. My eyes were still shut; obviously AJ could tell I was a little dazed.

"Hey, earth to Liz, this is mission control, you can come in for a landing now." I slowly opened my eyes, catching a glimpse of AJ looking into my eyes and smiling. Though rather embarrassed for one brief moment, I was able to gain enough composure to give him a rhetorical response.

"Mission control, the Eagle has landed." Still smiling he gave me a wink. "Good, let's eat." My eyebrows arched in a serious query. I almost uttered aloud the words do we have to? I found myself barely able to move, still a little dizzy, and reeling from that kiss.

He guided me back to my chair, pulling the chair back out, so I could sit, I needed to sit. My legs were weak; they were like Jello, barely feeling them under me. Once seated, AJ went to the kitchen to serve up the food.

We started with a salad, lettuce with apples, grape sultanas, and a dice of pine nuts. Then came the main course. Rolled roast pork, stuffed with spinach, and mortadella, and baked potato. Dessert was an Italian chocolate cream cake, a recipe of his mothers, with an after dinner southern Italian Liqueur, Mandarino.

"I must tell you AJ that was an exquisite meal, my compliments to the chef." "Thank you Liz, I'm glad you enjoyed it." "Tell me though chef Antonio Juliann Giovanni, there had to be aphrodisiac properties in the meal?" I realized what I had just implied. AJ began to chuckle. "Well Liz, they say pine nuts are an aphrodisiac." He paused for a moment.

"Are you still feeling up to continuing from where we had left off before supper?" "Well that all depends AJ, are you referring to our dancing or that kiss?" Giving me another wink. "Perhaps a little of both Liz."

I momentarily drifted back off into space, remembering how captivating his kiss was. Suddenly catching myself. "Ah, perhaps I should help you clear the table and help wash the dishes AJ." "I don't think so Liz, I can do the dishes later." "But, AJ." "No *buts'* about it Liz, besides we have some more dancing to do." Extending his hand. "May I have this dance?" I took his hand and followed him back into the living room.

The way AJ was holding me, as we moved across the floor, I could feel an increasing sexual desire. Perhaps it was the pine nuts, contributing to how I was feeling, but I doubted that. AJ alone was the aphrodisiac. Or was it the music or perhaps the wine or the after dinner liqueur. No, it was AJ. He was the cause of the chills running up and down my spine, and the goose bumps forming on my bare skin arms. Of course, the meal, the pine nuts, the music, the wine, and the liqueur were probably contributing catalysts in how I was feeling. What a romantic night this had turned out to be. I didn't want it to end.

"What time is it AJ." He glanced at the clock sitting on the mantle over the fireplace. "It's almost 1:00 Liz." "Oh no, I forgot all about Goldie." "Don't worry about Goldie Liz. I asked Leslie if she wouldn't mind taking her out for her evening stroll." "Huh? You did? My, you have thought of everything, haven't you AJ?" "Well, I told her I was having you over for a nice quite supper, alone. She was ecstatic to know and told me not to worry about Goldie. She and Tom would be more than happy to take her out for her evening walk, along with Blackie and Chocolate."

"Wow! Where has this night gone? It's late AJ and I have to work in the morning, do you?" "Well, no, I don't have anything to do, until the afternoon. I don't have structured hours like you do Liz."

"I have had such a wonderful time AJ. Everything was perfect. Thank you for everything." "I suppose this means it is time for me to take you home Cinderella?" I smiled. "Yes, I suppose that's what it means. My fairy Godmother must have extended the time without me realizing it, before everything was to change back. This Cinderella better find her glass slippers though. But, I don't recall when or where I had taken them off?"

"They're over next to the couch I think, come on, sit on the couch while I get them, then I'll slip them on your feet Liz." "My, what a gallant and noble prince you are, and they say chivalry is gone. However, I better put my boots back on AJ."

"Here are your shoes and boots." I sat on the couch and AJ knelt in front of me. "I need your left foot Cinderella." I was obliging and extended my foot. As he took my nylon-clad foot in his hand, instead of slipping on the boot, he placed it back on the floor, and began to massage the top surface of my foot. Then taking his thumbs, in a slow, firm stroking motion starting at my toes, he moved up to the ankle. Once he reached the ankle he followed the same line back to the toes, applying lighter pressure towards the toes than the ankle. He continued to repeat this several times before he performed the same technique to the sole of my foot.

"Ohhh, that feels so good AJ." My sensitivity to my feet caused me to squirm. It wasn't long before I was in a supine position and lying half off the couch. AJ stood and reached down scooping me into his arms. He was kissing me again. Something I had been waiting for, starving for since the first kiss, which seemed so long ago.

"Liz, if, if you would just stay, I would promise you that the rest of this night, I, I would give you all the love that's burning in me. I'd give you everything that I am, if, if you'll just say that you'll stay." His words were music set to my ears, as I studied his face for a moment. Hesitantly, I took a deep breath. "I, I thought you were never going to ask AJ, yes, yes I'll stay, I'm all yours."

As he disappeared momentarily into the on-suite bathroom, the thought did cross my mind. The chances of me regretting this when I came to my senses, was a risk I was willing to take? This was a moment of happiness, however fleeting. It was well worth it, up to this point my heart was soaring. I quickly had to block, push those or any negative thoughts aside. Not to show him even the slightest of pretense or back away now. Oh, what he had me doing and feeling. I had to remain as I was, continuing to focus on the joy and desire he had already been able to stir within me. Surrendering completely to what was obviously something we both were earnestly longing for. Our relationship was definitely moving to another level.

As he returned, my wide-eyed gaze was now holding his. We were but inches apart.

I reached up to remove the hair accessories that were holding my hair in place and then passed them to him. AJ stood staring for a moment as I wrestled my hands and fingers through my hair, until it was free flowing, and shoulder length again. AJ leaned over towards the night table to place the hair accessories on it.

I gathered my hair, lifting it up. "AJ, would you mind removing the pearls?" "Not at all." As I turned around, he removed the necklace. He again leaned over to lay the necklace along side the hair accessories.

Regaining his stance, I was facing him again. I slid my hands beneath his suit jacket. I could feel the heat of his chest through the thin fabric of his shirt. Moving my hands from his chest to his shoulders, his arms dangling by his side, I slipped the jacket from his shoulders, easing it down his arms until it dropped to the floor.

Drawing me nearer and without hesitation he began to kiss me softly. I whispered. "Ohh, oh God. Don't stop, please don't stop."

His kiss deepened, exuberating passion, and warmth that was penetrating my mind, body, and soul. There was something more intoxicating about this kiss. The more he gave the more I wanted. The sensations he was stirring consumed me . . .

When I came to my senses, I felt the hot weight of his body still clinging to me. We remained, as we were in silence, sated and weary. AJ quickly shifted his body away once he realized his weight was becoming unbearable for me to continue to support. "How about we get under the covers Liz, snuggle up, and we both try to get some sleep." "What time is it AJ?" "I don't think you really want to know, but it's almost 6 o'clock." I laughed. "Oh well, I guess I'll be phoning work to say I won't be able to make it in, until sometime this afternoon."

"What time are you expected into work Liz?" "Around 9:00 a.m." "I'll set the alarm clock for?" "Set it for 8:00 please, I'll call then to make arrangements to go to work later. Oh and by the way AJ, we didn't figure out what we are going to prepare and serve for Saturday night when we get together with Leslie and Tom. Do you have any suggestions?" He crooked his head to look down at me, giving me a mischievous grin, which revealed his dimples. "I suppose for this Saturday darling, we could do take-out or have home-delivery?"

I snickered. "True, I suppose." Once under the sheets I snuggled up against his chest, tucking my head under his chin my nostrils drew in his masculine scent.

Chapter Fourteen

Another winter storm was beginning to brew. I was working late due to not getting into work until the afternoon. I hoped I could make it home safely before the already snow-covered roads would become impassable.

I turned on my car radio in the hopes of catching a weather up-date. The meteorologist was bleak, calling for heavy snowfall warnings, with high winds, causing drifting snow, and whiteout conditions throughout the province. I was unable to catch the actual amount of snowfall expected. But gathering from the conditions already, it was going to be a doozy of a storm. The snow was now falling heavier and making it hard for the wipers to work properly. The ice forming on the windshield wasn't helping matters either it was obscuring my view.

I could barely make it out but there was a snowplough up ahead. It sure was a welcoming sight. I followed the plough as it turned down my road trying to keep a safe distance behind and remain in his tracks. I breathed a sigh of relief as I turned into my driveway. Good thing for four-wheeled drives.

As I was getting out of my vehicle the snowplough was passing-by on the other side of the street. He gave me a honk. I waved back, unsure if he could see me waving.

When I got closer to the porch I noticed there was a rather large object propped-up against the front door. The snow hadn't covered it completely yet. It was a parcel, wrapped in Christmas paper. This was an unexpected but pleasant surprise. An envelope was taped to the top of it with a bright red Christmas bow. I recalled Leslie mentioning something about the church wanting to send me a Christmas hamper. A little token of their appreciation for all the volunteer work I had been doing with the after school program. Perhaps, I could invite some of the single people I knew who didn't have any family commitments for a Christmas dinner.

As I opened the door, and as usual, Goldie was there to greet me, jumping up, and down, wagging her tail, vying for my attention. The phone began to ring. It had startled me for a moment. Glancing at the kitchen clock I struggled to make my way through the door with the parcel. I wondered who would be calling me now it was nearing 1 o'clock in the morning?

The parcel was heavy and awkward. I was beginning to lose my grip with the parcel. Goldie wasn't making matters any easier. I had to quickly find a place to put the parcel down and maneuver around Goldie to get to the phone that was still ringing. I managed to grab the phone before the answering machine kicked in, sitting down in the recliner in the living room.

"Hello." "Hi Liz, it's me, Kerrie." "Kerrie! Do you know what time it is?" "Yes Liz, it's 1:00 am, I'm bored and need you to come and get me." "Kerrie, have you looked outside there is a nasty storm brewing, how could I come to you now? Besides, it is very late and I barely made it home because of the storm."

"I know it's late and snowing Liz, I'm on Lemarchant Road calling you from a payphone." "Kerrie! What in the world are you doing on Lemarchant Road at this hour, and in the middle of a blizzard?" "Calling you to come get me." "Kerrie, you should be at home and in bed sleeping. How in pray tell do you expect me to come and get you at this hour of the night, and during a snowstorm? Does anyone know where you are Kerrie?" "Yes, you." "No, Kerrie, I mean from the house?" Kerrie's response was a barrage of ugly epitaphs. Her contempt had no limits.

"Oh, Kerrie! I am sure they are aware that you are missing in action, and are frantically worrying about you, wondering where you are at this hour, and especially during a storm." "Well Liz, I hate them, I hate them all, and as I said, I don't care what they think, I just want you to come and get me now."

Man oh man; it was moments like these when one wanted to throw in the towel, when Kerrie would pull a stunt like this. She could be so demanding, unrealistic, acting inappropriately, and at the most inopportune times – impeccable timing. It didn't take much to set her off. It certainly wasn't going to be an easy task for me to convince her to return home and wait-out the storm, until I could come to her aid when the weather, and road conditions improved.

Whatever the reason, surely it could wait. Kerrie was known to call-wolf. Acting out and seeking any type of attention she could get. It was rare for it to be good attention. As long as she got what she wanted and it suited her that was all that mattered. She would resort to just about any trick in the book to get what she wanted, no matter what the cost.

"Kerrie, listen to me, I don't know how I can get to you now? I just got home and the roads are treacherous. So much snow has already fallen, it would be ludicrous for me to even try and it would take forever, and probably I would end up getting stuck, and stranded somewhere. It's dangerous for anyone to be outside including you, you must be freezing." "Well, I refuse to go back to the house and if you don't come and get me Liz." Kerrie paused, mumbling under her breath something inaudible. "Well um, then I'll do something to have the police come and get me and go to lock-up."

"Kerrie! You know that won't be a good thing. Please go home and try to get some rest. When the storm is over and the roads are cleared, then I promise I'll come to you." "So you won't come to get me now Liz?" "It's not a matter that I won't come to get you Kerrie, you know I would, I just can't, due to the storm, it's out of my control." The phone went dead. Kerrie hung-up.

Just great, this was going to be one of those nights. I could feel a headache coming on. I was looking oh so forward to climbing into my cozy bed for a good night slumber. Provided of course that Goldie didn't decide to hog most of the bed. I had a gut-wrenching feeling that getting a good night sleep wasn't going to happen now. Good thing I didn't have to work in the morning.

Charlene, one of my co-workers wanted to return a favour. Her eight-year-old daughter was thought to have had some kind of a debilitating and life-threatening hereditary condition. But with swift and accurate medical attention, and treatments, her chances of survival, and beating it were in her favour. About a month ago, her daughter was in the hospital for approximately a week, having more difficult routine tests and procedures done. Glad to report she did receive a clean bill of health once the test results came back negative, and now is an active, normal, little eight-year-old girl again. A number of us were only too glad to help. Re-arranging our work schedules to cover Charlene's shifts were a lot easier than what trauma and fears her little girl had gone through. Knowing how stressful it was for Charlene, she needed to be with her daughter, and her daughter needed her mommy by her side.

Charlene had approached me in the afternoon, thanking me for covering one of her days, and offered to work for me tomorrow. I told her it wasn't necessary for her to return the favour, but she insisted. So, I took her up on her offer. Knowing I could use a day off.

Goldie was in front of me, looking at me with those dark, gorgeous, beady brown eyes, wagging her tail, and holding part of her slipper in her mouth. It was obvious she had been chewing it as I reached out to grab hold of the other end. Yuck, how slimy and wet it was as I tried to hang on to the little bit I had in my hand. She was stingy in giving me enough to hold on to.

Goldie began tugging and pulling, growling more each time she tugged or pulled a little harder. She was a character. A seesaw motion ensued, the harder she tugged, and pulled, the weaker my grip was becoming. This seemed to be an evening ritual. She was frisky and wanted to play whenever I came home. Goldie had her teeth sunk into the slipper; it wasn't going to be an easy task to get it from her. Suddenly, I realized that the slipper we were wrestling over wasn't hers it was one of mine.

"Goldie, you little rascal, give me back my slipper." Goldie ended up winning the tug of war over my slipper. She was such a little stinker. Oh well, another slipper to add to her well-chewed collection. Anyway, I liked the distraction. But as soon as Goldie headed off down the hallway with my slipper in tow, I was back to worrying about Kerrie. Wondering what has transpired since she abruptly hung-up on me. I decided that no matter how late it was I had better phone the house where Kerrie was living.

Jane answered the phone. "Jane, sorry to call so late, it's Liz." "Hi Liz, it's ok, I'm on night awake anyway." "Kerrie just phoned me." "Oh Liz do you know where she is?" I could hear the worry in Jane's voice. "Not really, but at the time of her call she mentioned she was using a pay phone somewhere on Lemarchant Road. She wanted me to come get her. There was no reasoning with her. I won't be going anywhere until the storm is over and they get the roads ploughed. I don't know what condition she is really in and what's in store. But I have a gut-wrenching feeling she is in the process of doing something to get arrested. Lock-up is one of her favourite places to be, as you know Jane. It might be a good thing for you to call the police and see if they can pick her up and return her to the house. If we're lucky that's what's happening now as we speak. I just wish we weren't in the middle of a blizzard."

"I know Liz, it's been a very stressful night. I have already been in touch with the police, but at that time they told me there was nothing they could really do. She hasn't been considered missing long enough. However, they are aware of the situation and know who she is, and told me they will keep an eye out for her. Grant it, the storm just adds more frustration to the situation. Sorry for this Liz, but I'll call the police again to see if they know anything more, at least tell them she contacted you, and where she told you she was. Thanks for the call Liz." "Okay Jane, and call me to let me know how things go." "Sure Liz, I'll call you as soon as I can." "Thanks Jane, bye for now." "Bye Liz."

Kerrie was a middle-aged mental health consumer, a lady with severe behavioral problems who had a long history of being in, and out of jail for misdemeanor violations that included petty theft, and vandalism. However, some of her offences exceeded these general misdemeanors, verbal threats, and acts of physical violence, some with weapons against others. Upping the antes to felony offences, which landed her in prison on the west coast of Newfoundland's Clarenville Correctional Centre for women. It opened in 1982, and houses all provincially sentenced female offenders, as well as low-risk female offenders sentenced to federal time, and those awaiting transfers to the federal women's facility in Nova Scotia. There was no federal prison in Newfoundland, at that time.

Abused as a child she grew up knowing only violence. Social Services, along with agencies that provide supervised homes, and the judicial system were all frantically trying their best to make things work for Kerrie. But she didn't make it easy to help her. Everyone was running out of options. It wasn't easy to befriend her or gain her trust. She loved to intimidate and threaten people, usually alienating herself from anyone who only wanted to help her. She easily intimidated others towering over most; she stood 6'2", and weighed around 300 pounds.

I had somehow managed to befriend her and became an advocate for her through the Department of Social Services, with a residential case manager, Mrs. Helen Taite. During the transitional period of helping Kerrie gain trust with residential staff always proved to be a challenge, to say the least, even at the best of times. She never took too kindly to anyone who was employed to work with her, especially social workers or residential support staff in the homes she resided in. As far as she knew, I was a volunteer advocate.

The residential staff's primary function was to provide, assist, support, and monitor her overall re-integration into the community. In hopes of her developing enough skills and social graces necessary for the re-integration process to be successful. The burn out rate and turn over for anyone working with her was astronomically high. It was hard to keep her happy and in a home for any length of time. Always referring to prison as her home. If she didn't threaten or attack someone, then she would run away.

My phone was ringing again. Perhaps it was Kerrie or Jane with an update. "Hello!" I answered in a concerned pitch. "Hello, may I please speak with Ms. Elizabeth Sulis, this is Constable Johnson with the Royal Newfoundland Constabulary."

The police were calling me? I hesitantly replied. "Speaking." "Ms. Sulis, sorry for calling so late, we have Kerrie McDermott here in lock-up. I just finished speaking with Jane Dicks, Ms. McDermott's worker at the house she resides in. Ms. Dicks said it would be okay for me to phone you. I know it's late, but she assured me it was okay, and you would want to know what's going on." "Yes, thank you for calling constable." "I understand that you're Ms. McDermott's advocate. We were hoping you might be able to help us out?" "Sure Constable, if I can." "Great Ms. Sulis." "You said Constable you have Kerrie in lock-up?" "Yes, we were able to locate Ms. McDermott tonight, but not before she apparently threw an object in the Dominion Market Store window, which set off the alarm, and she continued to vandalize the premises until we arrived on the scene." "Oh damn it . . . sorry Constable. Did she try to hurt any one?" "She only tried to assault the officers, but they were able to apprehend her, subduing her until they were able to get her safely into the paddy wagon, and bring her here. So, Ms. Sulis, we have to keep her in the city lock-up, in custody until she will be transported to court for her arraignment, which is scheduled to take place later today, at 2:00 p.m."

The St. John's City lock-up is the temporary detention centre for those awaiting appearance before the courts. Most are detained under the Mental Health or Detention of Intoxicated Persons Acts, those locked up in the *drunk-tank*, all of which are short-term detentions. It is located in the basement of the Supreme Court of Newfoundland, which was built in 1901. The lock-up has been operating from there since 1981.

"Constable Johnson, I guess she got what she really wanted after all, the thought of prison has always been a haven, of sorts, for Kerrie. The time or history she has spent in prison is a testament of how she would rather be back on the inside. It's a sad thing to say, but that is really all she knows and wants. I'm not sure what really happened this time, leading up to this, but I was worried that she was going to try, and do something tonight, after I spoke with her earlier. However, her actions tonight might land her in a mental health facility, other than the residential home she lives in now or worse, prison. After tonight, I'm sure the judge will review her history of previous charges, behaviour, and perceived risk of violence or elopement. No matter what we have tried to do to help her, she continues to demonstrate, being a danger to herself, and others. This is definitely not a good thing for Kerrie, but when it comes right down to it, it's her choice. I'm so sorry for the trouble Kerrie has caused, especially on a night like tonight, and for the storeowner. I might have been able to prevent this from happening, if the weather wasn't so terrible, and I could have gone to her aid. But I can't control the weather Constable."

"Excuse me for a moment please Constable?" "Sure Miss Sulis." I took a moment to reposition myself in the recliner, before continuing my conversation with the Constable.

"Constable Johnson, you mentioned you were hoping I might be able to help you out, what is there that I can possibly do right now?" "Well, Ms. Sulis." "Please, call me Liz." "Sure . . . Liz. Ms. McDermott is not being co-operative and continues to cause quiet a raucous here in lock-up. We have ourselves here, one very unhappy lady. She is adamant in seeing you and I'm not sure if she will settle down any time soon, until she can see you."

"I don't know how that is going to be possible, until the storm passes, and the roads are cleared. I tried reasoning with her earlier constable. But to no avail, she wouldn't listen to me. She's a good one for causing so much havoc and in the most inopportune times. But that's why we call them crisis I suppose. But the weather is so treacherous. The snow is still coming down hard and blowing around, causing whiteout conditions out here Constable." "You're right, I doubt we will be able to get you here until the storm has blown over, and the driving conditions improve Ms. Sulis . . . Liz. That's the best we can do, wait out the storm, then we will make sure a plough can clear your roads so we can pick you up, and bring you to her."

"Yes, I'll need to be there Constable. But, right now, all any of us can do is wait out the storm. Hopefully you will be able to calm her down. I'm sure she will eventually settle, at least she is safe where she is. Tell her that I will be there as soon as possible, but for now I want her to relax, and try to get some sleep. Neither of us will be able to function without sleep. I know I can't. By the way Constable, her social worker or case manager is Helen Taite with the Department of Social Services. She will need to know what is going on." "I got that information from Ms. Dicks, when I was speaking to her. We will be contacting Ms. Taite in the morning. Anyway, I won't keep you any longer Liz, it's very late, and you must be tired. Thank you for your time." "You're welcome Constable Johnson, thank you for calling me. I just wish there was more I could do right now. But, I will need to be there for her arraignment tomorrow." "We will do our best to get you here as soon as possible, but for now, you better get some rest. We'll contact you when it's feasible for a patrol car to be able to pick you up. Parking will be limited tomorrow due to the snow. Good night Ms. Sulis, sorry . . . Liz." "Okay, thank you and good night Constable Johnson."

I sat mulling over the events of the evening. Really, there wasn't anything anyone could do until the storm was over. I was so tired. I guess I better get to bed. I didn't even notice that Goldie had returned and was lying in the corner, next to the woodstove. "Come on Goldie, let's go to bed girl." Even Goldie seemed pooped, as she stretched getting back up, and scampered over to my side.

Out of the corner of my eye, I caught a glimpse of the Christmas hamper still lying on the kitchen counter. With all the commotion I had forgotten about it.

"*Wow!* There's enough here to feed an army Goldie, the turkey's huge." As I was trying to find a place for the monstrosity of a fowl to fit in the freezer, the phone was ringing again. It had startled me. "Gesh, it's like Grand Central Station, now what?" Making the assumption it must be Constable Johnson phoning back. There was just enough room on the side of the freezer for the turkey to fit. It sure was heavy as I struggled to lower it into the freezer. In haste, the freezer door slipped out of my hands and made a loud thud as it closed. "Oops." Rushing towards the phone, as fast as my weary body allowed me to move, I collapsed into the recliner, answering the phone a little out of breath.

"Hello Constable Johnson." There was a brief moment of silence on the other end of the phone. "Liz, this is AJ, who is Constable Johnson, are you okay, what's wrong, were you in an accident, do you need me to come over?" "Oh sorry AJ, I'm okay, and no I wasn't in an accident. I just finished speaking with the constable and thought it must have been him phoning me back. I wasn't thinking that anyone else would be calling me at this hour. I'm fine though, really, I made it home safe and sound. It is nasty out there and I'm freezing. I'm going to tend to the woodstove right now. I need to get this chill out of my bones."

"Oh, would you like me to come over and stoke your fire Liz?" I grinned at the thought, my mind, tired or not, briefly drifted back to the events of the evening before. However, if it was any other time, I would probably welcome him to come over, but right now, I was tired, and wanted to go to bed, to sleep.

"Liz, you okay, what's going on, what's with this Constable Johnson?" "Oh, ah, well the police want me to come to the station, to deal with a crisis, regarding a client of mine." "I hope they aren't expecting you to come to their office now Liz?" "Well, sort of, it's just this weather is complicating matters." "What, are they frigging nuts Liz, out of their freaking minds? How on earth are you going to get there in this storm? It isn't safe." "That's why I suppose they are called crisis AJ. They can happen at any time or come in the most inopportune time. It's the nature of my job. But, I do think it is sweet of you that you are so worried about me. But, you can relax. They're waiting until the storm blows over and the roads get ploughed, before they send a car to pick me up. Anyway AJ, I would love nothing more than for you to come over, but." "That's what I was hoping you would say Liz, I'll be right over, and I'll take care of the woodstove." "AJ wait!" He hung the phone up, before I could elaborate.

I loved the thought of him coming over, but I was so exhausted, all I wanted to do was go to bed. How would I be able to go to bed now and get some sleep? Grant it, AJ would be a welcomed distraction from the problems weighing on my mind about Kerrie.

I heard him at the door. So did Goldie, as she began barking. "Relax Goldie, its just AJ." It sure didn't take him long to get here. I opened the door, struggling to hold onto it, due to a gush of wind, and blowing snow.

"Let me brush off the snow before I come in Liz." I was amused and began to giggle at the sight of how much snow had covered him, with such a short distance to come. He shook and brushed the snow off from his head and jacket, trying to get enough off from his boots before entering.

"Wow, this sure is one *hell* of a storm Liz. I could barely see anything in front of me as I walked over." "Yes, it sure is nasty out there AJ." He reached out to me, drawing my body into his, and wrapping his arms around me. "I missed you Liz, I had to come over and see you. I was glad when I saw you pull into your driveway earlier. It was a relief to know you got home safely. I saw your light was still on, but when I called, all I kept getting was a busy signal."

"Yeah, the phone has been rather busy since I got home." I barely got the words out of my mouth, when he leaned over, and kissed me. He reluctantly released me in order to slip off his wet jacket and hang it up in the closet.

"You're shivering Liz." "It's so chilly in here AJ." "Let me take my boots off so I can take care of it." After he placed his boots on the mat by the door he made his way over to the woodstove, where Goldie was lying, with my slipper in her mouth. Rubbing Goldie behind the ears he told her that he couldn't play with her right now, but managed to pull the slimy slipper from her grip, and gave it a toss down the hallway. After he dealt with the woodstove, he joined me in the living room where I was sitting in the recliner. AJ realized that I was barely awake.

He knelt down in front of me, taking me by my hand, and rubbing it. "Come on Liz you need to go to bed. I really doubt you will be going anywhere for a while. The storm isn't expected to be over until later in the morning and the rate of the snow coming down, it will take time to get the roads ploughed, and salted properly." "You're probably right AJ, but knowing my client, I'm sure the police have their hands full, and were wishing I was there right now. I'm sure once the storm is over, they'll have the ploughs help them make their way to me as fast as they can." "I'm sure the police can handle things for now Liz. Meanwhile, me pretty lady, you need to go to bed, and try to get some sleep. I know you didn't get much sleep last night" "That's true AJ, can't argue with you there." Giving AJ a wink and a smile.

Still holding my hand, he helped me out of the recliner, and led me down to my bedroom. He pulled back the bed sheets. "Now, little lady, you climb into bed, I'll make sure things are okay here with the woodstove, and that the doors are locked, and the lights are turned off, I want you to get some rest Liz."

"I must admit I am exhausted. But, you need sleep too AJ. I don't really think I will sleep much, if I do, it will probably be a restless sleep, and if the storm stops, and the police can get the roads ploughed, then I don't want to miss their call." "If it makes you feel any better Liz, when, and if the Constable phones back, I'll wake you. I can sleep out on the couch." "No AJ, you won't get any rest on that old thing. I would rather you sleep." I stopped in mid sentence. AJ lifted an eyebrow as he studied my expression on my face. I was sitting on the side of the bed, barely able to keep my head up. "You can sleep here too, the bed is big enough for the two of us." It had been a long time since I had shared my bed with anyone. But considering what transpired between the two of us last night, it wouldn't really matter now; I just wanted the both of us to get some sleep.

"Okay Liz, you lay down and try to get some sleep, I'll go, and give the woodstove one last check. I'll join you in a bit, I'll try not to wake you though, unless you get a phone call." AJ leaned down and gave me a kiss, a kiss that once again quickly flooded my memories of what had transpired between the two of us the night before. "AJ, promise me that you will get some sleep too and please, if the Constable phones." "Yes, I'll get some sleep and don't worry Liz, if he calls, I promise, I'll wake you."

I watched AJ as he left the bedroom. Then desperately struggled to slip out of my clothes to put on my nightshirt. It might not have been the most glamorous, but it was the most comfortable. Crawling into my bed, I managed to reach for the lamp on the nightstand to turn it off, and covered myself up with the blankets. As soon as my head hit the pillows I was out like the light.

Chapter Fifteen

The phone rang. AJ tried reaching over me for the phone, before it would ring again, and without his movements jostling the bed too much, disturbing me.

AJ answered the phone in a whisper, but I was already awake, immediately worrying how long I had been asleep. I quickly glanced at the clock radio. It was shortly after 10:00 a.m. I turned looking at AJ.

"Yes Constable she's awake now, just a moment, and I'll pass her the phone." AJ muffled the receiver with his hand, lifting it into the air, out of my reach. Before I could say or do anything, he said good morning, leaned over, and planted a rather long, drawn out sensuous kiss. AJ stopped and handed me the phone, smiling.

"Here you go Liz." I had to take another moment to gain my composure before putting the receiver to my ear. "I'll go start breakfast Liz while you take your call." Giving me a quick peck on my cheek, which I returned with a smile, AJ jumped out of the bed. I was finding it difficult to concentrate when I finally spoke into the receiver. "Hello Constable Johnson." I was being distracted by AJ's antics of dressing in front of me. I got a good glimpse of how chiseled and gorgeous his body really was, and oh what a *butt*. Finally, I was able to focus more on the phone call once AJ had left the bedroom.

The Constable apologized for waking me. He said he could have left a message with my husband. It took me another moment to respond, once I got past the husband part. "That's okay constable." I realized that it was a simple mistake for him to make an assumption that AJ was my husband.

"I was just about to leave a message that I am going off duty soon, and to let you know that things settled down. Ms. McDermott actually got some sleep." "I'm glad to hear that Constable." "The storm has stopped and a plough has been working in your area, hopefully soon, we will be able to get a patrol car out to you." "That's great constable and thank you." "Okay Mrs. Sulis, someone will be in touch with you shortly and best of luck." "Thanks again Constable Johnson."

After I was off the phone with the Constable, I took a shower, got dressed, and joined AJ out in the kitchen for a tasty omelet he had prepared with toast, orange juice, and brewed coffee. I enjoyed having breakfast with AJ. Sure we have spent many a lunch, and supper together, but never breakfast, until yesterday, and today. This could be habit forming if I wasn't careful. I smiled at the thought, but even more, when I remembered Constable Johnson referring to me as a Mrs., an easy mistake.

"Do you have any idea Liz when you expect to be home?" "Huh, um, no AJ, I'm not really working today, but I'll have to see my client, and be there for her in court. To tell you the truth, I'm not really sure what is going to happen, but I hope to be able to get home by five, or six that's if everything goes well. Of course I won't have my car, but I'm sure I'll find a way home."

"Well Liz, I could pick you up, perhaps we could go out for supper tonight?" "Oh AJ, do you mean go out to an actual restaurant or do you mean your house?" "Good one Liz, but I actually meant a real restaurant for tonight, let someone else do the cooking. Perhaps we might even be able to take in a movie that's if you're up to it?" "That sounds like a wonderful idea AJ, I would love that. But, I guess we'll have to wait and see." "Okay Liz."

I grabbed a piece of paper, scribbling down quickly my pager, and phone number, and the street address to where Kerrie lived, where I hoped I would be later, and handed it to AJ.

"What's this Liz?" "The phone number and the street address to where I expect I'll end up after the hearing. So, if you try to communicate with me later, hopefully, you'll be able to reach me at this phone number. If that's not the case, I also included my pager number." "Oh okay, good Liz."

When AJ took the piece of paper I said dryly. "If you can't reach me there or by using my pager AJ, then I've been abducted by aliens." AJ laughed as I got up from the table to head to the sink.

"Since you made breakfast AJ, I'll do the dishes. "The dishes can wait Liz, I'll do them before I head into the office." I looked up, turning my head, catching AJ reaching around me, removing the dish I was holding, and placing it down on the counter, next to the sink.

"AJ that's not fair, you cooked, I'll clean up?" "I have something else I'd rather we do, before you have to leave Liz." "And what would that be AJ, as if I have to guess." "I just want to." "You just want to what AJ?" "Turn around for a sec, will you please." Obliging, AJ asked me to close my eyes. "Close my eyes? What is it you are up to AJ?" "Just close your eyes Liz, *please!*"

I was leaning against the counter of the sink, as I sensed AJ's body closing in on me. His arms were stretched out on either side of me, resting on top of the counter. "Keep your eyes closed Liz." Next thing I felt his wet tongue and moist lips lightly touching the nape of my neck. His breath was warm against my skin, adding to my heightened senses. I began to squirm beneath his touches. He began to slowly move upwards, gliding his tongue, and lips along my skin, and contours of my neck, until he reached my ear lobe. Continuing with his exploration he moved along so gingerly until he reached my quivering mouth. My lips were posed for his.

"Oh AJ, I can't, not now, this isn't fair, the officer will be here soon." AJ didn't give any heed to my words. He swiftly engulfed my mouth with his, ravenously plunging his tongue deeper, and deeper. I was helpless I couldn't resist his kisses. His strong hands moved to support the upper part of my neck, under my shoulder length hair.

The doorbell rang. I almost didn't hear it due to the trance AJ had me in with his powerful kisses. "I guess one of us should answer the door Liz." "I suppose so AJ." AJ released his hold he had on me. I briefly gazed into his eyes. "Oh what you do to me when you kiss me. You're kisses are lethal AJ." AJ smiled. "I promise you Liz, there is more, but I'll save the best for later." "How could there be anything better AJ?"

I regained my composure and answered the door. "Mrs. Sulis, I'm Constable Devlin and I'm here to bring you to the station. Sorry I didn't call first, it just took me a bit to get out here." "Yes, thank you Constable, but it's Ms. Sulis or Liz. Give me a moment to get my things, I'll be with you momentarily." "Fine Ms. Sulis, I'll wait for you in the police cruiser." "Okay Constable Devlin, I'll be right out."

"Here's your coat, gloves, boots, and purse Mrs. Sulis." I nudged his shoulder. "Oh AJ, it's a simple mistake." AJ held my coat while I slipped it on. My boots were easy to slide into. "Thank you AJ, you have a great afternoon and call me later." "Sure Liz, I hope things go okay." "Thanks AJ." I shouted back as I ran out the door.

~

As I was walking down one of the many narrow corridors of the Department of Social Services, I noticed Helen Taite's office door was open. Helen was sitting behind her desk, hunched over with her elbows resting on the desk. I studied Helen for a moment, watching her hold an arm of her glasses in one hand, twirling them around her fingers, while with her other hand she rubbed her eyes with her fingers. It was obvious, due to the pile of paperwork and folders that were scattered over Helen's desk, she was one busy lady, and looked tired.

Helen didn't notice me standing in her doorway. Her office was rather small, dark, and dinghy. The lighting wasn't the greatest, florescent lights, and no windows. It was an old heritage building, which could have used a face-lift. But for now, this was the best they had. The fire, a year ago destroyed their original office building. The investigators proved it was arson, but to this day no one had been caught or arrested. A new building was in the process of being built.

I was surprised to actually find Helen in her office. She was a rather stout person, always on the go, dedicated to her job as a social worker. "You look like death warmed over Helen." Helen looked-up.

"Yes, I guess I do, I feel like death warmed over too." Helen chuckled. "Come on in Liz, I have been so busy lately that I have gotten behind with paper work. This has been such a busy trying time with the scandal, the looming possibility of a province-wide strike, with all the residential support staff, the situation with Kerrie, and all these other cases I am dealing with. It's hard to believe that in a couple weeks it will be Christmas.

Sometimes, there just doesn't seem to be enough hours in the run of a day to get everything dealt with."

"I can agree with you on that one Helen." "So, what can I do for you Liz?" "Well I see that you are rather busy, I won't keep you, I only have a few minutes myself, I decided to try for that Live-In Supervisor position. I just finished the first part of the interview process and the Board members asked me to step out for a few moments so they could talk amongst themselves. I asked them if they would mind if I quickly dropped off something to one of the social workers in the building. They said no problem that they would need about 15 minutes before we would start the second phase of the interviewing process. I know that you are swamped with things. But, since the holidays are approaching, I hope you don't mind, but I wanted to drop off early my month end summaries, and Jane asked me to drop off the information you requested in regards to Kerrie. Entertaining reading material and more paper work for you Helen, as if you need anymore."

Helen rolled her eyes. "Thanks Liz and thanks for your help yesterday too, I know that staff appreciated it, especially Jane. We were lucky that the judge was lenient, once we were able to work out a deal with everyone to have all the charges dropped. I just hope Kerrie will cooperate and abide by the conditions regarding her release back into the home. I'll be making a home visit to her later this afternoon to have a talk with her." "It isn't going to be easy Helen, she sure doesn't like it there. I plan on going there too, once I finished up here, so perhaps I'll see you then. I won't keep you any longer, besides, I'd better get back, I'm sure they are wondering where I am."

"Wait Liz! Since you're a candidate there's no reason for the interview process to continue on any further, that's if I have anything to say about it. I didn't realize you were interested. I really should have known better, but I've been so busy. Anyway, my point is, I usually have input when it comes to making the final decision, since I am the social worker for that house. I can't see why the job can't be yours if you really want it Liz?" "Are you kidding? I do want the job Helen." "Come with me then Liz."

The Board Members were still sitting behind closed doors, but that didn't stop Helen from knocking, and entering the room, with me in tow. Mrs. Fitzgerald, chair of the Board greeted Helen.

"Hi Helen." "Hello Grace, everyone. Listen, I just found out that Liz is here for the Live-In Supervisor position, stop the interviewing process, and hire the girl." Everyone started to laugh. Mrs. Fitzgerald glanced at me, smiled, and then glanced back at Helen.

"It sure sounds like you strongly believe Ms. Sulis is the right person for the job Helen?" "I sure do Grace. It will be a pleasure to work with Liz in this capacity, and without a doubt, she will make a fine supervisor. Liz has been apart of our team, working for us in the community with many of our Mental Health consumers, as well as others. She meets all the necessary requirements, so she definitely qualifies, but most of all, I know she will bring a lot to this job, filling every aspect of the position well. We would be fools not to hire her."

I was pleasantly surprised of Helen's kind words and support. I know it probably also helped having Mrs. Poole sitting on the Board. She was the one who made me aware of the opening and told me that I should apply. She attended the church where the after school program was going on, and also was one of the volunteers.

"Well, we are glad to hear your recommendation and approval Helen. Ms. Sulis had already impressed us and we unanimously agreed that she is the best person for the job. I guess that clinches it, but perhaps we should ask Ms. Sulis if she accepts the position?" "Thank you everyone, I do accept Mrs. Fitzgerald, but, please call me Liz." "Congrats Liz, I better return to my workload that's piled up in my office, I'll talk to you later Grace, bye everyone."

Mrs. Fitzgerald and the other Board members said their good-byes to Helen. "Again, congrats Liz, I'll see you later this afternoon perhaps." "Yes Helen and thank you for everything."

While I was visiting with Kerrie that afternoon, I received a phone call from AJ. "AJ, how did you know I was here?" "I took the chance Liz, it was the phone number you gave me with the address you wrote down on the piece of paper yesterday, and I hoped I would be able to track you down." "Well obviously you found me AJ." I was a little perturbed. He was a no show the other day. I tried calling, but couldn't get an answer. He didn't even call.

"I know you must be upset with me for not being there for you Liz, and not calling you, but I've been at the hospital." "At the hospital, are you okay AJ?" "Yes Liz, I'm fine, it's Tina." *"Tina!"* "Yes, my ex-wife Liz, she got into a serious car accident during the storm. After you left, I cleaned up, and when I went back to my place, her mother phoned. She was hysterical and asked me to come to the hospital, she didn't know whom else she could turn to. It's really only the two of them Liz. She's a mess Liz, it's been touch, and go, they had to perform life saving emergency surgery, and she's been put into an induced comma. It doesn't look good for her Liz, it really doesn't. All the wires and tubing coming out of her, oh God Liz, it will be a miracle if she actually pulls through this. We might be divorced Liz, but I certainly would never have wished anything like this to have happen to her."

"I know AJ, I know you wouldn't, I hope she'll be okay too." "Thanks Liz, but, I'm so sorry, I just didn't get a chance to phone you until now, and was hoping I would somehow reach you, luckily I had the number on me that you gave me, hoping you would be there. Please forgive me Liz."

"AJ it's okay, really I understand, I was just worried that's all." I could hear commotion going on in the background, inaudible noises, and voices. "I better get back Liz, I'll try to phone you later tonight okay." "Sure, I hope she pulls through AJ, I really do. If there's anything I can do" "Thanks Liz, but all anyone can do right now is pray." "Ah, sure AJ." "Okay Liz, I'll talk to you later." "Bye AJ."

Chapter Sixteen

A month or so had passed. AJ's ex-wife had pulled through. But now, she was facing a lengthy road ahead of her, with months of difficult, and challenging rehab, and physio, in the hopes of her to have a full recovery. It just wasn't going to be a speedy one.

AJ told me that the doctors were optimistic and encouraging. They just couldn't give a time-line or predict what the full outcome would be. It would all depend on her . . . her spirit, drive, and determination. But most of all, how imperative it was for all the people in her life, who meant the most to her . . . to be there every step of the way, giving her their unfailing love, morale support, and continued encouragement. Especially, during those tough times when she wanted to give up, there would be those days rest assured.

During her stay in the hospital and when they transferred her to a rehabilitation facility, AJ spent most of his time, day and night with Tina, and driving her mother back and forth. Her mother lived further outside the city, so AJ offered for her to stay with him. He had already used up all his family sick days, vacation, and holiday time, and now was taking a leave of absence.

Just great . . . there was a part of me that could understand why AJ felt it was necessary for him to be so involved with his ex-wife's rehabilitation process, and to be so gracious, and accommodating to his ex-mother-in-law. But, another part of me, the selfish part of me, didn't want to understand. I had to ask myself, did AJ still harbor feelings for her, did he love her . . . was he still in love with her? After all, the doctor did tell him that all the people in her life that meant the most to her, who loved her . . . needed to be there for her.

Time just kept slipping by. It seemed like we were drifting further and further apart. A few weeks earlier, on my first day on my new job, there were forms to fill out, and issues to discuss, one being legal strike action that was scheduled to commence a week Tuesday, at midnight, if the last ditched effort at the bargaining table wouldn't pan out. It didn't look like either side was going to budge. The problem wasn't over money, but over seniority, and hours of work.

The midnight hour on Tuesday rolled around and legal strike action did take place. The province-wide strike was now entering its sixth week. Not the easiest position to be in, when in a new job. It was beginning to look as if this strike wasn't going to end any time soon.

Most residents, who were pulled out of their day programs, sheltered workshop environments, and homes, were sent to foster parents or wherever they could be housed secretively, to avoid picketers. The system was already bogged down, due to one of the most infamous Canadian child-abuse scandals that had reared its ugly head. Sexual abuse allegations were surrounding an orphanage home for Boys, operated by the Catholic Church. The Christian Brothers of Ireland in Canada, the defunct Catholic teaching order who ran the notorious Mount Cashel Orphanage in St. John's, where dozens of boys were raped, and beaten by a series of Christian Brothers between the 1960's, and the late 1980's.

Everything was turned up side down, inside and out, through an on-going police investigation. The media worldwide was having a field day with this. As the strike continued and when there were no other placements available, signs of cabin fever were evident for those residents who had to remain in their homes, feeling trapped, and isolated. Picketers were complicating things, intimidating any worker who crossed the picket line. All supervisors and social workers ended up staffing the houses that remained open.

Things were escalating; tempers were flying. Any shift changes were becoming more and more confrontational with verbal taunts, jeers, and jostling, making it difficult for anyone to cross the picket line. A few fights broke out, so the Police had to be called in, to help escort those of us who had to cross the line, to and from the premises. Parked cars, even if they were parked a distance away had air taken from the tires or they were slashed. I was happy that only the air was let-out of my tires. A few other cars were reported to have had other minor damage done to them.

The Province was pretty much at a standstill. News coverage, worldwide, continuously reported and up dated any arrests or allegations made against clergy believed to have abused their positions of power, and trust. It felt like you were part of a three-ring circus. The scandal would rock the church, but not to its very essence, the core of its foundation. All faiths, denominations under the umbrella of Christianity were faced with lessons in moral contradictions, and hard truths. The church and clergy were vulnerable to the innuendoes, ridicule, jokes, and sometimes death threats. These were the types of things books were written and movies or documentaries were made of.

The home I was responsible for, both residents were whisked away to a temporary foster home, before we really had any chance to get to know each other. I actually couldn't move into the house until Mr. Bryson returned from Florida, but he was due back the first week of April, which was now, only a few weeks away.

I had been squeezing in time to keep an eye on the empty residence, while covering shifts at homes that were still open. At night, I would drive to the foster home, where my residents were placed, hoping all was well with them during this disruption, and to spend some time with them.

I moved into the house at work, a couple days before Mr. Bryson returned from Florida. At least I could get my things in and settled. Leslie and Tom took care of Goldie until he got home. I was going to miss living there, especially Goldie, being near Leslie, and Tom, but most of all, being so close to AJ. But I knew this day was coming.

AJ had asked me to stay with him, whenever I would be off duty. Things were pretty much the same, at a standstill as far as the strike went. But, considering the situation, with his ex-wife, especially with his ex-mother-in-law still being there, we both realized that wouldn't be a wise move. I met Mrs. Dempsey, Tina's mother, at Christmas, when I had a get-together with a few friends, asking AJ, and her to join us. After all, it was Christmas and I needed to cook the turkey. I wasn't sure if they would show up, but somehow AJ convinced her to come. It probably had something more to do with the fact that she knew AJ would come, with or without her.

Leslie helped me prepare the turkey and all the fixings. Of course she made the desserts too. For the most part, Mrs. Dempsey was cordial to me and my other guests. But, I knew she really didn't relish the thought of AJ and I being together. She wouldn't let AJ out of her sight, remaining by his side during the entire evening. It sure didn't take an *Einstein* to figure out that she was championing the cause for her daughter's, and AJ's reconciliation. Obviously, to her, the chances of that happening were greater, if I wasn't in the picture.

When Leslie asked Tom to carve the turkey, she pulled me aside, and told me to not pay any attention to what Mrs. Dempsey had been saying or doing in trying to keep AJ and I apart. For the remainder of the evening I socialized more with my other guests. Occasionally, our eyes would meet, across what seemed to be a crowed room. AJ would smile, but it didn't take long before Mrs. Dempsey would draw his attention to someone or something elsewhere.

AJ and I didn't get too many opportunities to see each other after the Christmas party. Between the times he spent at the rehab with Tina, and her mother, and my busy work schedule, it seemed like we were just two ships that passed in the night. One morning on my way to one of the houses, my pager was going off. It was AJ, so I called him once I arrived at the house.

"Hi AJ, what's up, I got your page." "I was just wondering Liz, what's your schedule like for today?" "Well, I'm at a house until 4:00 or so, then planning on grabbing a bite to eat, before heading out to see the girls for my nightly visit . . . why AJ?" "Well, since I'm on your way out to see the girls, do you think you can drop by Liz, come here for something to eat?" "Do you think that is wise with Mrs. Dempsey being there AJ?" "It's okay Liz, I had other things to do today and she is going to be at the rehab with Tina. I don't have to go pick her up until after 8:00 tonight." "I'll come out around 5:00 then AJ." "Okay Liz, see you then."

~

AJ looked up and caught me studying him, his eyebrows quirked, as he grinned. "Anything wrong Liz?" AJ's grin faded at the bluntness of my question. I came right out with it. "What are the feelings you have for Tina, AJ, your true feelings, and I want you to be completely honest with me?"

He didn't answer me and there was an expression on his face that I couldn't read. "You have to work out your feelings, what you have for Tina, and what you actually are feeling for me. I don't want to be misled up the garden path AJ."

I knew that I had put him on the spot, with what was and had already been a difficult situation, and a trying time. "Liz, you think – you think I've been just amusing myself with you, leading you on?" "Have you AJ?" "No Liz, I could fall in love with you very easily, in fact, I'm half in love with you already. It's just that" "It's just what AJ?" "I got to be there for Tina, see her through her healing process." "Well you're doing a great job at that AJ, you've been by her side almost 24/7."

All I knew, was that I didn't want to have my heart bruised any more than what I felt it already was. It was right then and there that my tunnel vision I had of our relationship had cleared up. Perhaps AJ was having a difficult time deciphering what he really was thinking, feeling, and wanting. But I knew, I knew. "It's obviously a no-brainer AJ. You might be half in love with me, but you're still totally in love with Tina." *"Liz!"* He shouted out, as he reached for me. I quickly took a few steps backwards, extending my arm, and holding up my hand, gesturing for him to stop.

"I need you to listen to me AJ, it's okay. Really it is. You and Tina have a past, a history together, husband and wife. I realize I don't know what the circumstances were around your divorce, but obviously, you still love her, because of her accident, and the fact that you almost lost her, for good. Well, right now, you have to be free, free to travel through the labyrinth of your own mind. Have a chance to be honest with yourself AJ. I don't think your intentions are to hurt me. But, I just can't jeopardize getting hurt any more than what I already am. I can't hang around to wait, while we might become more involved, only to find out that some day, some day, you'll finally realize, I was right . . . you're still totally in love with

Tina." *"Liz!"* "Let me finish AJ! I want you to know, I believe we have had a marvellous time together, so marvellous in fact that for a little while I'd known what it was like to live in an enchanted world, and I thank you for that. So, AJ . . . we need to stop seeing each other."

I left. Okay, ran before AJ had a chance to really say or do anything. I was a hurting girl. AJ followed me out to my car, but I didn't let him stop me. As I was pulling away, I glanced in my rear-view mirror, I remember seeing AJ, just standing there. That would be the last time I would see him again. Under the circumstances and no matter how much it hurt, I knew it was the best thing to do.

Chapter Seventeen

The strike was still lingering and everyone was being stretched to his, or her own limits. When both sides agreed to get together again, for another attempt at further rounds of talks or discussions at the negotiating table, there had been another offer made by the employer, and government. But their offer was rejected. So, before another impasse was reached, the minister responsible stepped in, demanding both sides accept an appointed arbitrator to help resolve the outstanding issues.

If the strike was ever to end, whenever that would be, I figured I needed to have somewhere to go for my days off. Christine Sparks was a girl I had known through Emma and she heard that I was looking for a one-bedroom or room to rent. She had asked me if I would be interested in sharing a flat downtown with her. Just to help offset costs or expenses, and it would give me my own space when I needed it, getting away from the house when I could.

Christine didn't want to live with her boyfriend, not yet anyway, unless they were married. But that wasn't going to happen any time soon, they both had a couple years left, attending Memorial University, both working towards getting their Bachelor of Education.

Tracy was a 16-year-old, going on 30. She was removed from her abusive and neglectful family situation when she was younger. Going from one foster home to another . . . she kept running away.

Certain schools and other institutions were shut down during the police investigation, one of which was a school Tracy was attending. It had reached a point, during all the chaos, and upheaval around the scandal, and now the strike, when the Department of Social Services was at a loss. They had run out of places of where they could place Tracy. They needed to find a place that she would agree to stop running away from. They asked her what would it take for her to stop running away if they found her another place, she told them she wanted to stay with me.

Tracy was one of the girls I had befriended and had taken under my wing, with the after school program. The Department was hesitant to ask me if I would consider being a temporary foster parent, of sorts, taking Tracy in, knowing it would add more responsibilities, and challenges to my goings on. But they were desperate. At least Tracy would be provided with the basics of food and shelter, the Department helping with meeting these needs financially, and any other financial needs that might pop up.

As far as dealing with Tracy's psychological needs, I would probably be the one who might have a better chance of handling those too. The fact that I already knew Tracy, was aware of her background, and she wanted to stay with me started the wheels in motion. We all were hoping that things would start to settle down soon, in regards to the scandal. That the police would finish their investigation so everything could return to some sort of a normalcy.

However, Tracy would have to stay with me at the flat that's if Christine would agree. I knew it would be asking a lot of her. As long as the strike was still going on, I only had to check the house, not actually stay there. I talked it over with Christine and out of her appreciation for the situation, her kindness, and love for kids, she agreed for us to take Tracy under our roof . . . temporarily.

I certainly had my hands full, juggling my schedule for shifts, keeping an eye on the house, and visiting with my residents, all the while, trying to be there for Tracy. I couldn't have done it though without Christine's help. We certainly needed eyes in the back of our heads when it came to Tracy's antics.

She somehow managed to get herself into a local bar downtown, with a fake ID. One night, there was a knock at our door. As I answered the door, there standing before me was a middle-aged man asking if Tracy was home. I was curious as to who the man was. He said he met Tracy at the bar a few nights back and wanted to see if she would go out on a date with him.

"Oh you do, do you?" This was going to be interesting. What was Tracy doing behind our backs? Giving men twice her age our address or our phone number no doubt. It was apparent that we were going to have trouble with Tracy if I didn't nip this in the bud. Putting restrictions on Tracy's activities and whereabouts at all times wasn't going to be an easy task.

Tracy was in the living room. I told the man to wait a moment while I called out to Tracy to come to the door. Tracy was embarrassed to say the least. Once I told Tracy to tell the man her actual age, I told him if I ever saw the man again on our doorstep, and if he was ever caught with Tracy, I would press charges, she was a minor. The man quickly left saying he didn't want any trouble.

Tracy was good at throwing things that was one of the ways she acted out when she was mad, especially at me. Pretty much anything she could get her hands on was sure to come my way. I became good at ducking or catching things. Anything that missed me would usually end up hitting the wall, maybe causing minor damage, nothing that a little Poly-fill couldn't fix.

I had found a case of beer that Tracy had purchased at the corner store, with one of her fake ID's. The fake ID was now in my possession, along with all the other fake ID's I had been confiscating. I had quite the collection too, I might add.

I guess some things, or generations, never really change, remembering when my Mom use to have to do the same, when I was Tracy's age. As for the beer, well Christine opened each bottle and poured it down the sink. The next time Tracy and I went to the corner store, I made a point of telling the storeowner that Tracy was under age, so it would be greatly appreciated if he would no longer sell any beer to Tracy.

No matter how miffed Tracy got with me and at times with Christine, especially when we had to lay down the law or how we dealt with any of her inappropriate behaviors or shenanigans, she couldn't stay mad at us forever. No matter how hard she tried to remain mad at us . . . she would get over it. I was the only person really that Tracy had developed any trust, emotional attachment or bond with, prior to her stay with us. But, I was glad to see now, the rapport that was developing between

Christine and Tracy, especially for shopping, the occasional movie or out for a bite to eat, when I was busy working.

Christine and I both knew that she liked being under our care, and supervision, accepting what stable home environment we both were trying to provide for her. No matter what the circumstances were that brought her to us in the first place, how temporary her stay with us might be, and how rebellious she might have been at times, at least she never ran away.

I gave Tracy some responsibility during the after school program, to keep her busy. Tracy seemed to like helping out, participating, and feeling she was important. I made a point of praising her for the positive things she did and thanked her whenever she helped, no matter how big or small the tasks were.

It didn't really take long before Tracy was able to return to the home she had been living in, prior to the scandal, and all the chaos. But this time, I told her she had to stay put, not to keep running away. I knew she didn't really want to leave us, but Christine and I told her we would still be here for her, we weren't far away. Perhaps we might even get to go out for the occasional supper or go to a movie once, and awhile. Christine even added, going shopping. I knew she definitely was an avid shopper, liking that idea. And of course, I would be seeing her at the after school program. Which brought up school. I knew that she liked school, so encouraging her to keep up with her grades, once she was settled back in school, wasn't really going to be a problem. That's if everything else was okay in her life.

The arbitrator was finally successful in helping both sides settle their disputes and put an end to the six plus months strike. Things were beginning to run more efficiently and on an even keel at work. Of course, it would take time for a healing process, for everyone to let go of all the frustrations, and animosities that were created or built up, during this rather nasty, and long drawn-out strike. At least now, there were some positive signs of this happening, people getting along, and working together.

Finally, it was my first real weekend off, to be away from pagers or phones from Friday at 4:00 p.m., until Sunday at 4:00 p.m. I went to stay with Karen and Bill, where no one from work would know where I would be.,Besides, Christine had family visiting at the flat for the weekend.

Karen and Bill had plans of going out that Friday evening, so I told them to go and have fun, and I would look after the kids. No need of hiring a babysitter. I just wanted to stay put, relax, and watch some TV. I could watch the kids and put them to bed at their bedtime.

Another friend of ours, Bailey, decided to bring her daughter Madison over to play with the kids for a bit, and it was a good thing she did. I was sitting in my PJ's on the hide-a-bed with my legs crossed. The kids were playing, while Bailey and I were chatting. The next thing I knew, I was waking up to Katie, Karen and Bill's three-year-old daughter jumping on me, nudging me to wake up. She wanted to see if I would like to go shopping with her and mommy.

Bailey ended up being the babysitter. I had passed out from exhaustion. Apparently, I was mid-way through a sentence when I passed out on the hide-a-bed. Bailey figured I needed my sleep and didn't have the heart to wake me. So she put the covers over me and took the kids, and went up stairs until Karen, and Bill came home. I had passed out somewhere around 6:00 p.m., now it was 11:00 a.m., Saturday morning. I didn't realize how tired and exhausted I really was. A fine babysitter I turned out to be.

Karen laughed, telling me it didn't really surprise her that I had passed out and slept for as long as I did. I probably would still be sleeping, if she didn't get Katie to come wake me up. She was an operating room nurse and told me that one could only go for so long without proper sleep, hard to function properly without it. On the other hand, she knew the situation and the havoc we all had been through, over the past several months. The very long and stressful hours I worked, and other things, without getting much proper sleep, had finally caught up with me. Most of us were, without a doubt, working, and surviving on adrenalin.

I got up, showered, and dressed, grabbed some breakfast, and we were off to go shopping. Can't remember how long we had been shopping, but I was still feeling rather tired. Karen and Katie were in the process of going through a check out. I told them I would go over and stand by the mall door entrance. As I was standing next to a pillar, I ended up somehow slithering down to the floor, leaning against the pillar, sound asleep. Karen said all she could do was keep from laughing. She asked mall security to help carry me out to the car. They took me out by a cart they usually use to lug large boxes with. I was placed in the car and Karen helped me into the house, and put me in their bed to sleep, while they slept in the hide-a-bed.

I slept until Karen came to wake me. I had to return to work, it was the following day, around 1:00 p.m. Wow, what an embarrassing weekend, but I definitely caught up with sleep.

~

Where did the weekend go? I was back at work. Something was brewing. It didn't take long for all hell to break loose. The two girls who lived at the house were at each other. Once the relief staff had left it didn't take long for things to escalate further.

It started out with verbal bickering. I knew one of the girls was so easily provoked and would lash out at the other physically if their spat escalated any further. I had to intervene, but trying to separate the two wouldn't be easy.

All of a sudden, Sarah walked off into the living room in a huff, sitting down in a living room chair. She was the more timid and shy one, usually non-verbal or only spoke clearly when she was mad; using every curse word she could think of, with a thick Newfoundland accent. This of course would antagonize Nancy more.

Nancy ran off to her bedroom. But, it didn't take long for her to return. I was in the living room with Sarah. I redirected Nancy to go back to her room, as I stood between the two, keeping a distance between them.

Sarah jumped up out of her seat and reached for me, unsure why, it was as if she wanted me to move. But, somehow her dangling, charm-bracelet, she wore on her wrist, got stuck in my hair as she reached for my shoulder. I took my eyes off Nancy for one brief moment to pull my hair from the jewellery. As I was doing so, Nancy moved swiftly, putting me at a disadvantage. She came behind me, grabbing hold of my hair in her fisted hands, pulling me straight to the ground, and landing on top of her.

It all happened so quickly. However, as Nancy pulled me down, I heard a strange, and wretched sound. I had to maneuver myself to keep Nancy from putting me any further into what was already a compromising position. It wasn't an easy task. Something was wrong, but I couldn't let Nancy know I was hurt. I tried desperately to manipulate myself, pinning her so she couldn't move.

Sarah sat back down cursing up a storm. Good thing I was taller and heavier than Nancy. All I could do was to keep her from moving. Sometime had passed, I could barely move, and the sweat was pouring off me.

Eventually, Nancy wanted me to get off her so she could go back to her room. I slowly struggled to get back to my feet, everything felt strange. Nancy quickly got up and scurried off to her bedroom. I got Sarah to follow me into my bedroom. My movements were rather slow and awkward. I had to call for help.

When back up arrived, I quickly told Ben what had happened, and I had to go to the emergency. I don't really know how I managed to drive myself to the emergency safely. It was late Sunday the emergency room was full. As I was telling the triage nurse what had happened and starting to fill out the papers for Worker's Comp, I passed-out. When I came to, the resident doctor was standing over me. Now sensations were weird. Parts in my lower extremities were numb. I remember being panicked stricken. The doctor asked me a few questions, the next thing I knew I was being whisked away for x-rays.

The resident doctor and a doctor friend of Karen's, can't remember either of their names, soon returned, telling me they had some good news, and some bad news. I asked for the good news first. "I doubt you will be going back to work anytime soon Ms. Sulis, if at all." If this was the good news what could possibly be the bad news? The resident doctor continued giving me plenty of medical jargon before I asked him to explain, in laymen's terms what he was actually saying. He said I had a mild cervical fracture. I was going to have to wear a neck brace or collar to immobilize my neck for eight to twelve weeks or so, and be given medication for pain. But, he assured me that any bruising, swelling, tenderness, muscle weakness, and numbness I was experiencing would only be temporary. Luckily for me there was no damage to my spinal cord. Well, I always felt if it wasn't for no luck, I wouldn't have any luck at all. But, I should be grateful I suppose, it could have been much worse.

Of course I couldn't go back to work, wasn't sure when I would be able to return, if at all. It was a frustrating time for me. I hated having to wear that wretched collar around my neck. I didn't have much stamina for lying down, sitting or standing for any lengths of time. I was also advised against doing any exercise until it was determined I was ready.

Bill took a transfer back to the west coast, to Edmonton, with the retail company he worked for, so he, and Karen, and the kids could be closer to their family. It was a sad time to see them go. But, due to my situation and a short time later, the end of October of 1989, I decided to return home with my parents to finish my recuperation. After an initial period of time, my doctor recommended a rehabilitative exercise plan, and physiotherapy to increase my range of motion, and muscle strength.

With much dedication to my exercise regime, within the year, I finally had recovered, and was allowed to look for work. It was a gradual process, getting back into the swing of things. Starting out working only part time as a residential counsellor for a local Dartmouth agency.

The move was complete. Mom and Dad were settled into the house on Lake Banook and Bridgette had returned to Oakville. Dad asked me if I was up to selling tickets again, for his junior 'A' hockey team. Of course, I couldn't turn him down. It felt kind of strange, as if I hadn't even been gone for the past seven years. The team was in second place in the overall standings. Hopefully, they would keep doing well and make it into the playoffs, perhaps even to the finals. Who knows, maybe this would be the year they would be the league champs. But what worried me the most was the probability of running into Geoff. He and his brothers usually attended the games.

Geoff was in the line-up to get a ticket. Our encounter was brief. "Hi Liz, I heard that you were back, you're looking good." "Thanks Geoff." "You did something with your hair Liz. It's short, a lot shorter." "Yeah, I got it cut." "I like it Liz." "Thanks, how many tickets do you want Geoff, there's a line-up behind you." "Sorry Liz, I need two adults and one child please."

I had noticed that his right arm was in a sling. He passed me his money with his left hand. I didn't want to ask what had happened. But, before he left the booth, he asked if we might be able to find a way to talk, perhaps at some point during one of the intermissions. I didn't really give him an answer. I realized things were still unresolved between the two of us. The last time we talked was the night I had met him at the garage. We argued, I blurted things out and in the heat of the moment one thing led to another. I didn't believe there was any point in talking again, especially because of his wife and children.

I noticed from a distance, Geoff passed a ticket to a pregnant woman and a little boy, as he was entering the rink. They had been waiting for him by the door. It must have been his wife and son. The little boy was the spitting image of Geoff. I caught myself staring before my attention was redirected back to a customer wanting tickets.

Once I saw him with his wife and son, it solidified my decision. It was best that we didn't meet. Once I had finished selling tickets and handing everything over to my Dad, I went home. That night at the rink was the last time I would ever see Geoff again.

Tragically, Geoff's life was taken by cancer at age 30. Leaving behind his wife, two children, and a third on its way. I remember Geoff telling me he always wanted me to be the mother of his children. He never lived to see his third child. Sometimes I wished it had been my funeral and not his. No doubt he was a great husband and father. Not that I would want to be a widow and raise children without a father, but if things were different, perhaps we would have still been together. I didn't give us a chance, I just ran away, leaving him to marry another who would bare his children.

Shortly right after Geoff's diagnosis, my father was the one who told me he had cancer, and they didn't give him long. The news shocked me. That is why his arm was in a sling at the hockey rink, he had a biopsy done that day. It was in his lymph nodes and had spread.

I dwelled on the thought. If I could have had the time back when he wanted to talk to me at the rink, knowing it would have been my last, would I have grabbed it? Regrets, I have had a few. I was left with unfinished business and I would never see him again. I didn't get to say anything to Geoff that I really wanted to express. Now, his death froze my emotions, leaving me with lasting unresolved feelings. All along, my first instinct, as usual, was to pull away, and trust anger more than love. I am a living example of how the inability of giving or receiving forgiveness impedes releases for inner healing. Unforgiveness and harboring anger contaminates. Now I was faced with a lifetime sentence of missing him. Nothing would be the same. How can anyone really come to terms with things like this?

I remember all the love we did have and the moments we had shared, now only distant memories. Memories that no one can take away not even Michel. The opportunities were many to end this torment, but I always panicked, not wanting to have to face my fears or my true feelings.

Chapter Eighteen

The Church was packed. The turnout for the memorial was incredible. The Church choir sang and angels couldn't have done it better. The eulogies were unbelievably moving. The priest's message was comforting. But I hadn't heard a word of it. Not the songs, the eulogies, the message. As I looked around, there was Michel, sitting in a pew, a few ahead of, and to the right of, my parents and me. I'm sure the look on my face, as I stared at him, spotlighted like a deer caught in headlights. What was he doing here? I never knew whatever happened between the two of them, if anything. I hadn't laid eyes on him in years. It wasn't fair that we were attending Geoff's funeral. If Michel would have ever made eye contact with me and looks could kill, I'm sure he would have died on the spot. Talk about having an anxiety attack. My mother made mention that I became rather peaked looking during the service.

After the memorial service, I had joined in the receiving line to speak briefly with the family members. I had to get back to work. I didn't want to come face to face with Michel. I wanted to tell Geoff's mom and dad I was thinking of them.

The first person in line was Geoff's father. Mr. O'Donnell was holding up quite well, under the circumstances, trying desperately not to show his emotions. Quickly he thanked me for coming, his right hand was touching his wife's shoulder, in a comforting manner, and motioning me towards her. Mrs. O'Donnell took a step forward so she could hug me. It was a strange momentary encounter as we hugged; she whispered to me that she was so sorry. I didn't understand why she was saying sorry to me. I knew her loss was greatly felt, as any mother would feel for one of her own children to be gone. Geoff was a man, an adult, but was still her baby. As she released her grip from the hug, her hand moved to one of mine, taking hold. I gazed upon her face, her eyes were tear filled, but a comforting smile came across her face as she squeezed my hand. Before releasing it, she turned, guiding me towards the lady standing next to her in line. It was Geoff's wife. We had never actually met in person. A little redhead freckled boy was hugging her side. It was the woman and little boy at the rink, the last time I saw Geoff. When I looked down at their son, it was as if Geoff and I were back in elementary, and I was looking at him, but I was older.

Mrs. O'Donnell made the introduction. As I went to shake her hand and give my condolences, suddenly, this little redhead freckled boy reached out his hand for me to take, such a little hand. As I grasped it, he looked up at me; his soft voice uttered the words, "Thank you for coming to my daddy's funeral." I almost lost it. I continued along, Richard and Stephen, Geoff's older brothers were at the end of the line. His oldest brother Stephen was very close to Geoff. They apparently shared anything and everything.

Stephen leaned over, grabbing and hugging me tightly, burying his head in my shoulder, close to my neck. Crying, he whispered. "I'm so sorry, I'm so, so sorry for everything, Liz. Now I was at a total loss, who was supposed to be doing the consoling?

Stephen was the one who spent the days and nights of the last six months in the hospital with his brother in palliative care. He asked if we could meet sometime soon, so we could talk. This caught me by surprise. I was not expecting anything like this. I was so curious as to the reason why he wanted to meet with me. He slipped me a piece of paper with his phone number on it. "Call me, Liz please!" I called him a week or two later, we arranged a time to get together at his house. I realized Stephen had always been Geoff's confidant, visa versa.

Stephen felt it was necessary to share with me that after all these years his brother's love for me was still the same. He did love his wife too, especially his children. But, I was different, I was his first, and if things would have worked out differently, could I have been his only? Reality was, and in this case, we couldn't turn back to a certain point in time to start anew. Or even from this moment start over.

An important part of healing from the loss of a loved one is reminiscing, sharing memories, and stories of that loved one. I was glad that Stephen and I were able to give each other that opportunity. Stephen thought he knew everything there was to know about the two of us. Geoff had kept my secret to himself until the very end. Stephen was very emotional, reliving Geoff's emotions when he revealed to Stephen my secret.

Stephen commented that if he only knew then what he knows now, perhaps things might have turned out differently. He certainly would have tried to help. Stephen likened the cancer Geoff had to what I must have gone through. What a statement, I knew what he was trying to convey.

His brother had suffered greatly with the cancer, battling against it courageously. Geoff didn't want anyone to see him. The cancer and treatments had taken its toll. Soon, Geoff would succumb to this horrible disease, six months to the day of his diagnosis.

Stephen continued to tell me that several years' back, he caught Geoff, and Michel in the middle of a physical fight, and he had to jump in to tear the two apart. If not, Geoff probably would have ended up reducing Michel to a pulp. He had never seen his brother exhibiting so much rage towards anyone, especially to be directed at his best friend. Stephen said he never knew what they were actually fighting about, until Geoff was on his deathbed. According to Stephen, what made Geoff more irate, and full of rage was Michel's denial when Geoff had confronted him. As far as Stephen was concerned, and the fact that Geoff never said otherwise, he wasn't aware of any reconciliation between the two, and knowing his brother, it was highly unlikely for that to have occurred. He was surprised to have seen Michel at the memorial service too.

Stephen then alluded to the fact that the doctors might have ruled his brother's death due to the complications surrounding his cancer, but he believed his brother died more of a broken heart. I lost all of my inhibitions that day. I know I was sobbing, crying uncontrollably. Somehow it was to be some sort of cleansing, a closure so I could move on with my life, not succumb to it.

Geoff's last request was for Stephen to promise him . . . if the opportunity ever came for Stephen to talk to me, it would be for him to tell me that even in death, his love for me will never end. To rest assure, no matter what, he had never stopped being in-love with me . . . his love for me is eternal . . . and perhaps that someday, somehow I would be able to forgive him for all the hurt . . . forgive him for not knowing how to fight for me. But now, his greatest wish of all . . . is for some other man to be able to experience that same joy and beauty of falling in love with me . . . of wanting to spend the rest of his life with me . . . but that I would be able, in return . . . to trust his love, accept his love . . . and say "I do!" forever. For the greatest gift of all . . . is love.

I told Stephen that Geoff would always have a part of me, a part of my heart, there would always be memories that I would associate with the happiness of loving him, and being with him. More so than I even realized. I was blessed to have had Geoff's love. He had played a significant role in my life. I would always regret though that I didn't express my true feelings to him when I had the chance.

When I left Stephen's home, as I was driving along in my car, I was unaware of the song playing, until I started to listen to the words. I turned the volume up, so I could listen more intently, something began to move inside me, I had to stop driving. I pulled over in a clearing, but not before I realized it was Big Albro Lake, the lake that Geoff and I had spent lots of fun filled, and romantic times together at, years before . . .

I'm looking out, as the world goes by, all the sadness, Lover we tried. It used to be, you held me near, and I felt your touch, now I'm holding back my tears. Well I, I look back, and I close my eyes, to the blame, and the heartache, that we left behind . . . won't you take me, I'm falling I can't stop from loving you . . .

Now you were my world, and all that was real, now the memories are all I have to live for, 'cause you, you made me feel, the joy, and the pain, all the memories, I don't want to see fade away . . .

Every day, life is just the same, I'm looking in the mirror, trying to put on a face, of someone who's happy, someone who's strong, but deep down inside me, I know I was wrong . . . 'Cause you, you gave me more, more than you'll ever know, and I was such, such a fool yeah, to let you go . . .

> *Oh, won't you come back, I'm sorry, I'm standing here calling you, you were my world, and all that was real, now the memories are all I have to live for . . . 'Cause you, you made me feel, the joy, and the pain, all the memories I don't want to see fade away . . .*
>
> *Oh, if I could see you, see you now, I would hold on forever, 'cause time made me realize, we need to be together . . . so, won't you come back, I'm sorry, I'm standing here calling, take me, I'm falling, I can't stop from loving you . . .*
>
> *You, you were my world and all that was real, now the memories, are all I have to live for, 'cause you, you made me feel, the joy, and the pain, all the memories, I don't want to see, baby, you, you were my world, and all that was real, now the memories, are all I have to live for . . . 'Cause you, you made me feel, the joy, and the pain, now the memories, I don't want to see fade away, you were my world, I want you baby, come back to me, come back to me baby [Memories* by Taylor Dayne; Lyrics – Songwriters: Taylor Dayne, Lotti Golden, Tommy Faragher].

I talked to Geoff, observing him closely in my mind, to release my feelings, telling him everything I wanted to say, grieve, and say goodbye. I remember crying torrent of tears, sinking into despair, wailing out loud, and at times sitting in silence.

At first, I protested and refused to accept the truth, thinking that Geoff would magically return. Calling out his name. Imagining what he would say to me. I knew what I wanted to say . . .

> *Forgive me for the things that I never said to you . . . forgive me for not knowing the right words to say to prove that I will [wanted to] always be devoted to you, and me, and if you can't [couldn't] feel that in my love, then I'm sorry for not giving you enough.*
>
> *But I'm not sorry for my love, I'm not sorry for my touch, the way I made your hands tremble, and my heart rush. I would do it all again, wouldn't take back a thing, no, 'cause with you I've lived a thousand lives in one, and I could never be, I could never be, sorry for love. [Chorus]*

And baby, there have been times that I let you down. Looking back on all those moments, and know that I should have found, the best of me for you, and should have kept my promise to you, and if you don't [didn't] see that in my eyes, then I'll be sorry for the rest of my life. But I'm not sorry for my love . . . [chorus]

And we all make mistakes, no matter how hard we try, but hearts can only break, when sorry comes around, and oh, sorry comes around, but, I'm not sorry . . . I'm not sorry for my love, for my love, for my touch, I would do it all again, wouldn't take back a thing, 'cause with you I've lived a thousand lives in one, and I could never be, I could never be, I could never be . . . sorry for love [Sorry For Love by Celine Dion: Lyrics – Songwriters: Birgisson, Arnthor; Bagge, Anders; Dioguardi, Kara; Astrom, Peer].

I knew I would never see Geoff again, but if I could . . . I would hold on forever. I realized he wasn't coming back. He needed me before, but I wasn't there. I broke his heart so many times, now I was feeling his pain. Now that I see, back in his arms is where I wanted to be. I didn't know that I needed him. I had my chance, but I threw it away. And now my love was too late.

I was the abandoned lover mourning. All I could settle for was to finally say those simple three little words . . .*"I love you"* . . . from my lips to God's ears. Praying somehow now, for those words to be audible enough to reach Geoff's ears too . . . rest in peace my love.

CHAPTER NINETEEN

It was such a sunny day. My friend Laura and I had just returned from the other side of the harbour, completing an afternoon of doing what we women do so well, shop. We were co-workers for a Mental Health Agency. Laura was one of the Social Workers and I was a Program Assistant.

From a short distance I saw him, but he didn't see me. It had been a few years since Geoff's death. Just my luck our paths would cross again for a second time. With a feeling of dismay, he was the last person I wanted to see.

Stepping off the ferry, Laura and I decided to take in the Multicultural Festival happening on our harbour's waterfront, our annual celebration, and showcase of cultural diversity.

I would recognize him anywhere. I must admit he was a looker and he hadn't changed much in his appearance, just older. That was always a problem I had. What he did to me there was no need for since he was a looker. He could have had any girl he wanted. They were all interested in him, wanting to date him, except me, I had Geoff.

Anyway, he was with a woman and two small children. A good guess, to say this was his wife and children. He seemed to be so happy, they all seemed happy, one big happy family. I am sure they had their house with a little white picket fence too, perhaps a pet or two.

Now, to possibly come face-to-face with Michel was unthinkable. It took everything that I had, to simply walk away, not to go up to him, and make a scene. Why make his wife and children victims too? Or, have me escorted away in a straightjacket and paddy wagon, right into a mental institution. I'd always felt I was one step closer to that trip anyway.

I had so many things rushing through my head. Laura knew that something was definitely wrong. She literally had to drag me away and took me to her home. I was frozen again in time and all my blood seemed to have left my body or curdled.

As soon as we walked through Laura's door, her golden retriever, Sandy was at the door with her leash hanging out of her mouth, wagging her tail, begging to go for her walk. "You want to come Liz, I don't really want to leave you alone, something you saw or someone sure spooked you, but as you can see I better take girlie for her walk."

"That's okay Laura, if you don't mind, I just need a few minutes, and I don't think Sandy can wait any longer." "Well, are you sure you'll be okay, we won't be long." "Yes, go, I'll be fine, really." "Okay Liz, make yourself at home, I'm just going to go take her to the park across the street."

While they were out, I sat on the couch, and began to flip through the pages of the Chronicle Herald newspaper, a distraction to take my mind off things. I never was one for reading a newspaper, always seemed to be too much negativity reported, but I guess that's what sells.

All of a sudden I couldn't believe my eyes. There he was again, twice in one day. What was going on, wasn't seeing him earlier enough? I already had to lick my re-opened wounds? I read the caption and article under Michel's picture and name. He was given a huge promotion with some big Canadian corporation, and taking a transfer to South America with his family. My blood was beginning to boil. I couldn't believe that he seemed to have the world by the tail . . . that crass, predatory ape of a man.

All the accolades that were noted of his achievements and accomplishments were now being rewarded with a promotion . . . and a mighty big one at that. Everything seemed to be going his way. It is sad to think that one's fortune and ability to enjoy life comes at the expense of another. At least he was moving to some place far.

Exhaustion never tranquilized my dreams. Tossing and turning, restless sleep, dreams filled with anguish, not remembering clearly when I awoke, my body trembling in a sweat, and my heart beating violently continued to grip me with fear. Now, more than ever, I realized it had been crippling me to the point of not truly being free, and living my life to my fullest, living happily. Years had come and gone, and I became an expert of putting up barriers, living in my own prison I had created for myself. Which takes rise to the fact I have noted and kept asking myself over, and over, what are the causes of my character, and personality? Being serene, confident, even-tempered one moment, then irritable, nervous, unsure of myself the next or tense, brooding, emotionally frozen, and at other times being emotionally explosive, volatile, elated one moment, and depressed the next. What accounts for all of these differences?

To recognize my built up extreme anger, frustration, and hatred was one thing, but to learn how to properly deal with it would be another. All the mixed emotions and turmoil was like a ball, and chain attached to my feet or noose around my neck.

For some reason, I continued to punish myself for something I didn't do or deserve, and loosing out in so much. Letting myself go further into a downward spiral, into the abyss, and no longer taking care of myself. Up until now, all the words of wisdom and knowledge I had heard from others went in one ear, and right out the other.

This all had to come to an end. I needed to deal with psychological problems psychologically. I had punished myself in so many ways. Not letting anyone else truly love me or I them, believing that my first love would no doubt be my last, which was so long ago. Sabotaging any intimate relationship I did or would have.

My life began when I found Geoff and I thought it ended when my love for him was twisted, betrayed, perverted, and shackled to violence. But, I was wrong. Dean showed me that if I was brave enough to open my heart, I could love again, no matter how terrible my grief or how much I had been hurt. He made me realize that I was only half alive. It scared me and it hurt. A subconscious block forbade me from knowing how much I actually loved him, to know, it would have unlocked the pain of my past. And I didn't know how much I needed him until the night I watched him walk away. I felt something inside of me rip apart, and I knew I should have stopped him, but I didn't. AJ was a man who articulated with great intellect, a man of much character, and substance, romantic, warm, and gracious, with many surprises, and spontaneity. But, due to the situation with his ex-wife . . . I believed he was still totally in love with her, whether or not he was truly aware of that fact. I saw it, I knew it, so, I ended-up severing any further involvement we might have had.

If some lives form the perfect circle, others take shape in ways we cannot predict or always understand. Loss has been a part of my journey. But, it has also shown me what is precious. So has a love for which I can only be grateful. I have had the privilege of loving in my life.

I always had those what ifs playing in my mind. If this didn't happen to me, where would I be today, and would I have chosen the paths I took? If only I had gotten the help back then, what paths would my life had taken over the course of the past several years? And yes, I ask myself, would Michel have had the life he has had. At least not the cushy job he apparently has and would he have had a wife and children?

One can't remain living in all the *"what ifs."* In my desperate times of need, I remembered praying to the *God of Vengeance* that I conjured up that I knew didn't exist. Even the wicked get more than what they deserve. Some people seem to go through life unscathed. Getting a handle on things a lot easier, finding meaning, and purpose in his or her life. I am sure we all have our skeletons in our closets. I guess it comes right down to how each person learns to cope and handles all the twists, and turns life has to offer. Taking the good with the bad, turning the page, and moving on in the next chapter of one's journey through life. The further you get, a little easier it might be to make clear, sound choices that one can live with. You're the one who has to live with you.

I have been really fortunate in some ways I guess. I do take some things for granted. But when I look at other's lives, people who seem to have everything, a home, a good job, a family, is the grass necessarily greener on the other side?

I ended up being in a profession where I helped the underdog, so to speak. Being an advocate for others seems to be my destiny.

Unfortunately, I ended up being so busy, being responsible for everyone else, I didn't think about myself. Camouflaging the turmoil lying beneath. I guess that was the easy way out or the natural thing to do, help others instead of myself. I had denied myself the love and attention

I needed, although I was great at taking care of others, a workaholic, and co-dependent that must have been what kept me sane.

Most of the time I put myself under considerable stress. Any time I started a sentence with I feel that or I feel like, it was expressing a thought, not an actual feeling. A true expression of my feelings is when I feel angry, scared, confused, and anxious when I think someone is trying to control or hurt me. Perhaps, if I were able to learn to distinguish between my thoughts and feelings, it would give me a greater awareness of my own reactions, and improve my communication, and personal interactions.

If I was able to become more aware of my body sensations, perhaps I would be able to use the areas of stress to give me clues about what I'm feeling or thinking, so I could change my thoughts, and behavior, and react to events more effectively. I was not aware of what would make me happy, and I tend to remember my failures rather than my successes. The way I feel about myself determines how I'll react and act.

I had been going out of my way to make a good impression, but I had reservations as to the likelihood of succeeding. I felt that I had a right to accomplish all that I set my mind on, but I had become helpless, and distressed when circumstances had gone against me. The idea of failure was most upsetting and this could even mean utter dejection. I was attempting to escape into a world in which I could relax, feel at ease, and safe.

Chapter Twenty

Thoughts about hurting myself resurfaced. I had already survived the worst. What a terrible waste to die now. Therapy, psychoanalysis, counselling, call it what you will. I'd always called it a sham, a cop-out. Talk is cheap and highly over-rated.

Obviously I'm not the most perfectly sane and well-adjusted gal. But up to this point in my life, I'd tried to do what's right, I'd tried to live a good life, I'd done my best, I'd put everything behind me, so I thought. Somehow I'd stopped solving my own problems, I'd gone soft, maybe a bit or maybe I'd been hard-edged for too long.

Okay, so I needed help? But no matter how much I needed the help, I was reluctant to ask for it, especially from a *shrink*, the expertise, and insight of a so-called competent, non-judgmental professional. To me, requesting help showed my weaknesses and made me vulnerable. I had misconceived notions about Mental Health Services and its providers, working in the system, and watching how the system had failed so many. That's frustrating in it self. The thought of bumping into someone I might have known and worked with, wasn't settling well with me either.

Life without mental illness, now there's a powerful idea. No more severe anxiety or debilitating depression, no strange phobias or suicidal tendencies . . . so, everyone seems to be seeing a therapist these days. Of course Sigmund Freud first theorized that psychological problems are rooted in the unconscious mind. The techniques he developed to bring those problems to the surface have, over 100-plus years of refinement, become the foundation of modern psychotherapy.

My sadness, depression, and anxiety were becoming more constant, like before. My GP had me on an anti-depressant and sleeping medication. Therapeutic solutions and chemical cures, but they weren't really helping, and wouldn't, especially if my problems were not due to a chemical imbalance, but rather, were situational. Thanks to the introduction to Prozac and celebrities who erased the stigma attached to psychotherapy, like Oprah, by talking openly on her show about her weight problems, and history of sexual abuse, there's been an explosion of self-revelation; it's really quite extraordinary.

If there was no pain, no sorrow, and no suffering in our lives wouldn't that be wonderful!

But the fact that my old suicidal feelings were resurfacing was a sign that I had to finally deal with all my fears, emotions, and memories I had learned to suppress. Years had past by since my unsuccessful suicide attempt. I didn't want to reach that point of desperation again. Letting the suicidal tendencies reign over me. Somehow, my mind had been telling me something was seriously wrong, and I had to find a way to handle these issues, and do it now. I had to stop the urges before they got too great to stop. Laying them to rest once and for all, giving them their proper burial, before the rest of me followed suit. Was I really crazy and incurable?

What a process one has to go through in order to get the help he or she needs, for just walking off the street, so to speak, and asking for help. I ended up having to go through my GP, sending a referral, but it took about a year before I had my first appointment with a psychiatrist... going through the process, the system, being screened first by mental health nurses, and a social worker. I had requested a female psychiatrist, one of my many hang-ups, but ended up having to settle for a male. If I really wanted the help I had to somehow let him try. Lord only knew how long it would have taken if I had to start the process all over again, to wait for an available female psychiatrist. All their workloads, I am sure, are crazy.

Who doesn't have issues today? Maybe some are hardly head cases, most probably even spend their time ranting about scheming bosses or annoying spouses, while their therapist sit there quietly, feigning interest, fighting sleep.

I almost turned and walked out. A rather dingy, poorly florescent-lit hallway, and waiting area, in an institutional setting, there was no receptionist, so I took a seat. Magazines were scattered about on the coffee table. I picked-up a Reader's Digest book, flipping through the pages until I came upon the Laughter's The Best Medicine section, getting a few chuckles out of it.

"Elizabeth." I looked up. He was smiling. A very tall, lanky, balding, but distinguished man, with a pleasantly disarming smile. "I'm Doctor Alan O'Leary." I shook his hand and followed him to an airy office at the end of the long hallway. He pointed me toward a seat, *what no couch*, as he sat down in a chair facing me. I'd dreaded this moment. It wasn't an easy task, but if there was going to be any progress I had to somehow open up, and talk, and let him in. Otherwise, what is the point of getting help if you won't open up and talk?

But how do you confide in a complete stranger? How do you share the thoughts you've never really shared with anyone else? Yes, this man was trained and paid to listen. Yes, it was supposed to be easier to talk about your life with someone outside of it. But I didn't actually buy any of that. I mean, seriously, the entire setup was so artificial. How should I play along? Where would I begin?

He hadn't asked me to lie down or recount dreams, etc. No, we just started talking, about this and that. Occasionally, he asked a pointed question. Sometimes he wrote things down. I was never really one for talking about myself. My comfort zone was challenging to find, overcoming feelings of awkwardness, and being fidgety, and rigid most of the time. He pointed this out to me on several occasions.

The first few sessions we had delved a bit into my unconscious, he had poked, and prodded. At some point, I remember him saying. "I'm not sure we've reached your unconscious yet Liz, but we have awakened some of the bats that were sleeping."

I hated the adolescent in me. It was weak and vulnerable, afraid of feeling helpless again. I had to make the adolescent inside me feel safe and loved.

I was asked to start coming about 15 or 20 minutes earlier to our weekly sessions, so I could fill out some paper work before the sessions actually started, a rather extensive questionnaire. Questions I was asked to answer truthfully of course. Mostly repetitive multiple-choice questions, different scenarios, relationship questioning, activity levels, how I was actually feeling at that particular moment in time, to how I had felt during the week, how I had handled certain situations, and giving them a rating.

My third or forth session he asked me if I would mind being videotaped, so he, and a team of his associates could study it, and analyze it. But if at any time I didn't want it to continue or if our therapy sessions were to ever stop, the tape would be destroyed. It was a rather strange and an uncomfortable feeling of having a video camera taping our sessions. I hate even getting pictures taken of me. I have lots of friends who are camera happy. Thanks to digital technology, any friends who usually try to sneak a pic of me, I usually confiscate their camera, and erase it. But even more disturbing, strangers were going to see the video, and analyze me. I reluctantly agreed. It took several sessions before I would stare dully into the awful memory of it, a lifetime worth of stifled emotions exploding.

Excerpt from Doctor O'Leary's notes: Ms. Sulis has been experiencing increased anxiety, frustration, and anger. Anger, which has been culminating, directed at her in the form of physical symptoms, exhaustion, depressiveness, and anxiety. Ms. Sulis had a lot of mixed feelings towards key people in her life that has resulted in mixed feelings towards herself. She does not experience anger and rage, and painful feelings about what has happened, but rather she turns the rage inward, to herself, to depression, and a variety of other mechanisms.

The five main contributing factors to how well an individual is able to adapt include their genetic makeup, physical condition, learning, and reasoning, and socialization.

I decided when I was younger, a part of me was not safe to be happy, and destroyed any happiness I felt. I was responsible for sabotaging relationships and other experiences of happiness, fearful thoughts in my mind when I started to enjoy something. It was difficult to face the fact that I had been preventing myself from being happy. Knowing myself required becoming aware of all the parts of my mind and healing my wounds. Convincing this part of me that its actions were counter-productive. Self-awareness is liberating.

With help from Dr. O'Leary, I was able to search through the parts of my mind, where things originated, and what had happened to me. I soon discovered the reactions and behaviours I thought were irrational had a logical explanation. After releasing my feelings of rage and hatred, I realized I had been trapped in a pattern of victimization and low self-esteem. My subconscious feelings of anger and hatred kept me from feeling love, and accepting love. *Only through awareness of the truth can forgiveness and real feelings of love begin.* When I accepted and understood my own feelings it started the process of healing my past, eliminating the barriers that made me feel separate, different, and alone.

I was becoming aware that I was not ready to receive these truths until now. Besides, I wouldn't have believed the answers, might have misinterpreted them, and certainly would not have known what to do with them. I had to change my view of all things, people, and myself before I was ready. I had created this world, in which I lived, as a way of protecting myself. No matter how angry, hateful or misguided this part of me seemed to be, it helped me survive. Its purpose was to protect my conscious mind from feelings that were overwhelming at the time, and to insulate me from experiencing further pain.

I could be healed no matter how hurt or hostile this part of me appeared to be. The amount of rage I discovered terrified me. A rage and anger so wild, and fierce, that it destroyed common sense, and made me like an enraged wild animal, wanting to harm, and destroy.

Animals are considered to hold certain, powers, and represent different traits. A totem, emblem or symbol of such among many peoples throughout the world, that is associated with their ancestral traditions and is looked on with awe, and reverence by a tribe, clan or family. Many peoples never kill the animals that are their totems. Individuals' names were compared to something in nature that represented them. Sometimes during a vision quest, the individual would encounter the animal or other natural beings, which would protect them. That individual could then learn how to adopt the powers and traits of that animal. Some names would come from some event in life that would stand out and then the individual would be compared with a particular animal.

I compared myself to a Jaguar. The Jaguar is the 4th largest of the wild cats. It is stockier, with a shorter tail, sturdier legs, bigger paws, and a broader head than the leopard. Okay, maybe it's not one of the most glamorous of the wild cats to pick. But that wasn't the point. Like a Jaguar, I am a loner, although I do associate with other people. But, I am more comfortable by myself and at home. Usually, I tend to be drawn to others like me. The Jaguar has a wonderful gracefulness with the ability to move with ease or freeze entirely. I seemed to have learned how to adopt the powers and traits of this animal.

Jaguars are quiet when they are stalking, hunting or pursuing. They show silence is a powerful tool. They are excellent sprinters, but tire quickly. I have to learn to pace myself and learn to play as well as work. I should not push too far or too hard on any one task. Those with the Jaguars powers and traits are usually the first to respond, especially in the work environment where they respond effectively to pressures, and deadlines.

Jaguar's usually only stay together for a short period of time after mating. The female Jaguar being the domineering one in the relationship, and does all the rearing, not liking anyone else involved. I didn't have children, but I could relate to the short-lived relationships, and the fact I always had to have some sort of control, the domineering one.

Like a Jaguar, one never confronts someone angrily up front, for the Jaguar usually attacks from the back. They stalk patiently, waiting until close enough to strike strong and hard, more ferociously. Lacking the build or stamina for high-speed chases, the Jaguar hunts instead by patience and brute strength. Picking off its prey by stealth or sudden ambush.

They don't play when they hunt. Unlike other big cats, the Jaguar is noted for killing prey by leaping on animals back with a crushing bite to the skull or one swift bite fracturing the neck. It also can shear the heads off of animals with a single swipe. Individuals with the Jaguar traits should be careful when responding for they can hurt without meaning to. The Jaguar helped me understand how to get good out of darkness and death, eliminating the fears of them both. The Jaguar awakened my inner passions and instincts.

Therefore, the Jaguar may be saying the old wounds are finally starting to heal or an old issue is going to be resolved. My journey back was beginning and the end is never as important as how you get there. A symbol of my awakening to the heroic quest and though depths of degradation appear, whether self-inflicted or influenced from outside, there is always the promise of light, and love to lead me back. The Jaguar holds the promise of rebirth and guardianship throughout, being the extra protection I needed in troubling times. It is the symbol of power reclaimed from whatever darkness within my life has hidden it. That which is greater, stronger, and more beneficial will replace whatever had been lost.

The Jaguar will try many different angles before attacking its prey, staying way out to the side to keep the prey from knowing they are moving. It has also been seen that the Jaguar will actually stomp its foot to confuse its prey while stalking. A belief that these traits can be compared to a person who can give the ability to cause others to see and think, as one desires them too, but this comes through self-discipline. The Jaguar can climb, run, and swim, even better than the tiger. A saying tends to go along with those of the Jaguars powers and traits . . . that which does not kill us, makes us stronger.

Once I was able to release that deep level of rage and anger with help from Doctor O'Leary that part of me no longer had any destructive desires, and was ready to be integrated. My uncontrollable temper was now controllable. No longer reacting angrily to situations that provoked my rage. I no longer had to argue with the adolescent in me who was unable to reason with the adult part of me. I listened to that hurt adolescent inside, listened to the stories, and allowed that part of me to release feelings.

Keeping a painful past event from my conscious mind was a heavy burden. It wanted to unload, let go of secrets, convincing it to give up destructive beliefs,. and behaviors. I had such an amazing control or power to sabotage my happiness. Now I could use this power in a positive way. Like, helping me find opportunities for success and happiness or helping me pick healthy relationships, and warning me to stay away from people who would hurt me. Although I am an adult, my adolescent part never had a chance to grow up. Now I can give the adolescent in me the compassion and understanding it needs. As an adult, I have the power to give the love back to the adolescent in me, the love it once starved for. Telling its story, releasing its pain, and being at peace. Now I know, by bringing my subconscious memories to consciousness, the parts of my mind that were blocked-off by trauma, the angry, hurt parts, and the voices I had heard in my head, the demons needed to be revealed, and allowed to tell what they suffered, so they can release their pain, and rage.

My subconscious memories determined my personality and how I reacted to present events. They governed my actions and what I experienced in my life. I no longer have to be a puppet to my past. By cleaning these parts of my mind, my life would change dramatically for the better. By bringing these parts to my consciousness, the memories they contain can finally be processed, and integrated into other conscious information. I can handle the memories and feelings now. I am no longer helpless and I now have the intelligence, strength, and ability to handle painful past experiences.

The humiliation, guilt, shame, and blame I felt were a form of punishments, and a way I felt inferior. Many people gave me negative messages because it was the easiest way to manipulate me. Instead of inwardly agreeing, yes, I'm guilty, I must do what they say, I had to start asking myself. "What is it that they want, why are they doing this?"

I learned how to live under a cloud of humiliation, guilt, shame, and blame. I always felt wrong or I was not doing the right thing or apologizing to someone for something. I didn't respect myself and couldn't forgive myself for things from the past. I had to let the clouds of humiliation and guilt, shame, and blame, dissipate.

I didn't need to live this way any longer. I don't have to play people's games anymore. It isn't easy to say no, but when people see that manipulating me doesn't work, they will stop. People will only control you as long as you allow them to.

I discovered that I held on to beliefs that prevented me from having what I wanted most, although well intentioned. Never to love anyone because something awful happened when I was happy or the love I had hurt. Never to be successful because I didn't want anyone to be proud of me, besides I didn't believe I deserved to be successful. Not to remain physically fit, thin or attractive. There were endless reasons of why parts of me contained destructive decisions that were sabotaging my life. It was a shock to my system that my own unconscious beliefs controlled my life, and prevented me from being happy. But, to finally accept the truth was the *beginning* of accepting responsibility for my life, and real healing, a phenomenon of sudden insight or inspiration.

Love, spirituality, and beauty are everywhere, but I didn't see it because my unconscious beliefs blinded me. I am supposed to be happy and enjoy the blessings of life, but I had pushed away what I wanted because of these beliefs. Exploring myself has been an exciting and dauntless task. Although at times, it was difficult to accept this viewpoint when I was overcome by pain and despair. However, when I was able to recognize the creative and effective ways my mind protected me when I needed it most, I was able to thank myself for my intelligence, and my strength. I had much to learn from all the parts of my mind.

I remember the happy memories that existed before I was hurt and the lies I came to believe about myself. The pain, anger, and defences have been a veil that covered my true self, my soul. My true self, my soul can never-be destroyed. It was buried, but it survived no matter what was done to me and no matter what I did. I rediscovered it.

My subconscious mind has recorded every event and sensation I experienced so that all of my memories are always part of me the happy ones, as well as the not so happy ones or the traumatic ones. My experience of discovering my core self has been more powerful after I understood the pain I had suffered, and why I feel the way I do now. I see clearly who I was before the painful experience caused me to forget.

Understanding who I really was enabled me to accept my violent emotions, and the hurtful parts of me because I know that my happy, loving, true self, my soul, existed underneath. Happiness, harmony, and love are our true nature.

I tried to repress my anger, hatred, and scorn I felt towards Michel. By doing so it caused stress, and sickness. God knows how I hated him, detested him, and abhorred him. So much so that my deep fixed dislike caused me to shudder, and shrink away from anyone or anything that overwhelmingly caused me to have feelings of hostility, and often a desire to hurt or harm. I didn't realize that my anger was a signal that something was wrong and the hatred provided the strength to survive what Michel had done. I locked up inside me the anger and hatred where it continued to simmer, creating a deep, subconscious layer, of murderous rage. I remember telling Doctor O'Leary, if only, at the time of the incident, I could have been capable of shape shifting – metamorphosis – into a Jaguar, then the outcome of that fateful day might have been totally different.

Hate is a cancer on the intellect and pollutes the mind. I had to embrace the infuriatingly savage thoughts and feelings inside me, learn to acknowledge, and accept my anger, and hatred so it would no longer have control over me. Recognizing it, dealing with it, and releasing it in a safe way. If I could do this, then perhaps, I would find it easier to understand, and forgive Michel or anyone else who had hurt me. Forgiving Michel would take his power he had over me away, he would no longer be able to command my emotions. He would cease to be the eye of the storm, becoming a person like any other, human, and flawed, and misguided on occasion, therefore, rather like the rest of us.

~

I contributed toward the creation of every condition in my life, good and bad. The thoughts I dwelled on created my feelings and I then began to live my life in accordance with these feelings, and beliefs. This is not to blame myself for things going wrong in my life. There is a difference between being responsible and blaming others. Responsibility is about having power. Blaming someone or pointing a finger is about giving away one's power.

Responsibility gives me the power to make changes in my life. When I play the victim role, then I am using my personal power to be helpless.

If I decide to accept responsibility, then I won't waste time blaming somebody or something out there.

I always have a choice. It doesn't mean that I deny who I am and what I have in my life. It merely means that I can acknowledge that I have contributed to where I am. By taking responsibility I have the power to change. All of the events I have experienced in my lifetime, up to this moment, have been created by my thoughts, and beliefs from the past. There is no reason to continue beating myself up because I didn't do better. I did the best I knew how. I can't look back on my life with shame. Clearing out the parts of my mind that contained beliefs I held that I could never depend on or trust anyone would allow me to become closer to people, develop better healthier relationships, and have more caring friends.

The mind is a complex organ, so ingenious that biology and experience work hand-in-hand. After I saw what I had survived and coped with, I began to realize my strengths, and abilities, and the incredible power of my mind.

Things are not perfect. I still have times of anxiety, frustration, and anger. It is how I react to these feelings and emotions that make a difference. Everyday I am constantly learning to deal with my feelings and emotions, so that they don't control me and to love myself. It is not selfish to love myself. So many times I hid from myself and I didn't even know who I was. I didn't know what I felt and didn't know what I wanted. I said many times I don't care, but the truth is I did, and still do. I couldn't forgive myself, love myself or trust myself. *Wow!* Did I miss out on a lot. To love myself I have to accept all the different parts of me, the whole package, unconditionally, my peculiarities, the embarrassments, the things I may not do so well, and all the wonderful qualities, and talents. Clearing the debris so that I can love myself enough to love other people. I still am not totally convinced yet that I have actually been able to forgive and forget completely that is tough. I'm still a work in progress. But, I am well aware that unforgiveness contaminates, it does impede inner healing. Naturally, I would have resentment. I was bitter and unforgiving of the past.

I am not sure who told me this or where I heard this saying, but it is something I repeat to myself daily. *"If I am not willing to forgive myself and others that have hurt me, and love myself today, then I am not going to forgive myself, and others that have hurt me, and love myself tomorrow. Whatever excuse I have today, I will still have tomorrow, and life will continue to pass me by."*

I am a great one for placing conditions on myself or making excuses that I can't love myself until I lose the weight or get the job or get the raise or the boyfriend, husband, whatever. The key is to love myself as I am right now, with no expectations. When I love who I am, I will not hurt myself, and I will not want to hurt anyone else. We all have different opinions. You have the right to yours and I have the right to mine. No matter what goes on around me, the only thing I can work on is what is right for me. The hardships have served to make me stronger. I try my best to go through each day with my head held high and a happy heart.

Repression was a subconscious mental process that forbade certain ideas, memories, identifications, and evaluations to enter my conscious awareness. In repression, certain thoughts or memories do not simply fade away. They are actively blocked and inhibited from reaching conscious awareness. They are not ejected from focal awareness; they are prevented from entering it.

If the memory of that fateful day ever began to float toward the surface of my conscious awareness, it was blocked before it could go any further. A kind of psychological alarm-signal that was set off and the memory was again submerged.

The simplest type of repression is the blocking from conscious awareness of painful or frightening memories. In my case, the incident that was so traumatically painful or frightening when it occurred, and would be traumatically painful or frightening if recalled, was inhibited from entering my conscious awareness. I wanted to forget what had happened and was successful to a remarkable extent. Memories were barred from my conscious awareness because of the pain they would invoke. I exhibited something close to amnesia concerning my early years. If any questions about my past were raised, I felt a heavy wave of pain or depression.

Among the various factors that may have caused me to feel alienated from my own emotions, repression is the most formidable, and devastating. But it is not emotions as such that are repressed. An emotion as such cannot be repressed; if it is not felt, it is not an emotion.

Repression is always directed at thoughts. What is blocked or repressed, in the case of emotions, is either evaluations that would lead to emotions or identifications of the nature of one's emotions. A person can repress the knowledge of what emotion they are experiencing. Or, they can repress the knowledge of its extent and intensity. Or, they can repress the knowledge of its object, i.e., of whom or what aroused it. Or, they can repress the reasons of their emotional response. Or, they can repress conceptual awareness that they are experiencing any particular emotion at all; they can tell themselves that they feel nothing.

When I repressed, my intention was to gain an increased sense of control over my life. Invariably and inevitably I achieved the opposite. Repression led to my increased frustration and suffering, not to my betterment. Whether my motive was noble or ignoble, facts cannot be wiped out by self-made blindness. I merely succeeded in sabotaging my own consciousness.

Chapter Twenty-One

Everything as I knew it came to a screeching halt that one summer day as I was preparing to go to the lake and paddle. I now remember that morning as if it happened yesterday . . .

My parents were at work. I was awakened by the phone ringing. It was Michel on the other end. Michel wondered if he could come see me before I went to the lake. He said he wanted to come and discuss some things regarding a surprise party I was planning for Geoff. I didn't see why not, I thought it was great he wanted to help me with the party. Michel had always been nice to me.

What was about to happen I could never have imagined it, even in my wildest dreams. It was the furthest thing from my mind, but I guess the first thing on his.

I had just taken a shower, slipping on my shorts, and shirt, and finished getting my gear together, so I would be ready to leave when he left. Suddenly I heard him knocking at my door. It started out fine, he talked about some ideas he had. Nothing seemed to be wrong, but things shifted quickly, and went completely out of control. It wasn't a pretty situation.

I had excused myself to go to my bedroom to get my party planner book, and pen, lying on my chiffonier. I glanced in the mirror from my chiffonier. He startled me. He was standing right behind me. Rather strange that he had followed me. I certainly didn't invite him in.

Michel had the uncanny ability to appear perfectly ordinary, disguising his true intentions. Some people manage to lead a double life. Empathy, conscience, remorse were completely missing from his emotional makeup, he was hollow to the core, utterly evil.

How can a person who seems so ordinary, possess the heart and mind of a monster?

I had an ideal love, a one and only, a person that made me whole, a Mr. Right, my one true love that special someone, my significant other. I didn't have to wait in suspense until the handsome Prince arrived with an invigorating kiss. I didn't have to wait for the knight in shining armour to ride by. Nor did I have to wait for karma, fate or destiny or some other temporal God to send a likely partner my way or use Cupid's arrow. We didn't need a powerful love potion to be brewed or drank, while thirsty and unaware, to make us fall in love.

But, there is no greater power over another person than that of inflicting pain, such as sexual violence.

Facing him, Michel placed his arms on either side of my arms. Trapping me against the chiffonier . . ."What are you doing Michel?" I tried to move. Instead, I was pressed closer to him. His hands now disturbingly rubbing the sides of my breasts, I pushed his hands away . . .*"Stop! What do you think you're doing?"* He reached up to fiddle with a few strands of my hair. "Come on Liz, I know you want it . . . you give it to Geoff . . . I've been imagining you going down on me for quite sometime."

I forcefully pushed his offending hands away again and side-stepped . . .*"Don't! Don't touch me. Leave, I want you to leave Michel."* I was pointing towards the door as I said it. "Here's news for you *bitch*. I'm not leaving, until I get what I came for."

Michel threw me face down onto my bed, pouncing with demonic fury. His hands pinned my outstretched arms as I was forced to lie beneath him. He was much stronger than me. I couldn't believe what was happening, how could it be happening? Yet I knew it was.

This was the beginning of unspeakable depravity. Violated forcibly to have sexual intercourse, without my consent.

I struggled frantically, pleading with him to stop. He was hurting me. But, to no avail, he wouldn't stop. He wasn't listening to my pleas to stop, soundless words to his ears. I was at his mercy, being forced to submit and subjected to such intense appalling horror, spewing obscenities, and shouting out insane remarks referring to my relationship with Geoff.

Blood surged through my taut veins. He managed to strip off my shorts. He spread my legs apart as he eagerly guided himself between my legs. My cries broke from my lips again as I felt the painful sting of him thrusting himself into me. I clamped my teeth unto my lower lip, shutting my eyes. This was not sexual pleasure. I tried to lay still, helpless, and un-aroused, while he performed his beastly act. Submitting to the assault for fear of greater harm.

His chants mingled with grunts and groans, mounting in tempo, and pitch, superimposing my pleas, and screams. I went mad. Waves of nausea and horror swept through me. My face contorted in spasms as he pushed his way farther.

I never felt so defenceless. I never suspected that he was utterly capable of such a very cruel and brutal act . . . raping me. This was totally out of his character, as I knew it. He was a genuine Jekyll and Hyde, a clean-cut, attractive, charming guy, but now I was face-to-face with a monster, an insidious hidden evil within Michel. I had been duped. The monster inside him, his evil Mr. Hyde had taken complete control.

Michel left when he was done, but not before he warned me against ever saying anything to anyone about this. He had made it very clear never to say a word or next time it would be worse. I didn't want to find out what worse meant. Nothing at this point could ever top what he did or could he top it?

He didn't have a clue of the hurt he had caused me, of course why would he? He no doubt would be in denial and perhaps has forgotten about it, it was so long ago. Did he think I would just move on and forget about it like he apparently did? He must have found a way to be pleased with himself. In his own mind at that time he had the right to take what wasn't his to take. Apparently, he was a guy who could move on, expecting me to do the same. Rationalizing that it was okay for what he did to me. He was right I guess. I did absolutely nothing about it. There were not the right programs in place to handle it and the laws back then were archaic. In my mind, if I did or said anything, I would have had to defend myself against the implication that I either lied about it or must have somehow asked for it. Even if I told the truth I felt I had no one to stand behind me. I was horrified.

I remember sitting huddled in the corner of my room on the floor, feeling dirty, and nauseous, weeping without restraint, sobbing audibly with uncontrollable shaking. I wept to the point of exhaustion. When my weeping subsided I remained, as I was, listless, eyes closed, tears drying on my cheeks.

I didn't know how long I had been sitting there emotionally distraught. I searched for some kind of rational explanation. To me, Michel had resorted to the only kind of sex he was capable of, *rape of demonic intensity*. Undoubtedly, Michel's only remarkable trait was a staggering capacity for violence. *I prayed to God that he didn't continue to pursue or prey on other girls to rape.* I wanted to say Michel was insane, but I believed he knew the difference between right and wrong, and chose to engage in wrongdoing, at my expense. What he did to me indeed had an enormous impact on my life and was incomprehensible and reprehensible. It's this sort of conduct that cries out for a sentence that expresses denunciation and deterrence.

Eventually, I managed to clean up the mess. So exhausted, so weak, and trembling I stood beneath the shower, hoping somehow to rid myself of him. Every effort had to be concealed from this unspeakable wrong. This had to be the way it would have to be, keeping this secret from Geoff and everyone else. I was terrified of the consequences if anyone would have found out. It would have been embarrassing and humiliating for me, for others to know what had happened, a psychological reaction involving my feelings of shock and shame.

I tried to figure out, why me? There was no answer, only my belief that somehow I was at fault. The emotions of humiliation and guilt, which included anger, powerlessness, and fear, started immediately during the assault, and remained hidden with me for years, unresolved.

Because the attack resulted in my body responding literally against my will, the psychological repercussions were profound. To name a few, but not limited to, various phobias, and anxieties, depression, self-loathing, and anger [my heart was held hostage by my anger], severe neuroses, and abuse with alcohol, and/or drugs. Finding it very difficult to form any type of lasting relationship with a man . . . the assault caused me to despise myself, and deny myself of any normal, healthy, and happy long lasting relationship. All contributing factors or a catalyst for me wanting to commit the ultimate act of self-destruction: *suicide*. If one gives evil an inch, it will take a mile.

Michel's savage instincts were let loose on me that day. Pretty much all human beings have aggressive and anti-social thoughts or impulses from time to time. Thankfully, for the vast majority of people, this basic, brute nature is kept in check. Guilt . . . that is, our own sense of doing wrong, and shame, the belief that others would judge our actions as wrong, generally keep people from acting out their violent impulses. While disinhibition is the process that allows people to overcome guilt and shame to commit violence, a form of disinhibition takes place when potential perpetrators of violence construct rationalizations that justify their crimes. Depersonalization and dehumanization are well-known mechanisms that allow people to disinhibit violence by making the victim's suffering less problematic.

I have been told that acts of violence always come from people who were violated. Sex offenders often need treatment for troubled upbringings. Either they just weren't brought up properly or they came from broken families or they have deep-rooted psychological problems that need to be treated. But there are not many treatment programs available, then or now, and while stiffer penalties might deter some would-be sex offenders, they probably wouldn't give a psychotic person pause for thought. Not for somebody that's been driven by the hormones where they got this compelling need to rape, that's the least of their worries. If somebody [like that] is going to go commit a rape, they don't care about the consequences. They really don't.

It's hard to pinpoint why Michel chose me. But I do believe he got great pleasure in setting out to destroy my world, as I knew it, for no discernible reason. But, it has been said that some of the most blatant sexual acts have nothing to do with sex per se, but is an aggressive desire of power, anger, and domination over the victim, rather than an attempt to achieve sexual fulfillment; rape being an extreme example.

They say sexual relations are about mutual satisfaction and respect, not power, anger, and dominance. Instead of facing the vulnerability and complexity of a real relationship, Michel resorted to a substitution for intimacy, raping me. It was a malicious, cowardly act by him and a dehumanizing experience for me, to say the least. Apparently, Michel was so full of hate and self-loathing. In my eyes he was the unmanliness of men, a limp member of society, a worthless male. I did not deserve, want, nor asked for this, no one does. Now I was forced to somehow face and cope with my own deepest fears, alone.

To be human is to be emotional, to have a body that is regularly ransacked by emotions of many kinds, including love. For whatever reason, Michel spared my life, but derailed any train of pleasurable thoughts or feelings I had, as I grew older. Any that I did have, seemed to be short lived. I disabled love and repressed any true intimate feelings. It was taboo. I had lost a part of me, pathologically depressed by that younger girl inside and filled with reproach, garbling or distorting love relationships, sabotaging any relationships that would matter most to me. There have been many times I had wished Michel had ended my life.

But . . . strong character develops as you struggle through tough conditions.

Growth means change and change involves risk,
stepping from the known to the unknown.
—Author Unknown—

Chapter Twenty-Two

The Hammer, the File, and the Furnace . . . by Charles R. Swindoll

It was the enraptured Rutherford who said in the midst of very painful trials and heartaches:

"Praise God for the hammer, the file, and the furnace!" Let's think about that. The hammer is a useful and handy instrument. It is an essential and helpful tool, if nails are ever to be driven into place. Each blow forces them to bite deeper as the hammer's head pounds and pounds.

But if the nail had feelings and intelligence, it would give us another side of the story. To the nail, the hammer is a brutal, relentless master—an enemy who loves to beat it into submission. That is the nail's view of the hammer. It is correct. Except for one thing. The nail tends to forget that the same workman holds both it and the hammer. The workman decides whose "head" will be pounded out of sight . . . and which hammer will be used to do the job.

The decision is the sovereign right of the carpenter. Let the nail, but remember that the same workman holds it and the hammer . . . and its resentment will fade as it *yields* to the carpenter without complaint.

The same analogy holds true for the metal that endures the rasp of the file and the blast of the furnace. If the metal forgets that it and the tools are objects of the same craftsman's care, it will build up hatred and resentment. The metal must keep in mind that the craftsman knows what he's doing . . . and is doing what is best.

Heartaches and disappointments are like the hammer, the file, and the furnace. They come in all shapes and sizes: an unfulfilled romance, a lingering illness and untimely death, an unachieved goal in life, a broken home or marriage, a severed friendship, a wayward and rebellious child, a personal medical report that advises "immediate surgery," a failing grade at school, a depression that simply won't go away, a habit you can't seem to break. Sometimes heartaches come suddenly . . . other times they appear over the passing of many months, slowly as the erosion of earth.

Do I write to a "nail" that has begun to resent the blows of the hammer? Are you at the brink of despair, thinking that you cannot bear another day of heartache? Is that what's gotten you down?

As difficult as it may be for you to believe this today, the Master knows what He's doing. Your Saviour knows your breaking point. The bruising and crushing and melting process is designed to reshape you, not ruin you. *YOUR VALUE is increasing the longer He lingers over you.*

~

Leon R. Kass, an American Bioethicist, is best known as a leader in the effort to stop human embryonic stem cell and cloning research. He was the son of Jewish immigrants from Eastern Europe and described his family as a *Yiddish speaking, secular, socialist family.* Below, is an excerpt I have taken from a paper he wrote on *Science, Religion, and the Human Future.*

> *"What kind of knowledge is science and how is it related to the truths promulgated [proclaimed] formally by biblical religion? Are these, as the late Stephen Jay Gould [a prominent American palaeontologist, evolutionary biologist, and historian of science] argued against creationism and proposed that science and religion should be considered two compatible, complementary fields or magisterial [showing authority], whose authority does not overlap – each with its own canons of evidence and legitimate claims, but – despite apparent contradictions between them – perfectly compatible domains, neither one capable of refuting or replacing the other. Or . . . should we rather insist that there couldn't be contradictory truths about the one world? For either the world is eternal or it came into being; if it came into*

being, either it was created by God or it was not; if there is divinity, either there is one God or many gods; either man is the one god-like creature – in the image of God or, he is not; either God has made known to man what He requires of him or, He has not" . . .

"And then, finally, there is that old chestnut, still hard to crack, of miracles. Few of us creatures of the present age believe in miracles, in occurrences that suspend the laws of nature, events that we must hold to be, according to the regularities that science describes for us, Impossible. In this respect, we are all children of science, at least regarding our contemporary life on earth. So little do we believe in the possibility of miracles that many of us even have trouble imagining any occurrence so unusual or momentous that would shake our faith in the impossibility of miracles" [http://www.aei.org/article/25908 – Leon R. Kass – Science, Religion, and the Human Future].

In 1982, somewhere around January or February, I was asked by a friend, if I would like to come to one of her church's evening, weeklong special services. To tell the truth, I had no real interest in going to church. But, due to a few other members of her congregation that I knew, and who had just recorded a gospel album, and would be singing, I decided to go.

However, just before Christmas, the lead singer of the choir, while on her skiing trip honeymoon, had a terrible accident on the mountain. Her injuries were extensive to her right leg; six breaks, including her femur. [The femur is the bone in the leg that extends from the hip to the knee.] The femur being one of those bones that one just doesn't want to break, if a person has to break anything.

She was air lifted back to Halifax, where she had undergone extensive surgery. The doctors were sceptical in how, or if, her leg would ever heal properly. "Only time will tell," the surgeon said. She was able to return home approximately two weeks, or so, after her surgery; I'm sure with plenty of pain medication, and a cast up to her hip.

However, she was the type of believer in Christ that nothing was going to keep her down for long, and her faith, and love in Christ was, lets just say, unshakeable, in fact, it was totally unyielding, unmoveable.

I remember arriving at the church, meeting up with my friend, Eleanor and her two boys. The sky was clear, so you could see the stars shining brightly. Grant it, it was still rather cold. It had snowed a day or so before Wednesday had rolled around, so there was plenty of snow.

But as soon as we entered the church, there was something noticeably wrong with the quality of the air. No one was able to really explain it. Someone had suggested that perhaps someone had been cooking something earlier in the kitchen that was located downstairs. But when they went to investigate, there was nothing found to be out of the ordinary. No one was experiencing any breathing problems and it certainly didn't appear they were going to postpone the service, in order to figure out what it was. There are really no words to describe it, other than the fact it was a noticeable, unexplainable, strange, odourless, somewhat hazy, and humid-like heaviness in the air.

The young, Texan, guest preacher had been introduced to the congregation Sunday night, but for those who had missed Sunday night and the previous two nights, he was re-introduced, along with his wife. He was a very tall, dark-haired, man, with glasses, somewhere in his mid to late twenties, with a very thick southern accent. After the introductions were made, his wife returned to her seat.

He began telling us that earlier in the day, while he was in prayer, and putting the finishing touches to his sermon for the night, the Lord had laid on his heart that he wasn't going to actually deliver the message tonight. God told him that something else was going to happen. The preacher admitted that he wasn't really sure what God had in store for tonight, and he seemed a little unsure as to why God laid this on his heart, but whatever it was, he was confident that God was going to do something spectacular. He asked the choir and band members to come back up to the front, to lead everyone into worshiping God again in song – God would do the rest.

Rebecca and her husband suddenly appeared at the back of the church. She was in a wheelchair with her leg extended in a cast. As they approached the front of the church, people were stepping out of the aisle to go to her, to give her a comforting hug and an encouraging word. The guest preacher joined the people to formerly introduce himself to her.

It is then that Rebecca made her intentions known. She told the preacher that she had her husband bring her, because she was going to be healed that night, and asked the preacher to have some people to come pray with her. Once there was a lull in the singing, the preacher asked everyone to keep singing, but if some of the believers would come gather around to pray with Rebecca, for God to heal her. He became very excited, knowing now what God had in store.

The choir kept singing, but pretty much the entire congregation came to pray with Rebecca. No matter what I have ever done or where I have ever gone, I have never forgotten about that night, and what took place a short time after people had started to pray for Rebecca.

I wasn't really paying attention; I remember I was gazing out the window I was sitting next to. When all of a sudden, I was startled, my eyes moved quickly to find Rebecca out of her wheelchair and worshiping God, praising God, and thanking Him for his healing power as she was trying to run, with the cumbersome cast, up and down the aisle. Needless to say, everyone went crazy, well crazy to me.

What happened next, some men went to find some tools so they could remove her cast. She was very adamant about this. At this point I wasn't really sure what to believe or think. I wouldn't have believed it myself if I wasn't there.

Once the men had returned with some tools, they worked on removing the cast. Once her leg was freed, the rest of the evening was unbelievable, but not as unbelievable as to what was going to happen the following day.

Her husband and mother took her to the orthopaedic clinic, at the hospital, to see the doctor who performed the surgery.

I wish I could have been there, to see the look or expression on his face, once he saw her, and realized who she was, without a cast and walking about freely, with no problem.

Apparently at first, he thought this was some sort of a cruel trick or mean joke, especially when he remembered Rebecca had an identical twin sister. But that thought quickly left him, once her sister walk through the clinic doors. Of course she was taken for x-rays and was thoroughly examined.

According to Rebecca, her husband, mother and sister too, when the doctor had returned with the results from the x-ray, scratching his head . . . he said he didn't have any medical or scientific explanation as to how her leg was perfectly healed . . . except to say . . . it must have been Divine Intervention – there was no other reasonable explanation.

What I didn't mention, instantaneously, as Rebecca jumped out of her wheelchair that hazy, humid-like air immediately evaporated. I noticed it, even as I was caught up with all the excitement and commotion going on around me. I didn't really know what to think, so I could only imagine what was going on in the doctor's mind and all the other people at the clinic that day.

Some time had passed and I don't remember how exactly I received this letter, but it was addressed to me . . . when I opened it up this is what it said:

Dear Friend,

I just had to send a note to tell you how much I love you and care about you. I saw you yesterday as you were walking with your friends. I waited all day, hoping you would want to talk with me also. As evening drew near, I gave a sunset to close your day and a cool breeze to rest you. And I waited. But, you never came. It hurt me, but I still love you, because I am your friend.

I saw you fall asleep last night and I longed to touch your brow. So, I spilled moonlight on your pillow and your face. Again, I waited, wanting to rush down so that we could talk. I have so many gifts for you. But, you awakened late the next day and rushed off to work. My tears were in the rain.

Today you looked so sad, so all alone. It makes my heart ache, because I understand. My friends let me down and hurt me so many times, but I love you. Oh if you would only listen to me. I really love you. I try to tell you in the blue sky and in the leaves on the trees, and breathe it in the colours of the flower. I shout it to you in the mountain streams and give the birds love songs to sing. I clothe you with warm sunshine and perfume the air with nature scents. *My love for you is deeper than the oceans and bigger than the biggest want or need in your heart.*

If you only knew how much I want to help you. I want you to meet my father. He wants to help you too. My father is that way, you know. Just call me, ask me and talk with me. Please, please don't forget me. I won't hassle you any further. You are free to call me. I'll wait, because I love you

Your friend,

Jesus

During my time in St. John's, Newfoundland, the churches that I became somewhat involved with through Turning Point, work, and the after school program, mentioned in the story, got together and had a faith healing week-long meeting. This was a big event actually. It was well advertised and they had rented a room at one of the hotel's downtown St. John's. All were welcomed. By the second or third night, the room had to be increased in size. They tried to squeeze as many people as they could inside. Crowds had even gathered out in the hallways and even outside the building.

The circumstances surrounding why I had been attending these meetings, was that I was asked to come help out with doing sign language. I had no real formal training, at this point. But getting the opportunity to use my ASL I had learned, and was using on a regular basis with clients I had or other deaf people that were in my life, helped me to be fluent enough in my delivery. I was a quick learner I guess. I also had been doing some occasional signing in the morning Sunday service for the main church hosting this event, and where we held the after school program.

There was a special faith healing minister that they brought in from Texas. Yes from Texas. I remember saying to myself, "There is a Santa Claus I do declare." He was a jolly, somewhat of a roly-poly man with a white beard, moustache, and white hair. All that was missing was the red suit. Without a doubt, he could have pulled-off a St. Nick impersonation.

All kidding aside, he was not Santa Claus or St. Nick; he described himself as a simple servant of God, a vessel, amongst other things. By the third night, he had been asking people to form a line, to come to meet him, while he instructed the rest of us to carry on worshiping Jesus in song.

I had just finished doing my turn of signing and sat down next to one of the girls I had known for a period of time. She was known to most in the city, born deaf, and somewhere in her mid twenties. So she had never heard a sound, not a peep, in her entire life.

Well, as I sat down next to her, she signed to me, asking me if I would mind taking her up, so she could join in the line up to meet this man. When we finally made it to the front of the line, I went to introduce her, managing to get her name out, before he told me to hang on, to stay put. He took her by the hand and proceeded to guide her across to the other side of the stage.

I thought this was strange, unless he knew how to sign, I was sure he would have difficulty in communicating with her, but of course she could read lips. The only problem with that was his beard and moustache. I wasn't sure if she could read his lips. But apparently, the two of them were able to communicate to each other without my assistance. He brought her back over to me, asking me to make sure she would be here tomorrow night. That was about it, to the extent of our conversation. We returned to our seats. I asked her if she was okay, she said yes, but appeared to me, to be somewhat preoccupied or was not sure perhaps of what was really going on or what had just happened. Of course I should have known better.

The following night came; I had just arrived, and was making my way through the crowd. As I opened the doors to enter the room, I was stopped, dead in my tracks. I couldn't believe it. There it was again. It immediately took me back to 1982, where Rebecca had been healed – it was the same, identical hazy, humid-like air. Not sure if this is something that has to happen every time God is going to do something like this, but this time around, He definitely got my attention.

I overheard others mentioning something about the air, but not many really paid much attention to it, I don't think. It was rather difficult to stay focused for when it was my turn to sign, but I managed to get through it. Shortly after I had returned to my chair, I hadn't really been paying attention, until I was centered out. I looked up; he was pointing to me, and once he got my attention, he asked me to bring the deaf girl, sitting next to me back up.

Okay, I thought to myself immediately, this isn't funny, what's going on. I turned to look at her, she was already rearing to go, and I stood, and led her to the stage. As soon as we climbed the few stairs, once again he stopped me, and told me to stay right where I was. He then took her by the hand again, but this time, he led her to the front of the stage. Once he began to speak, the crowd went silent. I think this was one of those few moments everyone was so quiet that you could actually hear a pin drop if you listened carefully.

Well the rest is history of what happened next. He had asked for everyone to start singing God's praises again, thanking Jesus for His healing power. He turned to her and cupped his hands over her ears.

I'll never forget the look on this girl's face, the exact moment she was healed, able to hear for the very first time. And yes, the air cleared – it didn't linger. This time, the air had me more captivated than this girl's miraculous healing. I watched it disappear.

Yes the place went crazy; she was hysterical, tears rolling down her face. She was pacing back and forth on the stage, running her fingers through her hair, to keep it out of her face. She looked out towards the crowd, not wanting anyone to stop, motioning to everyone to continue singing and clapping.

She then jumped down off the stage and started to run through the crowd, towards the door. Everyone moved out of her way to let her through. I ended up leaving the stage to go follow her, unsure where she was heading. Once I made it out to the hallway, someone told me that she had gone into the washroom. I went in, she was standing at the other end of the washroom, staring into a mirror over a sink. I called out her name. She turned to me immediately, running to me, throwing her arms around me. The words she so desperately tried to utter . . . I can hear, I can hear!

Well, the following day she had an audiologist test done. And yes, perfect healing, perfect hearing.

With man this is impossible but with God all things are possible [Matthew 19:26].

Elizabeth 'Liz' Sulis

BEGIN . . . start . . . commence . . . open . . . There's something refreshing and optimistic about these words, whether they refer to the dawn of a new day, the birth of a child, the prelude of a symphony or the first miles of a family vacation. Free of problems and full of promise, beginnings stir hope and imaginative visions of the future. Genesis means "beginnings" or "origin," and it unfolds the record of the beginning of the world, of human history, of family, of civilization, of salvation. It is the story of God's purpose and plan for His creation. As the book of beginnings, Genesis sets the stage for the entire Bible. It reveals the person and nature of God [Creator, Sustainer, Judge, Redeemer]; the value and dignity of human beings [made in God's image, saved by grace, used by God in the world]; the tragedy and consequences of sin [the fall, separation from God, judgment]; and the promise and assurance of salvation [covenant, forgiveness, promised Messiah].

God. That's where Genesis begins. All at once we see Him creating the world in a majestic display of power and purpose, culminating with a man and woman made like Himself [Gen. 1: 26, 27]. But before long sin entered the world, and Satan was unmasked. Bathed in innocence, creation was shattered by the fall [the wilful disobedience of Adam and Eve]. Fellowship with God was broken, and evil began weaving its destructive web. In rapid succession, we read how Adam and Eve were expelled from the beautiful garden, their first son turned murderer, and evil bred evil until God finally destroyed everyone on earth except a small family led by Noah, the only godly person left.

As we come to Abraham on the plains of Canaan, we discover the beginning of God's covenant people and the broad strokes of His salvation plan: salvation comes by faith, Abraham's descendants will be God's people, and the Saviour of the world will come through this chosen nation. The stories of Isaac, Jacob, and Joseph, which follow, are more than interesting biographies. They emphasize the promises of God and the proof that He is faithful. The people we meet in Genesis are simple, ordinary people, yet through them, God did great things. These are vivid pictures of how God can and does use all kinds of people to accomplish His good purposes . . .

Read Genesis and be encouraged. There is hope! No matter how dark the world situation seems God has a plan. No matter how insignificant or useless you feel, God loves you and wants to use you in His plan. No matter how sinful and separated from God you [or I] are, His salvation is available. Read Genesis . . . and hope [NIV]!

> *"The Biblical words about the Genesis of heaven and earth are not words of information, but words of appreciation. The story of creation is not a description of how the world came into being, but a song about the glory of the world's having come into being. And God saw that it was good. This is the challenge: to reconcile God's view with our experience . . . there is more. The purpose of the song is not only to celebrate. It is also to summon us to awe and attention. For just as the world as created, is a world summoned into existence under command, so to be human beings in that world is to live in search of our summons" [Rabbi Abraham Joshua Heschel – Who is Man? 1965].*

God's Word endures!

EPILOGUE

I can't describe God completely, but I can tell others what He has done for me. I don't want the indescribable aspects of God's greatness to prevent me from telling others what I know about Him.

It has been very difficult for me to believe much of anything or really trust anyone over the years. Michel wasn't the only one I loathed, and hated . . . God—Jesus. I was a person who thought I would believe in Jesus if I could see a definite sign or miracle. *Even when I stood in Jesus' presence and witnessed those two miraculous miracles, I still didn't want to believe, and continued to turn my back on Him.* I continued to alienate myself from God – Jesus; after all, I had a lot of practice. But Jesus says we are blessed if we can believe without seeing. We have all the proof we need in the words of the Bible and the testimony of believers. A physical appearance would not necessarily make Jesus any more real to us than He is now. Trust is the fruit of a relationship in which you know you are loved. Because I didn't understand what God was doing, I could not trust Him – I didn't know Him.

If only, we cry as we search our minds for a way out and look to the skies for rescue. With just a glimmer of hope, we would take courage and carry on, enduring until the end.

Hope is the sliver shaft of sun breaking through the storm-darkened sky, words of comfort in the intensive care unit, a letter from across the sea, the first spring bird perched on a snow-covered twig, and the finish line in sight. It is a rainbow, a song, and a loving touch. Hope is knowing God and resting in His love . . .

I recently admitted to myself and to God that I fit the human pattern and frequently fail to live up to my own standards [much more to God's standards]. That was my first step to this process of forgiveness and healing. I know I cannot please God without a proper relationship with Him, and I must make sure that my actions match my words. If I am to claim to be one of God's people, my life should reflect what God is like. When I disobey God, I dishonour His name. But my relationship with God is not about performance or me having to please Him. He is not a bully; He is not some self-centered demanding little deity insisting on His own way. He is great, and worthy of my praises, and His desire is only what is best for me. He is now my best friend, who has transformed *my* life.

I have a very strong support in a Christian Church I attend, with trustworthy pastoral leadership, which I am grateful for.

A friend of mine told me that He couldn't stand hypocrites, especially in churches. He told me he would never ever enter the sanctuary of a church again. I could certainly understand that . . . and to my friend . . . you are not alone.

> *The caller to the radio program mentioned religion, so the radio talk show host began to rant about hypocrites. "I can't stand religious hypocrites," he said. "They talk about religion, but they're no better than I am. That's why I don't like all this religious stuff."*
>
> *This man didn't realize it, but he was agreeing with God. God has made it clear that He can't stand hypocrisy either. It's ironic though that something God opposes, such as hypocrisy is used by some people as an excuse not to seek Him. The prophet Isaiah also criticized hypocrites [Isaiah 29:13], and Jesus applied Isaiah's words to these religious leaders. When we claim to honour God while our hearts are far from Him, our worship means nothing. It is not enough to act religious. Our actions and our attitudes must be sincere.*

The Pharisees knew a lot about God, but many didn't know God. It is not enough to study about religion or even to study the Bible. We must respond to God Himself.

Jesus told His disciples to leave the Pharisees alone because the Pharisees were blind to God's truth. Anyone who listened to Pharisees teaching would risk spiritual blindness as well. [Pharisees . . . in ancient times, a member of a Jewish sect that was very strict in keeping to tradition and the laws of its religion – in other words, a person who makes a show of religion rather than following its spirit.] *Not all religious leaders clearly see God's truth. Make sure that those you listen to and learn from are those with good spiritual eyesight – they teach and follow the principles of Scripture.*

I didn't know how to pray, but I am learning, I didn't really believe in God's word, but after asking Him to help me and teach me, He has opened my eyes – and my heart – a continuous daily learning process . . . from here on out. There is always something new and fascinating to learn.

We work hard to keep our outward appearance attractive, but what is in our hearts is even more important. The way we are deep down [where others can't see] matters much to God. When people become Christians, God makes them different on the inside. *He will continue the process of change inside them if they only ask.* God wants us to seek healthy thoughts and motives, not just healthy food and exercise.

Non-Christians who point out hypocrisy in us when they see it are right in doing so. They are agreeing with God, who also despises it. A Christian's task is to make sure his or her life honours the One who deserves our total dedication.

Hypocrisy is a common sin that grieves the Lord above; He longs for those who'll worship Him in faith, and truth, and love [Henry G. Bosch]. . . the devil is content to let us profess Christianity as long as we do not practice it.

I can say now, after 47 years, I have surrendered myself completely to the grace and mercy of God – Jesus, asking Him to show me the way out of sin and into the light of His freedom and His love. I'm really just beginning to grow in my knowledge of the Word, by studying God's Word because ignorance has made me vulnerable to deception. Yes, I'm seeking to find God's truth . . . and will for my life. Without a proper foundation though, I will find it easy to quit during difficult times . . . all believers need a strong foundation.

I asked myself, what is the purpose of life, my life? It is that I should revere the all-powerful God. To *revere* God means to respect and stand in awe of Him because of whom He is. Purpose in life starts with whom I know, not what I know or how good I am. It is impossible to fulfill my God-given purpose unless I revere God and give Him first place in my life.

Jesus is always there to help, providing me refuge, security, and peace. Jesus' power is complete and His ultimate victory is certain. He will not fail to rescue *those who love Him.*

Jesus is my refuge and strength, an ever-present help in trouble – He is not merely a temporary retreat; He is my eternal refuge and can provide strength in any circumstance – and for anyone.

God *ALONE* knows and controls the future. We may never see more than a moment ahead, but we can be secure if we *trust* in Him. The human eye and ear are never completely trustworthy because distortions can creep in. But when God speaks, the communication is totally and completely 100 percent accurate.

Apostle Paul wrote in 2 Timothy . . . but mark this: There will be terrible times in the last days. People will be lovers of themselves, lovers of money, boastful, proud, abusive, disobedient to their parents, ungrateful, unholy, without love, unforgiving, slanderous, without self-control, brutal, not lovers of the good, treacherous, rash, conceited, lovers of pleasure rather than lovers of God – having a form of godliness but denying its power . . . Was Paul wrong?

I want to avoid punishment and live eternally with Christ. That I know is the smartest decision I have made yet. Of course God doesn't have to punish people for sin. Sin is its own punishment, devouring us from the inside. I don't think it's God's purpose to punish it; it's *His Joy* to cure it!

God has always respected human beings' choices. He has had to work within our systems even while He seeks to free us from them. Creation has been taken down a very different path than what God desired or intended. In our world as we know it, the value of the individual is constantly weighed against the survival of the system, whether political, economic, social or religious – any system. First one person, and then a few, and finally even many are easily sacrificed for the good and ongoing existence of that system. In one form or another this lies behind every struggle for power, every prejudice, every war, and every abuse of relationship. The 'will to power and independence' has become so ubiquitous that it is now considered normal – but it's not! It is the human paradigm – pattern. *It is a matrix, a diabolical scheme in which I have been hopelessly trapped even while completely unaware of its existence. It is an indispensable fact, like air is indispensable to life that in the absence of love for God resides a lust for power, a yearning to become God.*

Knowing I must depend totally on God's grace . . . I don't expect most people to approve of or understand my decision to follow Christ. It all seems so silly to them. Just as a tone-deaf person cannot appreciate fine music, the person who rejects God cannot understand God's beautiful message. With the line of communication broken, he or she won't be able to hear what God is saying to him or her. My faith now lies in the God who created the entire universe – my communication lines are open [1 Corinthians 2:14, 15].

God will not settle for my mere acknowledgment of His existence. I didn't want anything to do with Him, I gave up on Him; I alienated myself from Him . . . Because I blamed Him. Of course I couldn't make heads or tails out of anything, really. But . . . He never gave up on me. He is a God of second chances, and new beginnings. Those who *seek* God will find that they are rewarded with His intimate presence.

As believers, our true reward is God's presence and power through the Holy Spirit. Later, in eternity [entrance is by God's Grace alone], we will be rewarded for our faith and service. If material rewards in this life came to us for every faithful deed, we would be tempted to boast about our achievements and act out of wrong motivations. Instead, I want to focus on God's gracious benefits to me, and be thankful for what I have – anything else is just a bonus.

I wasn't promised that there is anyone or anything that will go back into the past and make my rape un-happen. But, despite the fact it happened, I could be made whole. There maybe a lot of work I still have to do – I'm still a work in progress. There are self-help books, counsellors, therapists, and psychiatrists, even pastoral counselling, and the most patient people in the world in my life, but that can only take me part of the way. The one who can heal me and make me whole is God. He made us and knows exactly where we need His help the most. He can restore me to a happy and fulfilling life. That is of course, if I choose God's help?

As difficult as it has been for me to understand, everything that has taken place in my life, it is occurring exactly according to God's purpose, without violating my choice or will.

There are millions of reasons why God allows pain and hurt and suffering rather than for Him to eradicate them, but most of those reasons can only be understood within each person's story. Although God is present everywhere, at times He may seem far away . . . causing us to feel alone and to doubt His care for us. God is not evil. I have been one who has embraced fear and pain. My choices are not stronger than God's purposes, and He will use every choice I make for the ultimate good and the most loving outcome.

As a hurting, broken human being, I have centered my life on things that seemed good to me, but that has not really either filled me or freed me.

Trials and persecutions make very little sense to us when we experience them. But they can purify us if we are *willing* to learn from them. After you survive a difficult time, seek to learn from it so that it can help you in the future. As Paul states clearly in 1 Corinthians 13: 13, faith, hope and love are at the heart of the [true] Christian life. Our relationship with God begins with faith, which helps us realize that we are delivered from our past by Christ's death. Hope grows as we learn all that God has in mind for us; it gives us the promise of the future. And God's love fills our lives and gives us the ability to reach out to others. God does not reveal everything to us in this life. We must be content with the partial picture until He wants us to see more. He will tell us all we need to know.

God knows each winding way I take and every sorrow, pain, and ache; His children He will not forsake . . . He knows and loves His own . . . God's love still stands when all else has fallen—[Henry G. Bosch].

I have been often very sensitive to what is right or wrong. What I should or shouldn't do. Never having much confidence in myself, I wasn't the smart one, and I found it so difficult to try to articulate. Believing God gave away all the special gifts and talents to others, not me. I was jealous of what God had given to another person. But that doesn't matter now; my gift to God is to honour Him.

Through God's Grace and Divine Mercy He is guiding me, supporting me, liberating me from the feelings of humiliation, and guilt of the past, and the fear of tomorrow. He gave me parents who never wavered in their unconditional love and acceptance. He brought great people into my life, especially when I needed them the most and continues to bless me with wonderful friends that enrich my life.

I have choices, I have a free will, and I am responsible for my own healing, increased self-esteem, becoming physically, and emotionally stronger, living in the present moment, and enjoying life. Remembering to turn the things I cannot change completely over to God, leaving them in His hands, and putting my *trust* in Him.

Looking forward to a future, free to live, and live happily, caring for my spirit, nurturing my unique potential, and celebrating life's many blessings. Not to say that sometimes I may not become discouraged with my progress, but I keep going.

My alter ego is the compassionate one, whose superpower lies in revelation of my life and worldly events. I reflect a sense of gratitude for my life and those involved, by showing humility, *forgiveness*, and charity. By doing so, I feel a strong redemption for past events, a great liberating feeling. I have punished myself enough and am free at last. Clearing the conscience through forgiving others *and myself* can bring an overwhelming sense of peace, and joy.

I no longer begrudge those who turn to God in the last moments of life, because in reality, no one deserves eternal life. Many people we don't expect to see in the kingdom will be there. The criminal who repented as he was dying [Luke 23: 40-43] will be there, along with people who have believed and served God for many years. Who am I to resent God's gracious acceptance of the despised, the outcast, and the sinners who have turned to Him for forgiveness. Yes I have forgiven Michel . . . but that is not all . . . I pray for him, and his salvation.

I pray for each and every one of you that God will give you His understanding that surpasses *ALL* things. A *faith* and *trust to believe* in Him and *lean on* Him, whatever your *needs* are, great or small. Instilling in you, always, an inner sense of His Grace, His strength, His wisdom, His peace, and His calmness, to lift your spirits up. Opening one's heart to embrace all the riches, love, success, and sheer happiness that one has always longed for. Remembering to give thanks to God in *ALL* circumstances, the *Author of Life*.

For the nature and fruits of faith. Now faith is being sure of what we hope for and certain of what we do not see [Hebrews 11: 1]. This is what the ancients were commended for. By faith we understand that the universe was formed at God's command. So that what is seen was not made out of what was visible [Hebrews 11: 3]. Two words describe faith: sure and certain. These two qualities need a secure beginning and ending point. The beginning point of faith – is to believe – in God's character – He is whom He says. The end point – is to believe – that God will fulfill His promises even though we don't see those promises materializing yet; we demonstrate true faith [see John 20: 24-31].

I know that without faith it is impossible to please God, because anyone who comes to Him must believe that He exists and that He rewards those who earnestly seek Him [Hebrews 11: 6]. I know that He wants my faith to lead to a personal, dynamic relationship. My goal is to let God's desires be mine. Being controlled by my own desires will stunt my growth.

Christians come out of all kinds of different backgrounds . . . I have had my life changed by Christ. I'm not perfect. I still make mistakes, and still have habits that are wrong, but I, with God's help, will overcome them, I will do my best to live Jesus' way, one day at a time, and He will show me what to do. I will trust in Jesus with all my heart and lean not on my own understanding . . . for He holds this day in His hand, as well as tomorrow, and all the tomorrows yet to come. I just need to remember to keep my focus on Jesus and He, in return, will direct my paths . . . make my paths straight [Proverbs 3: 5, 6]. Knowing that, I can step out in confidence and enjoy the experience the day presents.

Today people are still confused about love. Love is the greatest of all human qualities, and it is an attribute of God Himself [see 1 John 4: 8]. Love involves unselfish service to others; to show it gives evidence that you care. Faith is the foundation and content of God's message; hope is the attitude and focus; love is action. When faith and hope are in line, you are free to love completely because you understand how God loves.

Therefore, great faith, acts of dedication or sacrifice, and miracle-working power produce very little without love. Love makes our actions and gifts useful. Although people have different gifts, love is available to everyone.

1 Corinthians Chapter 13 defines real love . . . Now I know . . . Love is patient, love is kind, never jealous, boastful, proud or rude. Love isn't selfish or quick tempered. It doesn't keep a record of wrongs that others do. Love rejoices in the truth, but not in evil. Love is always supportive, loyal, and hopeful, and trusting. Love never fails [1 Corinthians 13: 4-8]. And now these three remain: Faith, Hope, and Love. But the greatest of these is love [1 Corinthians 13: 13].

Live, Love, and Laugh . . . As it is written . . . No eye has seen, no ear has heard, no mind has conceived what God has prepared for those who love Him [1 Corinthians 2: 9]. This world is not all there is. The best is yet to come.

M.A. Walker

God's love cannot be explained – it can only be experienced!

THE END

ACKNOWLEDGEMENTS

Yes, God most certainly does *use unexpected people in unexpected circumstances during unexpected times to demonstrate His power! I am humbled. I thank everyone who has helped me to bring this story to its final form.*

Dora Paige, publishing consultant with Xlibris, was the first to see a very rough, crude draft of my manuscript, and went out of her way to encourage me to go beyond what I had originally planned, or ever dreamed of doing. Dora, your continued and consistent kind words, enthusiasm, infectious laugh, and belief in a complete stranger, and her story . . . so many miles away . . . are all a part of the special qualities that you possess. I also want to thank you for hand picking, putting into place, an awesome, hard working, Xlibris publishing team . . . Extending my warmest regards and thanks to Athena Mallen – Submissions Representative, Frieda Lovett and Christine Tan – Author Services Representatives, this books' initial Interior Galley – Designed by James Mensidor, and Alberto Bastasa – Brian Sianson and French Pino – Marketing Services Representatives – and last, but not least, Meagan Arevalo, Xlibris Editor. It has been my honour, and pleasure in working with you all, thank-you!

A very special thank-you to a very special friend, Janet Pilon, who took time from her busy schedule to help me with the final tweaking process . . . you not only have a huge heart, you have impeccable talents and skills . . . in many areas. I truly appreciate you adding your insights into the ways in which God works, and in particular, what He is doing in your life . . . *You rock Pumpkin! Hugs, Chicklet* [a.k.a. M.A.]

To Susan [Sue] Demmons you are an inspiration. You are one of those people that anyone would be blessed, beyond words, in knowing . . . next to Jesus that is. With my heart-felt thanks, I am truly blessed to have you in my life, and corner . . . and praying for me. I look forward to many more Tim Hortons or Starbucks rendezvous.

Rev. Laura Sherwood, I want to reiterate that I am grateful . . . grateful for your overall trustworthy pastoral counselling, advice, support, and friendship you personally have given to me, and continue to give me. I know, without a doubt, that you are a leader with good spiritual eyesight, who teaches, and follows the principles of Scripture. We are a blessed church in having you, Pastor Peter, and the rest of the pastoral team, shepherding us into the future.

If, instead of a gem or even a flower, we could cast the gift of a lovely thought into the heart of a friend . . . that would be giving as the angels give.

TO: Linda Powell

In response to your note you sent me on March 1, 2009 . . . thank you!

Today you made my heart sing . . .

What you are is God's gift to you. What you do with what God has given you is your gift to Him.

Dear M.A.:

Today you made God smile! You made many of his people smile also. Thank you so much for sharing your talent with us this morning. The offertory added a beautiful musical interlude to our worship service.

I hope we will not have to wait too long for your return to the keyboard.

Love ya!
Linda

Get Published, Inc!
Thorofare, NJ 08086
18 September 2009
BA2009261